FOREVER HOME

Also by Graham Norton

FOREVER HOME

A Novel

Graham Norton

HARPERVIA

An Imprint of HarperCollins*Publishers*

FOREVER HOME. Copyright © 2022 by Graham Norton. All rights reserved.
Printed in the United States of America. No part of this book may be used or
reproduced in any manner whatsoever without written permission except in the
case of brief quotations embodied in critical articles and reviews. For information,
address HarperCollins Publishers, 195 Broadway, New York, NY 10007.

HarperCollins books may be purchased for educational,
business, or sales promotional use. For information, please email the
Special Markets Department at SPsales@harpercollins.com.

Originally published by Coronet in 2022 in the United Kingdom.
First HarperVia hardcover published in 2023.

FIRST EDITION

Designed by Terry McGrath

Library of Congress Cataloging-in-Publication Data has been applied for.

ISBN 978-0-06-333861-6

23 24 25 26 27 LBC 5 4 3 2 1

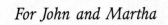

For John and Martha

The Back Quay of Ballytoor was where things used to be. That grey building on the corner of Twomey's Lane had been the Garda barracks long before it was upgraded to the glass and brick box up beside the hospital. Keogh's hardware shop used to be housed in the big double-fronted stone premises, the name still legible above the large windows smeared with the mysterious milky wash of abandoned shops. Few could remember it but the tall thin building with the narrow door had been the town's only bike shop; now it just seemed to be awaiting its own collapse. Cleary's Garage remained open, an apron of oil and grease spreading across the road, but these days most car owners gravitated towards one of the newer garages further out on the Cork road.

Peering over the shabby patchwork of roofs along the Back Quay was a strangely genteel terrace of houses. It looked out of place, like a guest who was hopelessly overdressed for the occasion. Formal in a way that made it unlike any other street in the town, Stable Row ran between Twomey's Lane and Barrack Hill. Just seven houses long, the small front gardens were all edged with the same metal railings, elegant rather than ornate. Most were well maintained. The people lucky enough to live in one of these houses took pride in their homes, aware of their good fortune. An ungenerous neighbour might have described them as smug. Doors were glossy, windows clean, the gutters weed-free. Originally built for the British officers who had come to the town as part of a small garrison, the short terrace still felt more Anglo than Irish.

At this time of the morning all was quiet. Mrs Buttimer, now widowed, from number one was away visiting her sister in Dublin. A poster for a missing cat, faded and damp, hung from the gate of number two, all hope now drained away. A bright plastic ride-on tractor toy was parked neatly on the path leading to the front door of number three, the children ferried off to school a couple of hours earlier. The morning light glittered as it struck the small crystals hanging in the windows of number four. Jenny and Arthur Beamish could never have been described as hippies – he was a retired accountant – but they embraced the trappings of middle-class bohemia. They had hung some wind chimes by their front door until Mrs Buttimer had complained of sleep deprivation. In number five, old Miss Cronin sat unobserved in the kitchen, a rug over her knees, the radio playing classical music she wasn't enjoying. One of the carers would return later to give her some lunch. Number six had just been sold. No one could believe the price they'd paid. Madness. A young couple apparently. They had yet to move in. He was something to do with the chemical plant out by Creenor. Next door at number seven a woman was standing by one of the first-floor windows. At first glance, a passer-by might have described her as young, with her slim frame and loose denim shirt. Her hair was pulled up into a messy bun, two plastic pens sticking out of it. A closer look would have revealed her drawn face, the dark circles under her eyes, her hair streaked with grey. This was Carol Crottie, almost fifty. Her gaze wasn't directed out of the window down towards the river, or across the roofs of the quays to the other side of town. Instead, she was bent over a folder, while she chewed the top of a third biro. Carol had lived in number seven for less than ten years and she wasn't ready to leave.

Living in an old house had been new to her. She had begun her life on a neat, modern housing estate in a suburb of Cork City. Her parents had christened her Carol. 'Were you a Christmas baby?' people asked politely. 'No,' she would reply, vaguely aware that she should have some sort of follow-up, an alternative explanation, but she never did. When she was ten, Brian and Linda, her older brother and sister, along with herself had been put in the back seat of the car and driven away from the city. Their new home was an ultra-modern bungalow on the coast, west of Ballytoor. This was their reward. 'Hard work, kids,' their father had beamed at them from the driver's seat. 'This is what hard work looks like.' He lunged across the car to give his wife an awkward kiss. She flushed, her eyes darting to the children in the back. Carol knew, as much as a child could, that her father's business was doing well. Her mother regularly reminded the children of how busy Daddy was, and how much he'd like to be at home with them all but he had to work. The small chain of cafés he owned in Cork had expanded into train stations, then into Dublin and finally the airports. Crottie's Cafés became well known, affectionately called Grotty's. Carol had spent her school years being referred to as Grotty Crottie, even by her friends.

Later, as a student, her home had been a small modern flat in Dublin. Her father had bought it as an investment. She was reminded many times, particularly in the presence of Linda and Brian, that she was not to imagine the apartment belonged to her. 'I know, Dad,' she would sigh. 'We all know. We get it.'

'Just to be clear,' her father would mutter.

What went unspoken was that Carol was indeed his favourite. Neither Linda nor Brian had gone on to university, and the fact that his youngest had made her a star in his eyes. But he hadn't bought her a flat. It was very important that everything was fair when it came to money. In his will everything would be split three ways. It was just love she had got more of.

When Carol began teaching English, she had shared an apartment with two nurses. On the north side of the town, it wore its newness as a badge of honour. Brightly lit corridors, donkey-brown carpet tiles. The street door had a security buzzer and a little camera. Carol's father had liked that. The two nurses shared one bedroom while Carol had the other. The three of them had got on well enough until they discovered that she was the daughter of the Crottie who owned all the Grotty's. It was never the same after that.

Carol had fallen in love. Alex taught geography and coached various sports teams. He wore tracksuits on and off the pitch and had a dark, neatly clippered beard. He was not the sort of man Carol would have ever expected to ask a bookish woman like her out on a date. That wasn't to say she hadn't found him attractive. On the contrary, her eyes were often drawn to him in the school staff room. From behind a pile of uncorrected homework she had observed him flirt and laugh with the blonde history teacher. Carol had seen how the older female students would hang around the door of his classroom, trying to think of questions to ask him about oxbow lakes or glaciers in the hope that he would notice them. Then one evening in the staff car park, he had casually called across to her an invitation to go out. His tone had been so familiar and unforced it seemed to suggest that this wouldn't be their first date. Carol had that feeling she got when she was watching a series on television and realised that she must have missed an episode, because the story had moved forward in unexplained ways. He had taken Carol to dinner, ordered wine without embarrassment, told her she looked beautiful. Her parents liked him. What more could she ask for? She married him.

They had bought a town house off plan when they became engaged. The large signs surrounding the development proudly declared that the homes were 'Architect Designed', as if most buildings were just constructed by builders using luck and a spirit level. 'Don't tell your brother and sister,' her father had cautioned when he handed over the cheque to help with the deposit.

They had been happy. Really happy. All the furniture had been chosen and bought without arguments. Quite often when Carol was cleaning or carrying in groceries, she would stop and admire what they had made. It was a proper home. They would laugh, swapping tales about students or mocking the television shows they were watching while they curled into each other on the sofa they had found together. 'Perfect,' they had said almost in unison when they'd spotted it in Caseys up in Cork. Carol became pregnant. A cot to choose. The small back bedroom to decorate. They had a son, Craig. He was six years old when Alex left. It wasn't the blonde history teacher, it was a new blonde French teacher. Carol hadn't been quite as heartbroken as she might have expected when he'd walked out. There'd even been a hint of relief – the thing she had been dreading, half anticipating, for so many years had finally happened. There were tears of course, and moments of wild rage when she wanted to track him down and cause him terrible, catastrophic physical pain, but she still had Craig. Sweet, untroubled Craig and the smart new town house. Carol's father had bought Alex out. There had also been a kind of comfort to be found in the news that the French teacher had dumped Alex after less than a year and he was now living with a physiotherapist in Drimoleague.

Being single didn't seem as bad as other people, certainly her parents, seemed to think it was. She found she preferred being with Craig in their little house without Alex in it. Then, just over ten years ago, after her baby boy had left home to work as an estate agent in London, she had met the second love of her life, her Declan. She felt almost ambushed by her newfound happiness. It was then that she had moved into this old house, with walls that swelled and floors that sloped. 1811 was the date embossed at the top of the long metal drainpipe that traced down the brick façade of number seven Stable Row. The terraced houses weren't large but they had ideas above their station. Three storeys high, with two small rooms on each, it wasn't really much bigger than a cottage but with its high ceilings, the delicate cornicing and imposing fireplaces, the house seemed convinced of its own fine breeding. The top floor was Carol and Declan's bedroom and the bathroom. The living room on the first floor had been the main bedroom but Carol had insisted, and Declan after much persuasion had finally agreed, that they move upstairs. She didn't want to lie with Declan where he had slept with his wife. Carol had also changed the small parlour on the ground floor into a dining room so that they no longer ate in the kitchen. She knew these changes irked Declan, but Carol felt it was important that she make her mark on the house. It was theirs now.

Declan's former bedroom became her favourite room. It was at the front of the house. Two long, floor-to-ceiling, small-paned windows looked out over the town, each fronted with a plain metal Juliet balcony. Carol enjoyed sitting in this airy room as the afternoon sun moved the shadow of the window frame across the worn oak floorboards. She liked to imagine that others had sat here before her, watching the light on its slow journey to the bookshelves on the far wall. Sometimes when she was preparing for a new school year, leafing through a Jane Austen novel, or Dickens perhaps, she wondered if these stories had been read in these rooms before. It wasn't creepy or unsettling to her. The thought of all the lives lived within these walls gave her a sense of comfort. No matter how busy or preoccupied she became with her life, it didn't really matter. The sun cast its shadows, the heavy shutters kept it out, the stairs groaned oblivious to who was causing the strain. This old house was far more than the sum of the lives it had contained over the years. No one could ever really own it. Certainly not Carol. That much, now, had been made very clear.

Boxes of various sizes were stacked in every room. Carol's handwriting was on most of them: Dining room #2 Glassware. Books. Pots. Miscellaneous. She held a folder where each box had a corresponding page listing the exact contents. The children were not going to accuse her of stealing anything. Not for the first time, she asked herself how she could love Declan so much yet have such an intense and visceral dislike for his children. She glanced at her phone. 10.45. They'd be here soon. It wouldn't surprise her if they were early, hoping to catch her out. What did they think she was going to do? Clank out of the house with the canteen of silver cutlery sewn into the lining of her coat?

The living room, where she now stood, was empty, but by looking at the darker patches of wallpaper where paintings had hung, Carol could still see them. The marks on the floor where the two small sofas had sat opposite each other. She could see him too. His legs crossed, the *Irish Times* held aloft, covering most of his body. A grunt when she had offered him tea. How was it possible that he was no longer here? The strange chemical scent of his anti-dandruff shampoo was still in the air. How could Declan, her strong ox of a man, be gone when a mere perfume remained. She felt her eyes fill with tears but she brushed them away with her hand. The children would not find her like this.

She heard the slam of a car door. Glancing out of the window down to the street, she saw that it was Killian. He looked up. Carol turned away quickly but she knew that he had probably seen her. Typical that he would have claimed a parking space right outside when most evenings after work she found herself circling the block on a fruitless search. She chanced another glimpse out of the window. Killian was now looking the other way, down the street. His large overcoat flapped ostentatiously in the wind, but his carefully styled hair remained unmoving. To Carol, Declan's eldest, now in his mid-thirties, still looked like a boy playing a businessman in a school play. He raised his hand to wave at someone. Sally, his younger sister, came into view. She was carrying a brightly coloured plastic bag with spray bottles and cloths protruding from it. Did she think she was going to clean the house? Was Carol not capable? She had never seen the inside of Sally's home but judging from her unkempt mousey hair and the state of her – was it a long cardigan or a knitted coat? – she very much doubted her commitment to cleanliness. Carol watched the siblings hug briefly. They had a huddled conversation, no doubt about her, and then started walking across the street. Carol hurried down the stairs, her footsteps echoing through the carpetless house. She would open the front door to them before they had a chance to use their key.

Declan had been an unusual figure at the school. The only single father bringing up children alone, he was usually referred to as poor Mr Barry. Carol knew him to see. Tall and broad-shouldered, his shock of silver hair worn a little longer than most of the other fathers, he would hover awkwardly at the edges of school events like sports days or parents' evenings. He was the sort of man who looked like he might crush his cup and saucer without meaning to. She knew that he ran the yellow-fronted chemist shop between the post office and The Cat and Fiddle pub, but that wasn't the pharmacy Carol used.

The first time they spoke was in the street. She had been standing outside Gallagher's shoe shop trying to figure out what shoes on display were included in their heavily advertised sale when a shadow fell across the shop window. She turned to find poor Mr Barry. He was holding a rolled-up newspaper. Later she would learn that this was his regular habit, to buy an *Irish Times* in Cassidy's on his way back to his car, having left Margaret or Orla to lock up for the night.

He lowered his head slightly and asked, 'Mrs Lawlor?'

'Miss Crottie,' Carol corrected him.

'Oh.' Declan looked confused, unsure of what to say next.

'I've gone back to my maiden name. I was Mrs Lawlor.' She smiled to show she was not offended and then added, 'For a while there anyway.' She gave a light laugh.

'I'm Declan Barry, Sally's father.' He held out his hand and she shook it.

'Carol. Nice to meet you.'

This encounter was nothing out of the ordinary. Parents of pupils often stopped her to ask a question or just to say hello. Carol had taught both Killian and Sally, though in truth neither of them had made much of an impression on her.

'Sorry to disturb you,' Declan glanced at the window display with barely concealed disdain, 'but I wanted to ask you something.'

'Feel free. Ask away.'

'It's Sally. She says she doesn't want to take Higher-level English in the leaving. I was just wondering what you thought? I don't want to push her if you don't think she's up to it.'

Carol wasn't quite sure what to say. Sally sat beside the window about halfway back. She had thick hair that never looked as if it had been cut or washed properly, but apart from that she was just one of those pupils who made up the numbers. Carol struggled to remember anything she had ever contributed in class or written in an essay. Perhaps she had never pushed her because of the whole 'no mother' thing.

'Well, Mr Barry, I always think there's no point forcing people, but she doesn't have to decide now. She has the summer. I tell you what I'd do. Get her a copy of *Wuthering Heights*. That's on the syllabus for next year. If she reads it over the summer and likes it, then I'd say she'd have no problem with Higher.'

Declan tapped the air with his paper. 'That's a plan. I like it. Thank you very much, Mrs, sorry, Miss—'

'Carol, please,' she interrupted him. They shook hands once more and he strode off down towards the quays. His whole body leaned from side to side as he walked, like a slow, heavy metronome.

They began to notice each other more often after that. A wave. A 'How's Sally getting on?' as they passed in the supermarket. Carol admired the way Declan held himself. He pushed his trolley without apology or embarrassment, and yet somehow the domesticity of the task didn't undermine his masculinity. Carol had noticed that most men finding themselves alone in a supermarket either behaved as if the chore was beneath them, the items they placed in their baskets beyond contempt, or they approached the aisles with hyper-confidence, a planned route through the store, a regimented system of packing at the checkout, all to demonstrate that this chaotic world of groceries would be much improved if it was only run by men. Declan wasn't like that.

Young Sally did manage to read the Brontë over the summer and while she would never have admitted that she enjoyed it, the fact that she finished it seemed to give her the confidence to take the Higher-level course. Carol noticed her in class and was pleased to think that her advice might have helped. One afternoon after the bell had rung, Sally lingered by the door to the classroom. She was stepping from foot to foot and her long arms swung by her sides. Unfortunate that her body had inherited quite so much from her father, Carol thought.

'Sally. Can I help you there?'

'Oh Miss Crottie, Daddy was wondering could you give me grinds at home? Thursdays would be best, he said.' Sally ran her words together as if she had learned them phonetically, with no real grasp of their meaning.

Carol didn't give students extra help out of hours. That was her policy. Many parents had asked, and some had even suggested very tempting rates of pay, but Carol had always said no. She knew other teachers at the school did it, but she always felt as if it was somehow admitting she had failed in the classroom, or been deliberately holding back information, waiting to exchange it for a fistful of euros. Why, then, did Carol find herself replying, 'I'd say we could probably arrange something like that. Give your father my number.'? She scribbled on a piece of paper and held it out to Sally. 'You'll be sick of the sight of me.'

Sally took the number, unsure if Carol had made a joke or not. 'Thanks, miss.'

On Thursdays, at eight o'clock, Sally and Carol sat at the kitchen table, the smell of the Barry family dinner still in the air, discussing the role of the fool in *King Lear* or the relationship between beauty and truth in 'Ode on a Grecian Urn'. How any of it related to a motherless girl with breath that still smelled of defrosted shepherd's pie, Carol didn't know. As the weeks went by, Sally gradually revealed herself to be more than the sullen girl Carol knew from the classroom. This version of Sally might have been the very opposite of an attention-seeker but it was clear that attention was precisely what she needed. The way she opened up if Carol showed any interest in her opinion, or encouraged her to expand on an idea, was heart-breaking. She gazed at Carol like a stray dog being promised a treat. When Carol had given her a slim notebook with a painting of Emily Brontë on the cover, Sally had been so pathetically grateful and excited that Carol almost regretted the gesture.

At nine, Sally would gather her books and head upstairs. At first she had tried to linger and join in with the adults when Declan came into the kitchen to deliver a discreet envelope of cash. Declan had quickly dispatched Sally back to her room, barking his command with a strictness that Carol found slightly intimidating. After Sally left the room, his demeanour was transformed. The first night he offered Carol a glass of wine, she refused. The next week, nothing. After their third session, the wine was offered again. This time Carol said yes. It became their routine: the envelope, a glass of red wine, and then she left. During the Christmas holidays, she found she missed her evenings at the kitchen table with Declan, their conversation flowing with an unexpected ease. Without consciously deciding to, they avoided any mention of their marriages or former spouses, but they happily chatted about what was happening at work or shared their thoughts about programmes they happened to have both watched. At first Carol had avoided any mention of the news or current affairs, fearing Declan's views might jar with her own, but he proved to be surprisingly moderate. Declan revealed that he was a fan of Leonard Cohen. They listened to his CDs as they sipped their wine. Declan seemed open and curious about the world; sometimes he was even funny, or at least flippant, and he was always eager to hear what Carol thought. She began to change her view of poor Mr Barry. There was a youthful quality to his conversation, a lightness to him that she might even have called flirtatious.

Carol mentioned the grinds to Craig when he came home for Christmas. She wasn't sure why. Had she been trying to prepare him? A seed planted so that if things developed it wouldn't come as a shock to him. Things? Was she losing her mind? Declan mightn't be old enough to be her father, but he wasn't far off. Is this what loneliness had driven her to? Craig had hardly looked up. 'What are you doing that for?' was his uninterested response. Unable to think of a reasonable answer, Carol had let the subject drop.

Things did develop. Had there ever been any real doubt that they would? One night as Declan showed Carol to the door, he stopped and gave her a dry peck on the cheek. He immediately backed away and apologised.

'I'm sorry. I shouldn't have done that.'

This struck Carol as a clever move on Declan's part. He hadn't done anything that he couldn't retreat from and yet it was now up to Carol to decide what would happen next. If she bristled and morphed back into Miss Crottie, then the matter was closed, but if she chose to say something softer, 'No. Don't be silly, I don't mind,' then surely that was his invitation to take things further. She opted for the latter and waited for him to move towards her, hold her, place a kiss on her mouth. Instead, Declan's arm came forward and opened the front door.

'Thank you,' he said.

She could feel her cheeks burning. How had she misread the signals? She hadn't. He had given the wrong signals. Had he changed his mind? She stumbled down the steps and rushed across the street to her car.

The following Thursday, she refused the wine and practically ran down the hall to the front door, calling goodbye with a degree of friendliness that was adequate but no more. The next week when Sally had gone upstairs, Declan came into the kitchen twisting the envelope of cash. He didn't just hand it over, so Carol was unable to leave.

'The other week,' he began. She felt herself become flustered.

Something was going to happen. For weeks she had been trying to convince herself that she had no interest in this man, he was too old for her, he was the father of a pupil, damaged goods, but in this moment all those arguments were lost.

'Yes,' she said quietly and waited for him to continue.

'The thing is . . .' He pulled out a chair and sat opposite Carol. 'It's been so long. I'm not sure how to do this.' He pushed a hand through his thick silver hair. 'Joan left us almost twelve years ago now.' He looked up at Carol. Was he looking for help? Did he want her to take over this speech? How could she when she had no real idea where it was going? Certainly, she had felt her hopes deflate when he'd mentioned Joan Barry. Was this all an awkward preamble to talk about his wife?

'I haven't since, you know.'

Carol was not at all sure that she did know.

'Last week I felt you were annoyed. Angry, maybe. And that wasn't what I wanted. I think I . . . I suppose . . .' He finally stuttered to a halt and looked directly at her. The room was still, heavy with the possibilities of what might happen next. She held her breath.

'Carol, can I kiss you?'

Even if she hadn't wanted to, she might still have agreed just to stop him speaking.

'Yes,' she said quickly and with a speed that took her by surprise Declan slid around the edge of the table and was kneeling in front of her, his mouth on hers. A poetry anthology fell from the table, landing with a slap on the floor.

'In case I don't see you.' Sally was brandishing a narrow bag covered with a rash of laughing Santas. Clearly it was a bottle of wine. Carol's first impulse was to knock it from her hands onto the floor. How dare she come in here, thinking that a mid-range bottle of rioja was going to make things all right?

'Thank you.' She willed her voice to be low and steady. Taking the bottle, she put it beside the two large suitcases at the foot of the stairs. In return Carol held out her ring binder.

'I think you'll find everything in here. It's all numbered. What time have you the movers?'

Killian reached forward to take the folder.

'Thanks. Thanks for doing all of this.' He indicated the boxes. 'I mean most of it is just rubbish really.'

Carol winced. It was as if he had struck her.

'Killian!' Sally admonished her brother.

'Sorry.' Killian shrugged. 'Poor choice of words.'

Sally put her plastic bag of cleaning products on the floor and the three of them shifted uneasily, as if they had all become aware of Declan's absence at the same time.

'Have you seen your father this morning?' Carol asked.

'I dropped in on my way over,' Killian told her.

'And how was he?'

'Fine. Fine. In good form.'

'Did he know you?'

'He did. Yes, in fairness to him, he recognised me straight away. He even asked after Colin.'

This was a lie. The truth was that his father hadn't taken his eyes off the television the entire time his son had been there. Killian had tried to make some conversation, but had quickly conceded defeat. It was too hard. That was the reason he preferred to visit alone. When he was in the room with Carol or Sally, it made him feel guilty and inadequate to hear the easy way they chattered on. What made it worse was that the silence between father and son couldn't really be blamed on Declan's condition; it had always been that way. Car journeys, breakfasts, walks to mass, all wordless. Killian could remember the great swarms of words that would fill his head at those times, all the things he wanted to say, to shout, at his father. The slab-like expression on Declan's face would make Killian furious, but incapable of expressing it. At least now that agony was over. All the answers were gone so there was no more need of questions.

'Well, I'll be off.' Carol bit the inside of her lip. She would not cry. These monstrous children had taken everything, but she would leave this house with her dignity.

'OK so.' Sally sounded keen, eager for this scene to end.

'That box is for your father. The one marked "Personal". Just a few things I thought he might like in his room.' She pointed to the corner. The cardboard box looked so insignificant. A life, an entire house, reduced to a picture of Declan with Joan and the children when they were toddlers, an extremely rustic ashtray made by Sally and a framed photo of herself and Declan looking windswept and carefree on a cliff top not far from her parents' bungalow.

Killian nodded. 'Thank you.'

Carol stared at him, his thin lips pressed together. She wondered how he was managing to cast himself as the hero in this scenario. Throwing the woman who had loved and cared for their father for nearly a decade into the street didn't seem like the right thing to do, but maybe their precious inheritance justified everything in his eyes. She was almost glad that Declan was so ill now that he would never know that this was how his children had treated her.

Carol pulled her two suitcases to the door. The wheels clicked across the floorboards, amplifying the awkward silence. She intended to just walk out, she knew there was no point in saying anything, and yet, she had to try one last time. She turned back to the children.

'Not for me, I'm leaving, but you both know your father was very clear. He never wanted this house sold.' She paused, looking for a flicker of understanding. 'You know that.'

Sally looked at her brother. Clutching the folder to his chest, Killian said, 'These aren't easy decisions, but this is a family matter now.' He stressed the word *family* with a bruising lack of subtlety.

Carol could feel the tears filling her eyes. She reached for the latch on the door.

'Carol.' It was Killian. His voice was softer. She allowed herself a hint of hope. A kind word to end things? A peace offering? She turned back towards him.

'Keys, Carol. We need the keys.' His hand was outstretched.

She broke. Her chin quivered and tears fell. She brushed them away angrily. As furious as she was with Declan's children, she was even more livid with herself for allowing them to see her like this. She fumbled with her key ring, hardly able to see.

'Would you like me to . . .' Killian asked helpfully.

'No!' she barked at him. Somehow she managed to extricate the house keys from the metal ring. She flung them on the floor and opened the door, dragging her cases down the three shallow stone steps. As she moved away down the short path she heard Sally's voice.

'You forgot your wine!'

Carol kept walking and heard the front door of number seven click shut.

Because of Declan, remembering felt like Carol's superpower. She sifted through every moment of the last ten years and treasured them. It was tempting to only focus on their best times or when things had settled down into a warm contentment, but Carol also remembered the harder times.

The beginning. That hadn't been easy. After that first scraping of chairs on the kitchen floor and their fumble of excitement, they had spoken in urgent whispers. A secret. Sally mustn't know – her attachment to the memories of her mother, the big exams coming up . . . Declan felt it was only fair not to upset her if they didn't have to. Carol was happy to agree. Not telling Killian or Sally meant she didn't have to explain her love life to Craig.

They met in the late afternoon or early evening, usually in Carol's house. Declan was able to park at one end of the development and then make his way unseen along a small service lane at the back of the houses, to knock at Carol's kitchen door. Remembering, Carol couldn't just play the memories in her mind; she found she had to pause and ponder, ask questions about what had really gone on. Had the clandestine nature of those early days made them both think that they had found a great love, when in reality they were just two lonely people, looking for someone, anyone, to cling on to? She blushed as she recalled the sex in her old bedroom, both of them performing for some unseen audience, each trying to convince the other that they were in a state of rapture. Had she really thrown her head back like some enthusiastic starlet and growled his name? Later, the physical side of their relationship had evolved into something perhaps more authentic, certainly more sustainable. It became brief and simple, more a way of confirming their connection than an act of unleashed animal lust. Sighs of contentment replaced the howls of ecstasy.

The following September, when Sally headed off to study catering at the tech in Waterford, Declan decided that he and Carol should go public. It felt like it was more his decision than hers but then he was the one who had wanted to keep things secret. Carol couldn't see why anyone would be particularly interested in her love life; it wasn't as if they were doing anything wrong. They were two single adults who had found a second chance for happiness. Perhaps predictably, the rest of Ballytoor didn't appear to see things in such simple terms.

The age difference.

The fact she was the teacher of his children.

That she was divorced.

That his wife had fled.

It seemed Carol's life was of much more interest to people than she had ever imagined. However, all the attention, gossip and judgement made Declan and Carol's bond even tighter. The excitement of their secret trysts was replaced by a sense of them having to shield each other from the rest of the world. It was around this time that Carol began spending more and more time at Stable Row until finally they had to admit that she had in fact moved in.

Carol found that she was increasingly reliant on Declan. Apart from a few teachers at work she really didn't have many friends, and those she did either seemed to disapprove of Declan or he found them irritating. Most of her old friends had left Ballytoor. One of the few who remained and met with Declan's approval was Eimear. She had left to study law and Carol had assumed that would be the last she saw of her – she seemed too sleek and sophisticated for small-town life – but she had surprised Carol and returned to join her family practice in Ballytoor. Hers seemed to be the lone voice of support for Carol and Declan's newfound love.

'Don't mind people. Haven't they little to be thinking about if they're that bothered by the two of you.'

'I know, I know.' Carol found it hard to take advice from Eimear. Everything in her life seemed so easy. Carol sensed that her friend really was above what other people thought about her. She wished she could be more like that.

'Oh, it'll all blow over soon enough – and haven't you both got your families?'

In fact, neither family had reacted well. Sally staged a sort of strike, refusing to come home in the holidays, while Killian had insisted on having what he called a 'man-to-man conversation' with his father. Declan had let his son vent his disapproval for a few minutes, and then, without apology or defence, began asking Killian about his own life. Robbed of the showdown he had wanted, Killian had slunk away, permitting them a grudging acceptance because he seemed at a loss for how else to react. Carol's son Craig had, at first, ignored the news, only acknowledging what his mother had told him when he revealed he wouldn't be coming home for Christmas. He used the phrase 'I don't think it would be right.' Carol was unclear about what exactly wouldn't be right, but reassured herself that Craig would stop caring once he understood that his mother's relationship wasn't going to impact him personally in any negative way.

After the drama of her divorce from Alex and then the wrench of Craig moving to London, Carol had allowed herself to think that her parents might be happy to hear that she had found love for a second time.

'Who?' her mother had snapped as if her daughter had just announced she was moving in with Donald Duck. 'Declan Barry? From Barry's Chemists? What age must he be now? Oh Carol, are you sure you know what you're doing?'

'Mammy, I love him.'

Moira flushed. Talk of any emotion, but especially something as intimate as love, was never welcome in her home.

'I mean what do you know about him? The first wife ran for the hills. What was her name?' she asked herself and then louder, 'Dave, what was her name?'

Her husband, who had been watching television, turned in his chair.

'Who?'

'Your one Barry. Married to the chemist. Ran off, left the kids.'

'I don't know,' Dave replied, but his response was too quick. Moira felt he wasn't really trying.

'You do. Dark hair. Never wore tights. The brother did away with himself. Walked into the sea out beyond Harbour View.'

'I never met the woman.'

This was too much for Moira. 'You *did*! She was in this house, for God's sake, looking for money for something or other. Was it new changing rooms for the GAA?'

'I don't know. I don't know her, her name or anything about the changing rooms.' This was a well-trodden conversational path.

Defeated, Moira turned back to her daughter. 'Well anyway, she must have left for a reason. He might be a drinker, or maybe he raised his hands to her.' Moira abruptly threw her own hands in the air. 'Dave Crottie. What are you talking about? Weren't you in the Chamber of Commerce with Declan Barry for years? You drove him to Limerick to play golf or something, didn't you?'

Dave pulled himself up in his chair. 'Oh, him.' Neither his tone nor his expression suggested he held Declan Barry in very high regard.

'What?' Carol snapped.

'Ah nothing. Nothing at all.' Dave had no desire to be drawn into this conversation.

'I just think you're moving very fast.' Moira folded her arms to indicate this was her opinion and it was very unlikely to change.

'Mammy, I'm not getting any younger. Can you not be happy for me? This is my second chance and I just think I've got to take it.'

Moira's pursed lips said more than any words could.

Even Alex bothered to text her, to inform her that she was embarrassing herself. Coming from him, after everything he had done, this almost felt like a badge of honour.

It struck Carol that they could make things easier for themselves. She tried out her idea on Declan.

'Couldn't we go away?' she had whispered in his ear one night after he had been complaining about all the unsolicited advice and judgement he had received in the chemist that day.

'Away? Where could we go?'

'Anywhere? Dublin? Up the country somewhere. A place we could just start again.' It seemed like a simple enough plan to Carol.

Declan furrowed his brow, unsure of how serious she was. 'What about here, the business, what would we do with it all?'

Carol shrugged. 'Sell it!' she replied with a breathy laugh.

Even as she said the words, she could see Declan's mood change. He became serious, any trace of whimsy or banter gone.

'Carol, I will never sell this house.' He paused. 'I mean it. I'll never sell. I couldn't.'

'OK, I understand. It was just a thought.' Carol wanted to get the conversation back to where it had been moments before.

'No. I should explain.' He took Carol's hands and spoke in a low, steady voice. 'I'm happy, so happy that we're together, and fuck anyone who doesn't like it.' He seemed lighter now, the atmosphere shifting. 'Fuck them,' he repeated and Carol smiled and squeezed his hands. 'It's just that after Joan left, well I can't leave too. I've got to stay here. I know the kids can be difficult but they've been through a lot, so you see I can't quit on them as well. This house, I want them to always be able to think of this as home. Do you understand?' He exhaled with relief at having had his say.

'Yes, yes I do.' She shook Declan's hands up and down to emphasise her words. Any mention of Joan made her tense. It was a subject she avoided and it seemed that Declan did also. She cleared her throat, knowing that if she had questions, now was the time to ask them.

'Do you . . .' She looked away from him. 'Do you still hope that she'll come back?'

Declan leaned in. 'No, love. Of course not. I could never forgive her for what she put us all through. And what's the other thing? Oh yes, I love you.' His lips found Carol's mouth, and when he pulled away, he looked into her eyes. 'What I'm talking about is the kids, not Joan.'

Of course, Carol had heard all the rumours about Joan Barry. She'd been put into an asylum with mental problems like her brother. A fancy man had whisked her away. Declan had beaten her. This seemed like the moment when she might have found out what had really happened, but none of the questions seemed fair. She felt as if they cast her in the role of gossip. She remained silent. Declan would tell her everything when the time was right. But then time itself became the problem.

Slow and swift at the same time. It had been only three years ago when the first signs of Declan's problem had begun to reveal themselves. Little things. He called her Joan when they were having an argument. He had accused the girls in the pharmacy of stealing when night after night he couldn't get the till to balance. Not knowing where the car was parked. They were all just isolated incidents, a shadow creeping across the landscape that neither of them wanted to acknowledge. It had taken over a year for Carol and Declan to admit there was a pattern emerging that couldn't be ignored. The diagnosis had confirmed their worst fears, and for Declan it was as if naming the condition had given his brain permission to embrace it without restraint. Things deteriorated rapidly.

'Who would have thought it would come to this?'

They were on their hands and knees in the bathroom, mopping up water with old bath towels. Declan had let the bath overflow. Usually when these things happened he railed against his illness or cursed himself, but tonight he seemed defeated.

'This wasn't the plan,' he said softly and reached out a hand to stroke Carol's arm.

'Shush.' She slid across the wet floor and held him. 'It's all right. No damage done.'

They stayed in their embrace on the floor for a few minutes and then Declan twisted his head to look into Carol's eyes.

'Don't feel you have to stay.'

'What?' Carol wasn't sure what he meant. Stay here, in the bathroom?

'Leave me. This doesn't need to ruin your life too. I mean it. Escape now.'

Declan's eyes had tears in them and as Carol gripped him tighter, she too began to cry.

'No. Never. Escape what? This is my life, you are my life – this is happening to *us*, Declan. I'm here, here for good.'

For nearly half an hour they stayed on the floor, hugging and weeping. It must have been what Declan needed to hear because he never mentioned her leaving again. Carol got him off the bathroom floor and took him across the hall to their bedroom. By the time she had dressed him in dry pyjamas, she doubted that he could remember the flood or even their conversation.

After the doctor had confirmed Declan's condition, Carol urged him to tell the children. At first he had resisted, not wanting them to worry, but Carol had insisted. Killian and Sally had a right to know. They would want to spend time with their father. Reluctantly Declan agreed, his only condition being that she had to be the one to tell them. He couldn't trust himself not to get upset if he tried to break the news, and that would only make matters worse. She phoned them both. They listened. Afterwards she congratulated herself on a job well done. She had told them the facts and without being dishonest had presented their father's prognosis as positively as she could. 'We'll have him a while yet, don't worry.'

As the days became weeks, she worried that in her attempt to sugar-coat the news she had failed to convey the seriousness of the situation. Neither of the children lived very far away, but even so, they didn't find the time to visit. They didn't even call to check in on their father. Carol knew that her arrival had driven a wedge between Declan and his children but surely this changed that? She tried to recall how close Sally had been to her father when Carol had first met them, but realised that back then all her attention had been on Declan. Sally had been a girl whom Carol suspected had had an adolescent crush on her before instantly despising her once she learned of the affair. As for Killian, she couldn't remember him being around very much even before she and his father had gone public with their relationship. She began to suspect that the Barrys had never been close as a family. How else could anyone explain their lack of interest now? It struck Carol that she and Declan had deliberately avoided speaking about their children over the years. To discuss their offspring might have been seen as acknowledging their former partners and Declan had made it very clear that he wanted no mention of Joan or Alex, unless absolutely necessary. Now Carol longed to ask Declan about his relationship with his children, but it seemed too late. Declan was busy losing himself; there was no point reminding him that his own children seemed to have abandoned him as well.

The first time his children saw what had become of their father was at Christmas. Sally was single, as she always seemed to be, and Killian brought his husband Colin. They had all made it very clear when accepting Carol's invitation that they wouldn't be staying long.

'Just a spot of lunch and give the old fella his new socks,' Killian had said breezily. Carol wondered if she had dreamed their phone conversation. Was her mind going, like Declan's?

Carol didn't want to see the children upset, but it was a gruesome kind of relief to see how they both reacted to their father on that Christmas Day. By then Declan's brain would get snagged on a single thought, like the pub bore near closing time. Usually it was a question he would ask for hours – 'Did you pay the phone bill?' – or a repeated snippet from the paper he still insisted on buying: 'They say tomatoes are going to be a fierce price.' Carol had become adept at nodding or giving a brief, non-committal reply. She knew better than to try to correct him or point out that it was just a few minutes since he had asked the same question.

That Christmas he was all about the lunch. 'What time did you put the turkey in?' At first the children found it funny: 'Are you starving, Daddy?' 'God, you're mad for the turkey.' But when he was still asking about it after they had eaten it and Carol had cleared away the plum pudding, their reaction changed. Sally went and sat by her father. 'Are you all right there? Sure we've had the lunch.' Killian followed Carol into the kitchen. 'He's not right. Has he been to the doctor?' Carol stared at him. She wanted to react angrily but somehow managed to remind herself how hard it must be for the children to see their father like this.

'I explained about his condition nearly nine weeks ago, Killian.'

He wiped at some grease on his chin. 'We just thought that you were . . .' He stopped himself. 'We didn't realise he was like this.' Killian looked genuinely upset. Carol's instinct was to give him a hug but she wasn't confident about how it might be received.

'He's still your father. Once you get past the repeating things,

30

your daddy is still in there. You can talk to him.' Carol hoped that she was saying the right thing.

The door burst open. Sally was crying. She grabbed Killian's arm. 'He thinks I'm Mammy. He's in there calling me Joan.' Her voice was an urgent whisper.

'Jesus,' her brother responded.

'He calls me Joan too.' Carol had meant this information to be reassuring but the children stared at her in horror.

'Sorry, no what I mean is, I'm pretty sure he doesn't think you are your mother. He knows who you are, it's just the name. It's the first one that comes up when he's trying to think of one.'

Had Carol imagined it or had Killian and Sally exchanged a furtive glance? Did they think that this was some sort of tiny victory for their mother? The woman, Carol reminded herself, who had abandoned her young family without a backward glance.

The door opened again and Colin stuck his head around it.

'Mm. Alone. I'm alone out here with him. Thank you very much.'

'Sorry.' Killian slid his arm around his husband's shoulders. 'I'll come out with you.'

They left Carol and Sally standing in silence on either side of the kitchen table where Carol had helped the seventeen-year-old Sally with her exams. They could hear Killian's voice coming from the dining room. 'Another glass of red, Daddy, or are you in the mood for a whiskey?'

The doctor had told Declan not to drink too much but Carol failed to see how a glass of wine could make things much worse.

Of course, things did get worse. She would be awoken by the sound of Declan screaming on the landing, trapped between the bedroom and the bathroom, not knowing where he was or where he was trying to get to. Begging him back to bed, knowing that as he finally fell asleep again he probably believed that he had been rescued by a kind stranger, his fluttering mind hopeful that when he awoke things would make more sense.

After she had stopped teaching to care for Declan full time, she tried to organise things so that the house and Declan were protected from each other. During the day she kept the bathroom locked to avoid any more floods, but then she found that he had been using the spare bedroom as a toilet. The rug was stained and stinking. She rolled it up and threw it out, as if removing the evidence meant that things weren't as bad as she knew they were. The air in the kitchen was acrid with the remains of smoke from all the pots he had let boil dry. Declan was not a man to do what he was told and his illness hadn't changed that. Carol realised that part of the problem was he had always been in control. They had always lived his way, but how were they to live now that he had lost his way? It was hard, coaxing him, often against his will, through the routine she tried to stick to.

Carol found scraps of joy where she could. Seeing Declan's face light up when she played a Leonard Cohen CD. Shuffling around the living room with him, swaying to the fairground rhythms of 'Dance Me to the End of Love'. She studied his face, his eyes squeezed shut, a faint smile tugging at his lips. Where was he? Who was he dancing with in his mind? Carol tried to think of each day as a small victory. She couldn't allow herself to think of how this story might end, or she too would be completely lost.

In a way the end came one night when Declan saw Carol as his attacker rather than his saviour. When she had tried to gather him in her arms on the landing he had fought her off. She fell backwards down the stairs, her head smashing through the bannisters. Dazed for a moment, she lay still, but when she tried to stand there was a searing pain in her ankle. She collapsed back onto the stairs and tried to push the pain to the back of her mind. She had to get up to Declan, who was now wailing into the space above her. Using her arms, she dragged herself up the stairs. She could see drops of blood falling from her forehead onto the carpet. Declan couldn't be consoled and she suspected that her ankle was broken. Phoning for an ambulance was the only option.

Looking back, she guessed it was the sight of her with her broken ankle sitting alone at the kitchen table that had set Killian's plan in motion. She just assumed that Sally had gone along with things. Sally wasn't where ideas came from. Seeing Carol living in number seven while Declan was in the nursing home receiving respite care, it was easy to imagine Killian's panic. His inheritance being occupied by this woman; what claims might she have unless he got her out? Obviously, his father would never agree so the only option was to move them both out.

It began gently enough.

'We're worried about you.'

'He's too much for you.'

Carol cursed herself for being so stupid. She honestly hadn't seen what was coming. Foolishly she had assumed that the children would just want the best for their father, doing what they could to make him happy. Clearly that was allowing him to remain in number seven for as long as possible. She had bought hospital bars to put on the side of the single bed in Sally's old room so that he would be safe at night. Covers were found so that he couldn't turn the knobs on the cooker. It broke Carol's heart but she found tiny shards of hope in trying to futureproof this house that Declan loved. So much of the man was slipping away but these rooms contained everything that remained. Take him away from Stable Row and he would vanish completely. Surely they all felt the same?

'I was looking for you. Where were you?' he would ask when she visited him.

'I'm at home in number seven waiting for you. You'll be back soon.'

His eyes widened like a young boy being reminded that his birthday was not far away.

'I just need to get rid of these things first.' She held up her crutches.

'Get rid of them!' he had shouted and the two of them had laughed. Carol pressed her lips against his and for just a moment things were as they had always been. Two people finding unexpected joy in each other. Carol told herself that when Declan got home, things would be better. He'd be happy, somehow he would find himself again. No more screaming into the night.

Declan never came home. Killian arrived at the house alone one evening when Carol had just got back from the nursing home and was throwing herself around the kitchen balancing on the backs of chairs and countertops. Her plaster cast was due to be removed early the following week, which meant Declan could be rescued. When she'd told him the good news that afternoon he had wept. He might not remember for long, but in that moment she knew he had understood and been overwhelmed by happiness.

Before she had a chance to tell Killian, he had slid a glossy brochure across the kitchen table.

'Great news, Carol. We've managed to get Daddy a place here.'

Carol glanced at the pamphlet. St Brendan's Residential Care Home.

'What's this?'

'It's only about half an hour away. On the back road to Macroom. Fairly handy really. We were all very impressed with it and they have a room available immediately, which is great.'

Carol felt her balance shift and she tightened her grip on the kitchen counter. She thought she understood what Killian was saying but was still having trouble believing it.

'What about here? I'm all set to look after him here.'

A slight twitch made Killian's lips pucker for an instant.

'We decided that coming back here would just upset him.'

'We?' Her voice was loud now. 'What are you talking about? Coming back here is the only thing that will make your father happy.' She sensed her anger had made Killian nervous. He smoothed down the front of his sweater as if brushing away invisible crumbs.

'It's just not sustainable, Carol.' The phrase sounded rehearsed.

'Killian, this is your father. You know he only wants to be in this house and I'm here to look after him. Happy to look after him.' Carol felt as if she was pleading for a man's life.

Killian turned towards the door. Was that it? Had he no interest in discussing his own father's future? Almost as an afterthought he said, 'Of course this means that the house will have to be sold.'

This was too much.

'Sold? Sell this house? How many times has your father said he never wants this house to be sold? And that was before all of this. That was when he just thought he might die first.' Carol pushed herself forward to lean on the back of a chair. 'Killian, you cannot sell this house. Your father won't stand for it.' Her mouth kept moving but there were no more words. If Killian couldn't understand what she was saying, the glaring truth of it, then there was no point in continuing.

'Carol, let's be real here. My father won't know if we've sold this house or if we've turned it into a petting zoo. He's lost his fucking mind. It's horrible. It's not what any of us want, but it's just the way things are.' A pause. 'So we will need you to move out.'

All at once everything made sense. This wasn't about Declan, it was simply the quickest way the children could think of to get her out. She stood as tall as her broken ankle allowed and told Killian, 'Your father would not want to see me without a home and you can tell yourself whatever you need to, but you know that is true.'

'Carol, you're hardly going to be homeless.'

'No? Well, where am I supposed to live?'

'I presume you must have lived somewhere before you . . .' He gestured to the room, unwilling or unable to describe her relationship with his father. 'So, I'd suggest you go back there.'

Carol had suddenly thought of something. Surely this would stop this wanton act of cruelty. 'Declan owns this house. It's his. You can't just swan in here and sell it out from under him.'

Disappointingly, Killian didn't look as if she had dealt him a killer punch – almost the opposite. His eyes sparked with what seemed like glee.

'Enduring power of attorney, Carol.' He said the words as if he was casting a spell. 'It's all legal and arranged.'

Carol felt dizzy, thrown off balance by this new information.

'How? When did Declan agree to that? He's in no fit state to agree to something like that. It'll never—'

'Eighteen months ago, Carol. It's all above board. It was your friend Eimear who did the paperwork.'

Her own friend? Why hadn't she said anything? Why hadn't Declan?

'I don't understand. I . . . I . . .'

'I guess when it came down to it, he didn't want you involved. It's a family matter.'

There was a steeliness in his voice, and Carol realised that he was enjoying this. Watching his father fade away might be a dark cloud in his life, but it was becoming clear to Carol that having an excuse to evict her from number seven was proving to be a very bright silver lining.

It was only in her teenage years that Carol had come to recognise how ill matched her parents and their sleek modern bungalow were. It crouched over the sea, a jumble of glass and concrete boxes. The architecture firm that designed it had won awards, and not just in Ireland. David Crottie, Carol's father, would mention this with pride to every guest, but while he considered the house a symbol of his success, neither he nor his wife Moira had ever figured out how to live in it. Overstuffed sofas covered in chintz looked like unwelcome visitors squatting either side of a suspended metal fireplace.

After the children left home Moira had developed an expensive interest in a certain sort of Irish art. Paintings by the likes of William Conor and Jack Butler Yeats in ornate frames now hung around the house looking ill at ease. Nearly half of one of the glass walls in the kitchen was blocked out by a pine dresser that seemed equally embarrassed to be there. The beautiful dark wood floors lay forgotten beneath acres of colourful carpets because Dave and Moira wanted the place to seem cosy. If it was a fight between the modern and the traditional, there were no winners here.

The Crotties themselves looked more like caretakers than owners. This was a house that was built for stylish willowy people, standing by the front door with their Afghan hound, a light ocean breeze giving them all life. The Crotties had never matched that description and now, in their late seventies, it seemed highly unlikely that they ever would. David Crottie, always less than statuesque, was now bent with age. He walked with his stooped head of thinning hair leading the way. He was one of those men who seemed incapable of controlling their own clothes. Ties worked their way to the side, shirt tails refused to stay tucked. No matter how much he spent on jackets he never managed to look like the successful businessman that he was. Moira had over the years become what some might have described as sturdy. Seen from the front she was almost square, her neat grey-haired head placed on her broad shoulders with no evidence of a neck. She had embraced the sexless fashion that being a woman of a certain age seemed to permit. A uniform of low-heeled shoes, slacks – heavy or light, depending on the season – and a thin padded gilet, no matter the weather. She was a woman who looked braced for action, in defiance of her age.

Carol was parked outside the bungalow, her cases in the back of the car. The engine was off but she couldn't face getting out and seeing her parents. Moving home at forty-eight, surely this was what failure looked like? What awful decisions had she made in her life that now brought her here? Her mother had always made it very clear what she thought and Moira Crottie had never softened her opinion of her daughter living with an older married man.

That's why it had been so hard to break the news to her parents about Declan and his illness. Sitting without Declan in the bungalow had felt like a cruel re-run of her years-earlier conversation about her new love. Moira didn't actually use the phrase 'I told you so', but she made sure to make her point.

'It's very sad I know, but that's what happens when there's a big age gap – isn't that right, love?' She turned to her husband for support.

'It's early onset, Mammy. You know that. There's no need to be cruel.'

'Cruel? Cruel?' She scanned the room, appealing to an invisible audience. 'Well excuse me for caring about my own daughter's future. You have no idea how long he'll live with this thing, and you stuck there, an unpaid nurse.'

'Mammy, this is the man I love. Jesus, can you not stop for just one second and see how awful this is for me. My heart is broken.'

Over the sound of sobbing, Dave Crottie tried to bring peace.

'Your mother is just worried about you, love. We're very sorry to hear about Declan, of course we are. Anything we can do to help you love, just ask.'

Beyond the bungalow the looming grey shape of a navy vessel made slow progress along the coast. The sky, sea and ship merged together to match Carol's mood. She checked her face in the rear-view mirror and gave a low moan. Heading into the house was going to be brutal but she couldn't delay any longer. As she opened the car door, the wind ripped it from her hand. She swore and bowed her head to tunnel through the storm to the house.

Her father greeted her with a studied cheerfulness, while her mother seemed oddly stooped and whispered her welcome as if it was Carol who was ill. Her teenage bedroom was unchanged except for all the cardboard boxes. These did not contain Carol's belongings; they were full of second-hand books and bric-a-brac that her mother was storing for the big charity sale she helped or-ganise every year to raise money for the hospice. Carol had asked her mother why they couldn't be stored in the garage that the car never entered. 'That place!' Moira had exclaimed as if their garage was in fact a portal to one of the circles of hell. 'You can't have the books smelling damp. No one will buy a damp book.' Carol just nodded. Given the number of boxes, it seemed not many people were buying dry books either.

'We'll clear them out tomorrow. Put the boxes in Linda's room.' Moira smiled and patted Carol's arm.

'What if Linda wants to stay?'

Moira raised her eyebrows. 'What? Come and see her parents? Maybe when one of us is dead, she might bother herself.'

'Mammy! Stop it. She's home every Christmas.' Carol chose not to elaborate and add that Linda loathed her visits and only returned once a year to prevent Moira and Dave visiting her in Edinburgh, where she was a social worker and lived with her girlfriend Rhonda. The fact that Linda was a lesbian was no doubt suspected but not acknowledged by her parents. They definitely weren't aware that Linda shared her home with a girlfriend who was a former nun from Ghana. Carol thought it was for the best.

'To be honest, we should have had them out of here already, but somehow we never thought it would come to this. Even this morning I said to your father that they wouldn't do it. I can't believe anyone can be this heartless. Poor Declan. Awful, just awful.' Moira shook her head.

'Poor Declan? Mammy, you never liked him.'

Her mother gasped indignantly. 'That is not true, Carol! I just didn't like him for you.' Moira shrugged. 'Do you think he knows?'

'Well I haven't told him and I'm sure the others haven't either.'

'What . . . what does he think is going on? Does he know where he is?' Moira's voice was low and hesitant, her curiosity tempered by not wanting to upset her daughter.

'He knows that he's been moved, but he still asks about coming home, back to Stable Row.'

Her mother nodded. 'And what do you tell him?'

'I lie, of course. Say he'll be home soon. Oh Mammy, you should see the way he smiles every time I tell him that.' Carol's face crumpled.

'Oh pet.' Moira hugged her daughter. 'May God forgive that pair for what they've done.'

Dave had made his way into the kitchen area and was standing by a vast chrome coffee machine that took up almost all of one coun-tertop in the kitchen. Dave saw it as a matter of professional pride that he had mastered the various steamers and valves. It wouldn't be fair to criticise his employees if he wasn't able to froth milk himself or strip the machine to be cleaned.

'Will you have a cappuccino, love?' he called to his daughter. Carol quite fancied one but the expression on her mother's face suggested she should decline.

'No thanks, Daddy. I'm fine just now.'

Moira studiously ignored the gleaming monstrosity, only referring to it as 'that thing' and pointedly brandishing the kettle if she was making tea or instant coffee. Moira liked to say to anyone who was available to listen, 'He pays more attention to that thing than he does to me,' while her husband fussed around the machine checking the pressure gauges.

Being back in the bungalow with her parents might have been more tolerable if she'd had any realistic plan of escape. How could she afford to leave? After the sale of her town house, she had paid off the mortgage and her father's debt, but she had given the remainder to Craig as a deposit for his flat in London. It was supposed to be a loan but as she sat in her teenage bedroom looking out of the window at a view of the garage wall, the chances of her son paying her back anytime soon seemed very remote. Carol tried to console herself by focusing on the fact that since Killian and Sally had forced her out of Stable Row and Declan into a nursing home, her mother and father now hated them more than Carol's relationship. The Crotties were united against a common enemy.

'Heartless.'

'If Declan knew that his own flesh and blood would turn on him like this . . .'

'You'd almost be glad he doesn't know what's going on.'

Craig finally rang her.

'Hello you!' She knew she sounded too relieved, overly happy, to hear from her son, but she couldn't help herself.

She didn't want him to worry about her so she asked him questions and they chatted about his life, the job, what he had been up to at weekends. Carol could sense the conversation was winding down to his standard sign-off – 'Well anyway, just wanted to see how you are' – so she volunteered a 'Granny and Grandad were asking after you.'

'Oh right. They're well?'

'Yes.' She purposefully didn't elaborate and allowed the line to go quiet. It was clear to Carol that her son had forgotten she was now living in the bungalow.

'Well anyway . . .' His sign-off. Carol quickly interjected.

'I'm living with them now, remember?' Another silence. She could almost hear the cogs of her son's mind whirring, then the click-clunk as it came back to him.

'Oh yes. Yes, of course. Declan. How is he?'

A flash of irritation and disappointment made Carol want to answer truthfully, to explain the full horror of Declan's situation, but she resisted. What was the point? Craig was young. Of course he didn't understand Declan's plight.

'Fine. Yes, just the same really.'

'Right. Well anyway, just wanted to see how you are.'

This time she allowed him off the line.

'Talk soon. Love you!'

When she hung up she wondered if Craig was a bad son, or maybe she was an overly needy mother or perhaps the problem was that every young person was now this selfish and self-involved? She wasn't sure. She doubted that Dave and Moira would ever have allowed her to forget what was going on in their lives. Was this all her fault? After the divorce all she had wanted to do was protect him, shield him from her problems. She never let him see her during a moment of weakness. If she wept, it was only when she was alone. She wanted Craig to think of his mother as happy and strong. Had she done such a good job that now he couldn't imagine his mother ever being vulnerable or in need of comfort or concern?

'Will you be going back to teach?' Moira asked on Carol's first night back in the bungalow. Dave cleared his throat, folded his paper and left the room. He evidently feared for how this conversation was going to go.

'I don't know.' Carol hoped that this might put an end to her mother's questions. The silence that followed was encouraging. Moira turned a few pages of her magazine, then without looking, up, said, 'It's just Declan doesn't need you now and you'd be as well being busy.'

Carol took a gulp of wine. This was her first night at home. She couldn't allow her mother to rile her so easily.

'I said I don't know, Mammy.'

The neat swish of a few more pages being turned.

'And you'll need money for rent, of course.'

Carol drained her glass and stared at her mother. Eventually Moira looked up.

'What?' she asked innocently.

'Mammy. I know you're trying to be helpful, but can you just, please, give me a chance? Today has been a lot. I had to leave my lovely home. I promised Declan that he was going back but now he's never going to set foot in there . . .' Carol's chin quivered and her eyes filled with tears.

'Oh Carol, love.' Moira heaved herself from her chair and came to comfort her daughter. 'You stay as long as you like.' She wrapped her arms around Carol, who let her tears soak into the wool of her mother's cardigan.

To call it a cottage suggested a degree of cosiness and charm that Sally's home sadly did not possess. Clad in water-stained grey plaster, it sat, featureless and box-like, just back from the road. Two squares of uneven tufted grass lined the short path to the front door. The windows seemed unnecessarily narrow, as if designed for a world where the sun was never expected to shine.

Sally was under no illusions about her little house. It had been rented in a rush after college, meant only to be a temporary refuge, to ensure she didn't have to move back into Stable Row with her father and that woman. Sally had seen it as her big statement, the gesture that would tell the world how upset she was, but it transpired nobody seemed at all concerned. Her father had accepted the news without protest or comment. Sally watched TV dramas where children and their parents had loud, tear-stained confrontations, followed by reconciliations and forgiveness. Why wasn't she capable of expressing her feelings in that way? She came to the conclusion that none of the people in her life had enough interest in her problems to listen, so why bother speaking up?

She tried not to dwell on the things that troubled her. Lying in bed when her thoughts threatened to overtake her, she would drown them out with reading or, more recently, listening to audiobooks. Still, there were nights when her anxiety lay in wait and crept up on her just before she could escape into sleep. Questions nagged at her like a faraway car alarm.

The central puzzle that kept her awake wasn't wondering about why she didn't have all the things she dreamed of, but rather, why she seemed to have settled for so very few of them. The house, her job, the embarrassing lack of friends or a social life – none of it was what she wanted. So why was she so accepting of it all? She knew she should be doing something to change her life but seemed incapable of taking any action.

Her problem, and she readily admitted it, was that she had always relied on other people to solve things. When she was a child, like everyone else, she'd looked to her parents. Then, when her mother disappeared, it was her older brother Killian who had tried to make things right. Then when Carol Crottie had come into her life, that was when she thought she had been made whole again, as if her wounds had finally begun to heal.

Thursday nights had been the highlight of her week. The evenings when she got to sit at the kitchen table and have the gentle attention of this bright, beautiful woman who would listen to her talk about life with all its dramas and romance. So many of the books and poems they studied were about love. Sally knew that if she had ever tried to explain her feelings to someone they would have dismissed them as a schoolgirl crush, but even now, Sally knew that wasn't true. There had been a bond, real, tangible, not just something that existed in her adolescent imagination. She could still remember how she had rushed her dinner on Thursday nights, so she would have enough time to brush her teeth and style her hair before Miss Crottie arrived. She had bought a scented candle from Cassidy's the newsagent to mask the smell of the family meal and give the room an air of so-phistication. She knew her father had noticed it, but thankfully he hadn't made a comment to embarrass her. Carol Crottie replaced everything that was missing in Sally's life. Her mother, her friends, none of that had mattered any more.

She couldn't pinpoint when she had felt a shift in their relationship, but imperceptibly a distance had grown between them. It was almost as if the kitchen table had begun to grow wider week by week. Sally had blamed herself. She'd lain in bed wondering what she might have said about the Earnshaws in *Wuthering Heights* to make Miss Crottie see her in a different light. It was only afterwards when she learned the truth that her hurt had been enflamed by fury. All that agony of self-recrimination when in fact she had been the injured party all along. Overnight, she realised she could only think of her father as a malevolent force in her life. Everything could be blamed on him. He had driven her mammy away and then stolen Miss Crottie from her. She felt tricked and humiliated by him.

Sally had never confided any of this to a single soul. To begin with she could hardly make sense of what had gone on and by the time she had understood, it all seemed so childish and long ago that it would be embarrassing to talk about it.

In her heart it felt like the defining moment in her life, worse even than losing her mother. She had been just a child then. This was different. The disappointment and betrayal she had suffered as a teenager because of Carol Crottie and her father, well, surely that was the root of all her problems? She knew that must be true, but still, she struggled to make a direct connection between the wrongs of the past and the dull limbo in which she now found herself. Why was she seemingly content to live in her draughty little cottage, getting to work by half past six every morning to feed sick people? She scrolled Facebook and saw the faces of girls she had been in college with, working in Dublin, Glasgow, London. Nights out at industry award shows, hen dos, babies. She envied them and knew that she did. Why couldn't she have the things they had?

Occasionally she would post messages of congratulations or a simple 'Looking good!' and sometimes the girls would even invite her to come and stay, or tell her about a job or a college reunion, but Sally always found some excuse to stay exactly where she was.

She wondered if Facebook was a part of her problem. Hours spent living vicariously through others, clicking through photos of weekend parties or big groups sat around tables in restaurants might have left her feeling inadequate and lonely, but instead of being shamed out of her inertia, she felt a comfort in watching the raised glasses and laughing faces of others. It was a social life devoid of anxiety or risk. Most of her friends on the site weren't actually people she knew. Some were mutual friends of people from school and college, others were just random friend requests. If people asked for her friendship she always accepted the request without question. Sally didn't care why they had stumbled into her timeline, she just enjoyed reading comments and seeing more photographs. Over time she had grown computer confident with these virtual strangers, liking more posts, wishing people happy birthday, even leaving the occasional complimentary message when someone changed their profile picture.

Sally posted nothing herself but happily reposted funny or heart-warming clips. She was careful never to post anything controversial or divisive. Others could post the diatribes from right or left; she preferred the clip of a monkey saving a kitten from a well. That had been her most popular repost. Forty-seven likes and lots of comments. That was how she'd come to meet Bindy. Her real name was Belinda but all her friends called her Bindy. Sally was one of them now. Bindy was no more active than other Facebook friends, but when they exchanged messages they weren't the usual brief and benign variations on wishing each other a nice day. With Bindy it was different. She seemed to feel able to tell Sally things about her life. She asked for advice, she shared her hopes and sometimes her worries. Nothing too extreme or emotionally taxing – the expensive weekend with work friends that she didn't want to go on, her landlord making comments about her cat, a haircut she hated. Sally found herself reciprocating. A few stories from work, just silly things about deliveries going wrong, or crazy complaints from patients. She mentioned her gay brother.

Recently, Sally had found herself typing messages about her father. His condition. The plan to put him in a home. She knew this stranger couldn't possibly care about any of it but just describing what was going on made Sally feel better. Bindy saw everything through Sally's eyes. When messages popped up, they were always so sympathetic to her. Suddenly her father's decline became something Sally was going through and not just a story that belonged to Killian and Carol with Sally lingering on the sidelines. She knew it was odd, maybe even unhealthy, to share things with a stranger when she had told no one in her real life, but that seemed to be how things worked on this site. Other people she didn't really know shared their woes with her too. A couple who were having treatment for cancer, a lady in the Midlands dealing with a flood. Even the aunt of someone who had lost her house in an Australian bush fire. Sally sent replies like the ones she got from Bindy. Sympathy, followed by words of encouragement. All variations on staying strong and things getting better. It was almost like the call and response during the prayers at mass, but still Sally meant what she said, and similarly she felt that when Bindy offered her cheerful platitudes, she too was being sincere.

When Sally watched movies where aliens invaded the Earth or monsters chased people through city streets, it reminded her of her life on Facebook. Like the creatures from space, her online friends were computer generated. She knew their friendship didn't really exist in the world she lived and worked in, but it felt real to her and, in the end, wasn't that the same thing?

On the brow of the hill, as the coast road left Ballytoor, was a small estate of semi-detached houses. Castle Heights, the misleading name of the development, was painted on a tasteful billboard. Killian and Colin lived two thirds of the way down a street called, for no obvious reason, Brook Drive. They had been there for a little over five years. They knew their neighbours to nod to, and might take their bins in if they were away, but they played no part in the residents' association, or community charities. This was not where they would put down roots. It was only a stepping stone to something nicer. Part of the reason they were still in Castle Heights was because Killian and Colin couldn't agree on what something nicer looked like. Killian imagined a Victorian villa out in the country somewhere, while Colin dreamed of a slick apartment with a roof terrace in Cork or Dublin. So they remained on Brook Drive.

Killian had never intended to spend his life in Ballytoor, but then Colin had happened. It had been an accident. Just a random encounter in a club in Dublin, his cowrie shell necklace glowing in the ultraviolet lights, smooth skin, just another fun one-night stand. But then in the morning when they discovered that they both came from Ballytoor, well, it seemed as if they were destined to be together. It felt like a real connection, a way of really knowing another person, when they lay in bed together shrieking with recognition.

'Of course I know Barry's Chemists!'

'No, your da is Hayes Travel? Mad!'

At first, Colin would come up to Dublin nearly every weekend. The idea of being a couple in Ballytoor seemed too daunting for both of them, but then as things continued Killian came back home. They met each other's fathers. Discovering that they were both motherless had been another *meant to be* moment. Colin lived rent-free in a flat above the family-owned travel agency, so when a job came up at the Ballytoor branch of the insurance company Killian worked for, it somehow made sense for him to give up on his life as a gay Dublin sophisticate and come back and settle down.

Colin had a theory about relationships. He thought they were like pot plants, so if you wanted them to grow you had to keep repotting them. Dating was the first pot, then they moved in together; after that, they bought Brook Drive, then the next pot was marriage and now Colin had decided it was time for another change in their lives. Killian agreed.

Killian was the older of the two, and yet he felt that it was Colin who made the grown-up decisions. Maybe it was because he had been to boarding school or it could have been that he'd started work in the family travel agency so young. He had a maturity and a seriousness that Killian sometimes envied. Looking back now, it seemed so unlikely that Colin had been in that Dublin nightclub. This was a man who always chose to rent them some cottage up the west coast for their holidays, while Killian looked longingly at pictures of Mykonos and Ibiza in the brochures that Colin brought home from work.

'What's wrong with these plates?' Killian was examining crockery stacked in a cardboard box by the back door.

'I'm restyling our formal table setting.' Colin said this as if this was something people did, like getting a new duvet cover.

Killian just stared at the oversized white plates, which he had in fact never liked. He exhaled through his nose. He had to decide if this moment was worth having an argument over or not. Could he really let this slide? Surely he had to point out to Colin that they never even had people over for a drink, never mind a dinner party, so why replace perfectly good, if quite ugly plates that he couldn't remember them ever using? Of course he could just have the row silently in his own head. Colin would claim that the old-fashioned crockery was the reason they didn't invite people over. Killian would then challenge his husband to reveal the names of these people that would sit around their dining-room table admiring their new plates. Colin would say Cath.

Cath was a single woman in her mid-thirties who worked with Colin at the agency. Killian imagined that she must be in love with Colin, because there was no other explanation for why she had agreed to a wage-cut and decreased working hours as the internet slowly stole their business. Hayes Travel these days mostly consisted of the rents from the flats upstairs, a few bus tours for Americans and organising the school trips abroad, and they only happened every second year.

Killian folded the flaps of the cardboard box closed. He was choosing not to have a fight tonight.

'Gin and tonic for my husband.' Colin handed Killian a glass.

'Thanks. What's this?' Killian pulled at a strip of green in his glass.

'Cucumber. It's much nicer than lemon. Really works with the gin. Try it.'

A slice of cucumber shouldn't be annoying, and yet Killian wanted to yank it out and slap it against the wall. Even the way it was cut was irritating, not as a simple round but lengthways. For fuck's sake. Moving as slowly as he dared, he followed Colin into the lounge.

His husband was making his rounds of the living room, brandishing a battery-operated lighter like a wand. He jabbed at the various candles, sparking them into life. Killian didn't dislike the candles and lamps, but it always struck him that Colin lived his life as if they were being observed, as if some omnipresent lifestyle guru was judging them at all times. If the TV was on, Killian really didn't understand why anyone would be looking at anything else. He sighed. Why was he quite so irritable tonight? He took a slurp of his drink to try to help himself relax.

Colin's lighting duties completed, he settled into the chair he always sat in and looked at his watch.

'Soon,' he said in a stage whisper and grinned at Killian.

'Soon what?'

An eye-roll. 'Soon Cath will be letting us know,' Colin explained over-patiently. 'She said it would be tonight or tomorrow.'

Killian lifted his drink and was surprised to find that it was empty.

Declan's new home must have been beautiful once: a large country house set among mature trees at the end of a curving avenue. When it had become a nursing home in the late fifties some trees had been felled to make way for a car park, but the house, on the brow of a gentle hill, had remained handsome. Sadly, over the years that had changed. A three-storey window-filled box added new rooms and then a long, low grey-brick building had been grafted to the opposite side of the house for a day-care facility. Each part of the present-day nursing home seemed surprised to find itself in such disparate company.

Visiting Declan had already become routine. Carol was familiar with every turn of the road and she found she could clear her mind as she drove there. She enjoyed the time she spent alone in the car. It was a respite from her parents and their oppressive concern. Even if they managed to edit what they said around her, their worry was a constant presence. Sometimes, even after the drive was over, Carol found she had to sit in the car park for a few minutes to allow whatever wave of anger or sorrow she might be experiencing to wash over her. It was best not to bring those emotions into Declan's room. His moods were unpredictable enough without her churning them up further.

Sometimes he would greet her with a smile. Those were the good days. He would use her name repeatedly and engage Carol in a form of conversation that was convincing, for a few minutes anyway. Then the endless loop of questions began.

'How are you keeping?'

'You're busy?'

'How's everyone?'

'You're keeping well yourself?'

His voice sounded interested and his face was alert. For a moment Carol allowed herself to believe that things were as they had been back in Stable Row. He might mention a red wine he wanted to try or some annoying customer from the shop. She smiled encouragingly as he asked his stock questions and then seemed to listen to her answers, but it was a performance. Carol wasn't sure who it was for. Did it make him feel better to appear capable, or was he just trying not to upset his visitors?

On other days, the bad ones, he sat impassive and cold. No questions or cajoling helped; even playing his favourite CDs failed to ignite a spark. Carol imagined that the man who knew her name was still in there somewhere but for whatever reason, he was refusing to appear. Maybe he was just tired, exhausted by the burden of his situation, or maybe the absence of even a spark of hope had shut the whole man down. Carol felt that the thought of returning to his true home on Stable Row had given him some strength. As Declan's hopes of that happening receded, so did the man. Once she had assessed his mood, Carol would sit with an unwavering smile on her face and chatter on, while Declan stared into the middle distance. Occasionally he would turn his head to look at her, and Carol couldn't help but feel a judgement in his eyes. She should have done more to stop this happening, or at the very least, she should be trying to help him escape. Maybe he was just willing her to stop talking so what was left of his mind could operate uninterrupted. If she was being totally honest with herself, and sometimes sitting in the car after her visits she was, Carol didn't really believe any of it. She was just projecting her feelings onto Declan, the way dog owners did to their pets. These days weren't good or bad, that was just her way of making some sense of them. They were all just the same, unforgiving and endless.

The staff knew Carol and she recognised most of the faces in the home. As she walked through the corridors, she heard the way the nurses spoke to visitors and she began to detect the hierarchy of pity. Children visiting elderly parents were at the bottom of the pile, then came elderly husbands or wives coming to visit their other halves, but as a younger woman she was awarded the greatest amount of sympathy. As soon as she stepped through the doors she became a tragic figure, but also an awkward one. No one seemed sure what tone of voice to use with her. Because of her age she existed in a limbo somewhere between a child and a spouse.

Declan, too, was an anomaly in St Brendan's. He wasn't one of the grey, broken-winged birds one saw being wheeled down the corridors towards the television room, not yet. His was not the wet gummy smile of so many of the residents. He sat in his too-tall chair, still broad, still strong, but for how long? His grey hair remained thick, but now it often lay dull and unwashed. Carol could see his face becoming gaunt. The grey patches of stubble on his hurriedly shaved cheeks gave him an abandoned look. Sometimes Carol saw him morphing into just another resident.

Killian and Sally were not frequent visitors but oddly, despite her antipathy towards them, Carol found she didn't blame them. These visits weren't easy for anyone. If you found yourself sitting by a hospital bed you could at least sympathise and assure the patient that they were looking much better and would be home soon. Alternatively, in the worst-case scenario, you held a waxy hand and whispered your goodbyes. But this, this was so much harder. No hope in sight nor any end.

Once, Carol's visit had coincided with the doctor making his rounds. After he had finished examining Declan, he turned to Carol. It wasn't clear if he thought he was delivering good news or just a fact when he said, 'He has a very strong heart.' Carol had felt her own break a little more.

Moira was beginning to worry. Carol should have been back by now. She had set off to see Declan just after lunch and it was now gone seven.

'That Mallow Road is lethal.'

'Would you stop it? She'll be fine. She probably just stopped in town or called in to see someone.'

'Who? Who is she visiting at this time of the night?'

Dave put down his paper. 'I don't know, do I? If she's going to be much later, she'll call. Would you sit down, woman? You're doing my head in.'

'If she's able to call,' Moira muttered and then announced, 'It's pitch black out there. I'll turn on the porch light for her,' before scurrying to the hall.

Through the frosted glass she thought she saw a dark shape. Opening the door, Moira saw that it was Carol's car parked outside. She stepped forward and peered into the night. There was someone at the wheel of the car. What was going on? Moira picked her way across the gravel in her slippers to the driver's door. It was Carol, her head bent forward, leaning on the steering wheel. Moira panicked and rapped urgently on the window. 'Love, are you all right?'

To Moira's relief, Carol sat up and looked at her mother, but then Moira saw her face. Her eyes were swollen from crying and her cheeks were wet with tears.

'What is it? What's the matter?' She pulled at the door and Carol opened it from the inside.

'Oh, Mammy. It was awful, just awful.'

Hours earlier she had set out to visit Declan. She had some clean shirts for him and a bottle of pomegranate juice she had found in the health food shop. She had read somewhere that it helped with memory. It was a crisp clear day, the trees silhouetted against a pale blue sky. Carol sang along to cheesy pop on the radio instead of replaying her usual inner arguments with Moira or Killian. Everything was awful, it was just that for a short time they seemed slightly less awful.

Carol parked the car and felt strangely unburdened as she strode towards the main entrance of the nursing home, swinging her plastic bag. Inside, she nodded to various members of staff. Past the nurses' station, at the end of a long corridor, there were some steps up to the right and that was where Declan's room was located. It seemed tucked away, as if the main action was happening elsewhere. Certainly that was what it sounded like when Carol sat beside Declan's bed, the clatter of trolleys and beeping of phones always quite distant.

On this day, when Carol stuck her head around the door of the room, Declan was in a chair, his head slumped over. She assumed he was asleep and made her way quietly to the other high-backed chair and sat down to wait for him to wake from his nap. She took out the folded shirts and reached across to put them on the bed.

It was then that she noticed that Declan wasn't asleep, he couldn't be, his eyes were open. She immediately feared the worst and fell to her knees in front of him, but he was breathing. A loose string of drool connected the corner of his mouth to his chest. She shook him gently.

'Declan.' Nothing. 'Declan love, it's me, Carol.' She tried to move his shoulder. Declan made a small groaning sound and his head flopped to one side. Carol stood and then, dropping the bag with the juice on the floor, raced from the room. She half ran, half fell down the short flight of stairs and headed for the nurses' station.

'Excuse me. I need help. Help!' There was no one behind the counter so her voice became louder.

'It's Declan Barry. I need help!'

A nurse came rushing around the corner. She looked like a child to Carol, with her cap perched on tight curls and her arms flailing.

'What is it?' she called and then she stopped, beaming. 'Miss Crottie!'

'Sorry. It's Declan, Declan Barry.' Carol pointed back down the corridor towards his room.

'It's me, Liz Quinn. You taught me English.' The nurse seemed delighted by this revelation. Now that Carol looked again, the wide little face framed with curls did seem familiar.

'Oh yes, of course,' she found herself saying. 'Please can you help me. It's my partner.' She pointed again. She hated using the word partner, but she was aware that she could hardly refer to a resident in a nursing home as her boyfriend.

The two women rushed back to the room together. The nurse crouched down before Declan.

'Mr Barry, is it? How are you doing? Let me just have a little look at you there.' She took his pulse. 'Seems fine.'

She said, looking up at Carol, 'Let me just run and get his chart.'

'OK.' Carol felt completely useless. She bent and kissed Declan on his cheek. Taking his hand, she knelt by him, waiting for the nurse to return.

After what was probably only a few minutes, but felt far longer to Carol, the nurse Liz returned with another woman who Carol recognised. She was older and wore business suits rather than any sort of nurse's uniform. Carol wasn't sure if she was the matron or some sort of manager. They'd spoken the day that Declan had been admitted. Her name was . . . Deirdre? Denise? Something with a D. Carol stood.

'Miss Crottie, isn't it?' A hand was offered and shaken.

'Carol, please. Nice to meet you again.'

'Miss Crottie used to teach me,' Liz offered brightly.

'Isn't that wonderful. Nurse Quinn, can you get back to the nurses' station there? Thank you.'

A chastened Liz crept from the room.

'Sorry about her. New.'

'Don't be mad. I think I remember her. Sweet.' She cleared her throat and reached out to put a hand on Declan's shoulder. 'He seems much worse today. Has the doctor seen him?'

The other woman bit her lip. 'He did – he saw him last night, in fact.'

'And what's wrong with him?'

'Oh, nothing. Well, he's no worse if you know what I mean? No, his medication has been changed, that's all.'

Carol was still confused. 'But why change his drugs?'

Deirdre or Denise seemed a little uncomfortable. 'The family felt Mr Barry was upsetting himself. This is just till he settles in properly.' She indicated Declan, his head slung low across his chest.

'You've done this deliberately?' Carol was appalled. 'What drug is he on now?'

The other woman winced slightly. 'Mm.' She paused. 'The family have requested that Mr Barry's medical care only be shared with his immediate family.'

'But I'm . . .' Carol began, full of righteous indignation, before the truth came crashing down on her. She was what? In that moment she felt like some crazy ex-girlfriend who refused to get the hint. It's over and you are not wanted any more.

Carol looked around the room, frantically trying not to cry.

'I left some clean shirts there.' She pointed at the bed. 'And a bottle of . . .' She began to form the 'p' of pomegranate but knew that before she finished the word she would be howling. She fled from the room without saying anything more. A voice followed her down the corridor.

'Talk to the children. I'm sure this can all be sorted out.'

Carol wanted to kick the walls and rip the pictures off their hooks. How dare those two humiliate her like this? Tears were falling freely now. She caught a glimpse of Liz Quinn behind the counter of the nurses' station. She looked appalled to see her teacher in such a state.

'Goodbye, Miss Crottie,' she called weakly.

Afterwards, Carol wondered how she had managed to drive home without crashing. Tears had streamed down her face the whole way, and her voice became hoarse from screaming obscenities at Killian and Sally. Once she had managed to get back to her parents' bungalow, she had collapsed onto the steering wheel, a sobbing heap. She had been there almost an hour when her mother found her and brought her inside.

Why was she tormenting herself? Carol was lying in bed with her laptop open looking at the pictures of number seven Stable Row. There was even a virtual tour, for God's sake. Stabbing at the mouse pad, she was able to move from room to room, but they looked drab and small without the things that had made the house somewhere that was loved. Carol was sure the estate agent had told Killian and Sally that it was a mistake to try to sell the house unfurnished, but such was their unseemly haste in wanting Carol out, they hadn't cared.

After all the tears of the previous night Carol felt, not exactly numb, but a sort of detachment. The house she had lived in, the man she loved, both still in the world but beyond her grasp. It was as if her old life was continuing in some parallel world and she had somehow slipped out of it, doomed only to glimpse it in shadows and hear its echoes for the rest of her life.

Worried that her mother would barge in and catch her wallowing in self-pity, Carol glanced at her phone. Not quite seven; Moira wouldn't be up yet. She noticed a message alert from last night. It must have arrived when her mother was putting her into bed and feeding her Night Nurse and warm milk. The message was from Eimear.

All OK? You seen FB? Killian enjoying his ill-gotten gains. Prick. Call me. E xx

Without pausing to consider if it was the best course of action,

Carol brought up Facebook on her laptop. Why was she still friends with Killian on this site? She must unfriend him, unless of course he had beaten her to it. No. Still friends. Carol checked his page and gave an involuntary gasp. Killian had posted the caption 'Christening Party!' above a photograph of himself and his husband in a hot tub, along with that red-haired woman who worked with Colin. Looking closer, Carol could see the side of the shed that Declan had paid for, and the back wall of Killian's house. His father was in a home he didn't want to be in, separated from the woman he loved, and this fucker was out buying hot tubs!

Carol jumped up from the bed and pulled on some jeans. She grabbed a sweatshirt from the top of one of her cases and stormed out of her room. Her father was in the kitchen standing beside the coffee machine, peering at a gauge. He turned when he heard Carol's footsteps.

'Good morning love. Coffee?' he asked brightly, obviously surprised to see his daughter up so early, given the state of the woman who had arrived home the night before.

'No thanks. I'll be back later.' Carol grabbed her coat and keys and pulled the front door shut behind her.

At this time of the morning, Carol was confident they would be there. As she reversed out of the driveway she sent an angry spray of gravel up in the air. She knew she was driving too fast but she didn't care. She opened her window. The chill morning air felt wonderful on her face, still tight from all the crying of the night before. Hunched over the steering wheel she spat out swear words and insults, all the things she would hurl at the smug faces of Killian and his milksop of a husband. It was only as the car approached the long hill into town and Carol was forced to slow down that her foul-mouthed monologue began to run out of steam. By the time she was driving around the market square, her voice had stuttered into silence. The anger she had felt was replaced by uncertainty. What was she doing? Did she really want these men to see her like this, unhinged and flailing on their doorstep? No. That was no doubt the sort of woman they thought she was anyway. She slid her car into a parking space by the bank and leaned back in her seat. If she was going to speak to Killian, she would do it on the phone. A brief surge of fury pulsed through her as she allowed herself to imagine that call.

Finally, she got out of the car and walked down New Street to The Koffie House, a small bakery and café run by a Dutch woman who had moved to Ballytoor for no obvious reason. Carol liked the coffee but she always found the owner, Noor, a little harder to warm to. She was so relentlessly cheerful, not in a friendly, pleased-to-see-you way, but in a glassy-eyed, frozen-smile, part-of-a-cult sort of way. Her blonde hair was tightly plaited and then tied around her rosy-cheeked face in a variety of styles that all managed to irritate Carol. Bracing herself for the usual blast of positivity, she opened the shop door only to be greeted by a Noor she had never seen before. Her brow was furrowed, her mouth turned down. A plastic-glove-clad hand was thrust across the counter and grabbed on to Carol's arm.

'How are you?' the baker asked, her head tilted to one side; she always sounded as if she was speaking through a mouth filled with saliva. It made Carol shudder. She looked down at the hand clutching her sleeve.

'Fine, thanks. Just fine.' She moved back to escape the caring grip.

'It must be so hard.' Large blue eyes, of the type one might find in a painting for sale in the art section of a department store, peered with feeling at Carol. She stared back for a moment and then broke the silence by asking for a large Americano.

'Of course,' Noor said, nodding her head as if to suggest she understood how healing Carol would find a freshly brewed hot drink.

As she walked back to the car with her coffee, Carol became paranoid that passers-by were giving her furtive glances. People had to talk about something and it made sense that it would be her. She hated the way that being a teacher in a small town made you a public figure. Her divorce and then her romance with Declan all deemed worthy of idle gossip, even among people who had never sent a child to the school or had any dealings with her, but this was worse. At least previously she had attracted attention through the vagaries of her love life, so that while it was annoying, it was also a little sexy, almost glamorous. Now, the looks on the faces of the people she passed made her feel pathetic. She got in her car and slammed the door. It was time for her to do something and fight back.

'Am I being a moron?'

Carol's friend Eimear, sitting across the wide slate tabletop, tried to summon some enthusiasm for the conversation that was about to occur. There was nothing new to tell her friend, and yet she understood she had to keep telling her, reassuring her that every avenue and possible solution had been explored and found wanting.

'Carol, stop beating yourself up.' In an effort to change the mood, Eimear stood. 'Look, is it too early for a Bloody Mary? I think I've got some mix in the fridge.' She tilted her head and smiled to cajole her friend into a better frame of mind.

'Oh, go on then. Not too strong. I've got the car.'

Eimear opened one side of her giant American fridge. Carol noticed that it appeared to be packed solid. With what? Eimear lived alone. Maybe the back of every shelf was just full of rotten vegetables and murky slime. Gazing around the large clinical kitchen, she doubted it. Eimear was one of those people who made living well look easy. Even at this time of the morning, away from her well-cut, expensive solicitor's suits, she had opened the door in a perfectly ironed blouse draped over jeans that appeared to have been made to measure. Her face looked fresh, with just a suspicion of make-up, and her bare feet sported a fresh pedicure. Carol had to remind herself that this was the woman with a full-time job, whereas she, the woman with hair fastened in an uneven wedge and wearing a sweatshirt with a very obvious stain on the left breast, was the lady of leisure.

'Pepper?'

'Yes please.'

Eimear twisted the large mill over each glass.

'Here you go.'

'Cheers!' Carol gave a feeble toast.

'To better days,' her friend replied and they clinked glasses.

The two women took a sip.

'So good.'

'Not too spicy for you?' Eimear asked.

'Perfect. Just perfect.'

They drank their drinks in silence. Perhaps Eimear was waiting to see if it was possible to change the subject, but clearly the Bloody Mary had not shifted Carol's focus. After a moment or two she sighed and asked in a vague voice, addressing the air as much as Eimear, 'Am I doing the right thing?'

Eimear put her glass down, her stock responses at the ready.

'It's not about you doing the right thing, it's about them doing the wrong thing.'

Carol looked at her friend.

'The wrong thing you helped them do,' she reminded her.

Eimear rolled her eyes. 'Carol, we've been over this a thousand times. I couldn't tell you, I'd have lost my job. I just assumed Declan would tell you. I'm only his solicitor because you introduced us. There is no way any of this is my fault.'

'OK, OK, but why? That's what I keep asking myself, why would Declan give that power to Killian, why not me? It doesn't make sense.'

Eimear rattled the ice in her glass. 'All I know is, they didn't force him. He chose to do it.' She hesitated. 'I suppose it could be—' She stopped herself. 'No. Nothing.' She took a sip of her drink.

'What? What were you going to say?'

'Well, and don't jump down my throat for saying this, but he wasn't exactly keen on you making decisions, was he? Maybe this way he thought he stayed in control. I don't know.' Eimear shrugged.

'I made decisions,' Carol said defensively.

'When they were the decisions Declan would have made anyway,' Eimear said quietly. She didn't want to antagonise her friend.

'That's not true.' Carol didn't sound convinced.

'What about holidays? Did you ever go abroad?'

'No.'

'Because Declan didn't want to. The party you wanted to have? That didn't happen. For fuck's sake – do you remember when you wanted to repaint the front door?'

Carol couldn't look at her friend. It was all true but not true at the same time. Eimear was making it seem a certain way and that was never how it felt to Carol.

'OK. All right. But even if you're right, we both know he didn't want this to happen. He must have thought Killian would respect his wishes. I don't know. Was I wrong not to fight? I feel like I just threw in the towel, not just for me but for Declan.'

Eimear had sympathy for her friend, but at the same time wondered how often she would have to reassure her in this well-trodden conversation.

'Carol, please listen to me. Anyone will tell you the same thing. If you pick a fight, it's going to cost a fortune and it's more or less certain you'll lose. There is no way to prove you lived in that house for more than five years. You're not on a single utility bill; even your bank account only changed to that address when you sold the town house and that was only three years ago. The same with the electoral register.' Her voice was low but firm.

'If only I'd—'

'Stop it. Just stop it, Carol,' Eimear interjected. 'There are a thousand "if onlys" and "what ifs" but they're no good to you now. You couldn't have planned for this, any of this. Not Declan's condition, not the reaction of his kids.'

Carol bowed her head. 'Yes, you're right, I know you're right.'

Eimear glanced at the digital clock on the microwave. She had a hair appointment at eleven o'clock. She drained her glass, hoping it might give her friend the hint.

'What you need to do now is focus on the positive.'

'The positive?' Carol sounded unsure.

'The things you can change. I know a solicitor over in Clonakilty, he owes me a favour. I'll get him to send a letter threatening legal action if they don't allow access to Declan's medical records. They'll change their minds, I guarantee it. It's not worth the legal fees to them. They were just trying to flex their muscles, show you who's boss. I can't believe they really care enough to fight you on something small like this.'

Carol finished her drink and studied her friend.

'It doesn't feel small.'

Eimear closed her eyes and bowed her head. 'I'm sorry. Of course, but you know what I mean, and I'm right.'

'I hope so.'

'Promise,' Eimear said with a smile as she showed her friend towards the door past the open shelves of books and random ornaments that looked as if they had never encountered a speck of dust.

'Thanks, Eimear. I'm sorry to dump it all on you, but it's hard to talk about, especially at home.'

'Don't be silly. Always here.'

At the door Carol stopped and turned.

'And just as a hypothetical, what would happen if Joan Barry came back into the picture?'

'Declan's wife? Are they divorced?'

'No. Well, not as far as Declan knows.'

Eimear considered the scenario for a moment.

'Well she'd have more claim on the house than you, even though she did abandon the family home. And the money from the sale. I mean it would be an almighty legal mess. Why? Have you heard from her or something?'

Carol shook her head and gave a short laugh. 'No. God no. Nothing like that.'

Her parents both looked at her with relief when she walked into the kitchen of the bungalow. Dave lowered his sunglasses and began to ask where she'd been, then he noticed the empty Koffie House cup his daughter was putting in the bin. Her father raised his eyebrows. Carol laughed.

'What? I like their coffee and there isn't a Crottie's in town.'

'We have the big machine in SuperValu,' he muttered defensively.

Moira patted a chair for Carol to sit in. 'You were out fierce early love. Where were you off to?'

Carol sat with a sigh.

'It was stupid. I got angry and thought I'd go and confront Killian and Colin.'

Her mother raised a hand to her mouth. 'You didn't?'

'I didn't.'

'Thank God for that.' Moira relaxed back into her chair.

After her experience in town, it felt comforting for Carol to be with people who were on her side, who could see how she had been wronged, but not judge her too harshly for it.

'I saw pictures,' she explained. 'Online. It looks like they might have already sold the house. They've certainly started to spend the money. A hot tub. I ask you, a hot tub, larking around in a new hot tub while their father is left to rot in that care home. I just lost it. Stupid, I know, but there you go.'

'A hot tub?' Moira asked. 'Is that the same as a jacuzzi?'

Carol wasn't sure why this information was relevant but also realised she didn't really know the answer to her mother's question.

'I think so. Something similar anyway.'

Moira rolled her eyes. 'Full of germs, those things.' She left unspoken her deep desire for Killian to catch some life-threatening disease. 'I would no more get into one of those . . .' Her voice trailed away.

'Well, fortunately I don't think we'll be getting an invitation any time soon.'

Dave stood and approached his gleaming colossus. 'Can I get anyone anything?'

'No thanks,' the two women replied in chorus.

His back still to the table, Dave said, 'The house hasn't been sold anyway.'

Carol waited for him to elaborate but he just stood at the machine. She looked at her mother for some sort of explanation.

'We've been talking,' Moira said, adding 'your father and myself.'

Dave turned back to face them.

'You tell her,' Moira instructed her husband. Dave cleared his throat.

'Nothing is settled and I don't know if we're doing the right thing, but' – he made eye contact with Moira for reassurance and then looked back at Carol – 'we've put an offer in on the house.'

It took a moment for the news to sink in.

'What?' Carol asked.

'An offer,' her father repeated, 'a serious offer. We've put it in and the agent thinks it will probably be accepted.'

Moira nodded, content that her husband had explained the situation properly.

Carol leaned forward.

'Daddy, there is no way they are ever going to sell the house to us, to you.'

Dave waved away her concern.

'I'm using a company name. It holds all the property leases. I'm not even listed as a director.'

Carol suspected nefarious tax arrangements so refrained from asking her father why that might be.

'They'll never put two and two together,' Dave continued, 'and why would they go looking? We're offering the full asking price.'

Carol felt a bubble of excitement rising; a glimmer of optimism she had not experienced for many months. But she knew she should be careful, not let her hopes run wild. Her life did not seem like one where things went well, so why should this be any different?

'When will we know?' she asked.

'Today? Monday at the latest. And to be clear, love, if someone else is after it or there is a bigger offer, we can't be going wild here. To be honest, I'd say it's overpriced as it is.'

Moira reached forward and put a hand on Carol's.

'And you're not to be worrying about Linda and Brian.'

Carol had not been giving her brother and sister a second thought. As if reading her mind, her father explained: 'This will be your inheritance. We'll get it all legal and sorted in a new will. Myself and your mother decided the money would be more use to you now than when we're gone.'

Carol simply nodded. As grateful as she was for this intervention, she hated how it made her feel. She had come back home as a last resort, and maybe for some comfort, but she hadn't really expected her parents to solve her problems. If this wasn't exactly humiliating, it certainly felt very similar. It was pathetic. She had a child of her own, she had watched her lover revert to childhood, what more did she have to do before she could finally feel like an adult?

Moira had got up from the table and was chopping mushrooms.

'We're going to have brunch.' The word was said as if it was a foreign delicacy sourced from beneath the waves or found by trained pigs.

'Eggs,' Dave said to his daughter as if translating what his wife had said.

'Lovely,' Carol said, a wave of gratitude washing over her. Even if everything fell apart, as she suspected it would, she knew it was just churlish pride to resent her parents' help.

Moira was cracking eggs into a bowl.

'Have you heard from Craig?'

Carol rolled her eyes. Her mother couldn't allow them all to just enjoy this moment. She had to needle her.

'Yes, he phoned the other day, actually.' She knew she sounded defensive.

'Big of him.' Moira's mouth tightened, expressing everything she felt about the transgressions of her grandson. It wasn't that Carol disagreed with her mother. She also felt let down by Craig. Sometimes she wondered if her son had disapproved of her relationship with Declan so much that he was pleased this was how the story was ending, but in her heart she knew it was worse than that. He just didn't care. He was completely wrapped up in his own life, whatever that might look like. His mother's dramas had nothing to do with him.

Carol went and retrieved the cutlery from the kitchen and began to set the table.

Another brunch, a different house. Killian Barry was toasting muffins while Colin was watching a YouTube video on his laptop that promised to reveal the best way to poach eggs.

'Did you talk to Sally about it yet?'

Killian didn't take his eyes from the toaster. He had already burned two muffins.

'No, not yet. No need. I'll wait till they view the place. See what they say then.'

Colin had paused the video and was holding two eggs.

'Killian! That's the whole thing. You never listen to me. The Jordan guy said it was a firm offer and they weren't interested in viewing the house. It's not even subject to a survey being done or anything.'

'Really? Jesus, well, we have to accept that then. Full asking price?'

'Full.'

'Seems too good to be true. There's got to be something fishy going on.'

'Jordan doesn't think so. Some property company from Cork apparently.'

'What would they want with number seven? It makes no sense.'

'Flats?' Colin sniffed the air. 'Are those muffins all right?'

'Fuck. Ah just fuck it.' Killian pulled more blackened muffins from the toaster.

This was the sort of small incident that could send Killian into a spiral of self-reflection and that never ended well. Of course the muffins were burnt, things always went wrong in his life. OK, maybe not wrong precisely, but certainly never completely right. His was a life in which perfection seemed just out of reach. Killian had very clear ideas about what he wanted, and he had managed to achieve many of his goals – or almost achieve them, anyway. And that was the problem: everything seemed to come up a bit short, so that he always found himself mired in disappointment. His sister Sally approached life very differently. She had no plan or ambition and yet somehow she always appeared perfectly happy. He had spent much of his adulthood looking down on his sister. Everything about her, from her job to her hairstyle, suggested a woman who was the very opposite of aspirational, but recently he had begun to envy her and her easy contentment.

He had tried practising gratitude as his various self-help books had instructed him, and he was grateful. He was, truly he was. Thankful to be married to Colin, happy he was a homeowner, it's just that he knew that if it was a nicer house, or if Colin hadn't begun to lose his looks quite so dramatically, then Killian would have felt more grateful. Even the new hot tub after two days was filled with water the murky grey of dishwater rather than the sparkling blue of the brochure. Killian was happy to be thankful, he just wished there could be a bit more for him to be thankful for.

On the other side of the room Colin observed Killian impassively. He knew better than to offer an opinion or comment. He had learned to navigate his way around his husband's moods, treading carefully when Killian drifted off into a wordless gloom. Sometimes

Colin wished that Killian could be as sensitive to his feelings, but no, Killian made his dissatisfaction with his life brutally obvious. The way he held open the kitchen cupboards and berated them for their cheap finish, the awed drooling when large expensive cars passed them in the street, even the way he looked at Colin and commented on the weight he had gained. Surely once you were married you were allowed to relax, to let your happiness show. Colin was puzzled that the unexpected windfall from number seven didn't seem to be having much of a positive effect on Killian. If their lack of funds made Killian morose and short-tempered, then surely the prospect of this money should bring some relief? It wasn't as if Colin didn't want more too. He did. It was just that from time to time, he worried their dreams might not be the same. Colin watched his husband reacting to some burnt muffins as if the roof had blown off the house, and fought the urge to tell him to cheer up. Who cared about the muffins? They were about to be rich! Naturally, Colin understood that it was a little difficult to celebrate their good fortune when it was so wrapped up in what was happening to Killian's father, and there was the slight shadow that had been cast over proceedings by its effect on Carol. Colin knew he was being disloyal, but he couldn't help feeling sorry for her. He could take no pleasure in seeing someone's heart being broken. Killian was at pains to justify his actions. 'I'm not a monster,' he had assured Colin. 'I know it seems brutal, but it had to be done.' Colin didn't dare to disagree. 'I was happy for her and Daddy, wasn't I? Wasn't I?' he repeated when Colin failed to respond.

'Yes.' His husband sounded doubtful.

'Love him, be his girlfriend, I didn't mind any of that. But she has no right to think he comes with a free house. The woman has a job if she could be bothered to do it, and anyway, she's part of Crottie's Cafés. She'll be grand. No need to worry about her. None. I'm not a monster,' he said again and to Colin it sounded as if Killian was trying to convince himself. Still, Colin wondered if there might have been a better way to deal with the whole situation. He knew only too well that his husband always saw the way to what he wanted as a straight line, but in life sometimes a more circuitous route was more effective. Most people understood that, didn't they? That achieving your goals shouldn't result in casualties along the way? Somehow it seemed that no one had ever taught Killian that.

'What about the other one?'

Colin wasn't clear what Killian was talking about. 'What? The other egg?'

'No,' Killian said impatiently, 'the house, the other offer on number seven.'

'Jordan went back to them but that was their best offer. Too low and they're in the UK. Full asking price and Cork is the only way to go. It's a result, I'd say.'

Killian shook his head. 'Weird, isn't it?'

Colin waited for a moment to see if his husband was going to make it any clearer what he was talking about. 'What? What's weird? I'm not a mind reader, Killian.' He tried unsuccessfully to keep an edge out of his voice. He didn't want this to escalate into a row.

'That the only offers we've got are from people who never came to see the house. That's weird. I suppose it might have something to do with the smell.'

'Smell? What smell?' Was Killian trying to irritate him on purpose?

'I'm not sure. It's like drains or something.'

'Old pipes. If you don't use them, they dry out. Run the taps, flush the toilet, that'll solve it.'

'Hey, not my problem now!' Killian seemed a little brighter. 'The lads from Cork can sort it all out.' He stepped forward and kissed Colin on his forehead. For once, something seemed to be working out.

The doorbell rang and Killian went to answer it. Colin was relieved. He wanted to start stirring the boiling water for the eggs and he needed to distract Killian from the cremated muffins. He heard happy voices in the hall. Killian ushered their friend Cath into the kitchen, her long red hair swaying as Killian pushed her forward. 'Look what Cath has!'

'I didn't want you cooking, so' – she held up some tinfoil-covered rolls – 'I made us breakfast burritos.'

'You're a life-saver, Cath!' Killian walked her through to the dining area on the other side of an arbitrary arch. Colin turned off the stove and followed.

'How lucky is our baby to have you for a mammy?'

How long had she been awake? Carol wasn't sure. Wine had meant that she'd fallen asleep easily but just as quickly she had been plucked back to consciousness, staring dry-eyed and thirsty into the darkness. She refused to reach for her phone, knowing she would be lured into its glowing embrace. Instead, she lay on her back, hands crossed over her breasts, and tried to will herself back to sleep. She practised her yoga breathing; she imagined endless still pastures. It was useless. Her mind was teeming with thoughts of the day before. Her initial excitement about her father's plan was now being chipped away by doubts.

She understood what her father was trying to do. He wanted to right a wrong and he thought that by returning the house to his daughter justice would be served. She had been swept along by his plan but now, lying in the dark, she imagined a future where she was installed in number seven like Daddy's little princess. It would be ridiculous. The whole town would think it was the house she had been after all along. Yes, it was true that she had wanted the place, but for Declan, not for herself. Now that was never going to be. Killian and Sally would never allow her to take their father out of the home and if by some miracle they did, who knew what state he might be in by then? Bringing him back to Stable Row might not be an option any more.

Her head hurt. She rolled onto her side and balled her fists to rub her eyes. This wasn't about the house. Her father had seized on the element of the story that money could fix, but there was no way to buy Declan's return. Her fight with Sally and Killian was just an unseemly sideshow. It didn't matter. The only thing that meant anything was her love for Declan, and he was never coming back. The bad thing had happened long before the children evicted her. They were caught up in their own dramas about their inheritance and probably some notion of Carol trying to replace their mother, but none of that mattered to her. Well, it did, but lying in her childhood bedroom she understood that it shouldn't. Buying number seven wasn't the solution, it would simply prolong her involvement in a story that she no longer needed to be a part of. She felt lighter, as if the release had already occurred. She would tell her father in the morning to call off the whole thing. No one fully appreciates the comfort of certainty, Carol thought to herself as sleep crept over her once more.

It was the best sleep she could remember having in months. When she woke, light was streaming around the curtains and there was knocking at the bedroom door. She glanced at her phone as she called for them to come in. Ten thirty. How had she slept so late?

The door opened and her parents peered around it. Their faces were beaming as if they were gazing upon the infant Jesus himself. Carol's heart sank. She knew at once what had happened.

'Great news, Carol, love! The offer is accepted. The house is ours.' Dave looked thrilled: this was business getting done.

Carol wasn't sure what to say.

Moira poked her head further into the room. She sensed all was not well.

'Isn't that great news, love? You must be over the moon, I'd say.' Carol roused herself.

'Sorry, yes. Great news. Sorry, I'm still half asleep. Let me get up and we can talk about it.'

She could see the disappointment on her father's face. This was to have been his moment of triumph.

'Right love.' Moira had one of her fixed smiles. 'Come on, Dave. Get out of here. Give the girl some privacy.'

Carol pulled the covers over her head. Fuck. What was she going to do? She had to say something. She couldn't let them buy a house she was certain she didn't want just to please her father. She got out of bed and her back cursed her for spending one more night on the sagging narrow mattress of her childhood. Carefully, she stooped to retrieve her jeans from the floor and pulled a light sweater from a neat stack of clothes.

She found Dave and Moira huddled by the coffee machine. Clearly they were discussing a problem and Carol would have bet good money that she was the source of it.

Dave noticed her first. He stepped away from his wife and called across the kitchen brightly, 'You'll have a coffee, love.'

'That would be great, thanks. And lots of frothy milk please.' She was playing the game this morning.

Her father beamed, while Moira eyed her suspiciously.

It was difficult to speak over the hissing and grinding of the machine, so Carol waited patiently at the kitchen table, her body silhouetted against the sun filling the glass box of a room.

'There you go. Oh, sorry – did you want chocolate on it?' Dave placed the large cup in front of his daughter.

'No, no. That's lovely, thanks.' She smiled at her father, bracing herself.

The three sat in silence before Moira simply stated, 'Dave.' It wasn't clear if this was her giving her husband permission to speak or merely a cue. Whichever it had been, he began.

'Carol, I was just saying to your mother there that you didn't seem too pleased about the offer.' He squinted at her, awaiting a response. Carol exhaled sharply and began to speak before she lost her nerve.

'Daddy, it's amazing. I hope you know how much I appreciate what you're doing for me. Both of you. I can't believe it. Really.'

'Does anyone else hear a "but" on the horizon?' Moira interrupted.

'Oh, Mammy.' Carol pushed her hands through her hair. 'Last night, after we went to bed, I started to think about things more. Why do I need the house? Without Declan, what is it really? And at this stage I can't see him ever living there again, can you?'

Moira bowed her head for a moment and then looked at Carol. 'That's not the point. It's your home and that pair had no right to turf you out. None.'

'None,' Dave agreed.

'I know, I know, but that was before, and now, well, I don't want to fight with them about money or the house. I couldn't stand it if they were able to walk away thinking that they'd been right about me all along and that all I cared about was the cash. You get it, right?' She looked at her parents for some sort of acknowledgement. 'I'm so sorry, Daddy. So sorry. I hate to waste your time and I know what you were trying to do. Do you mind? Daddy?' Her voice had taken on a whining quality, a much younger Carol begging her father's forgiveness for some misdemeanour.

Dave's tongue retrieved a tiny dab of milk froth from his upper lip.

'I don't mind,' he said stiffly. 'We were only doing it for you, but if it's not what you want. Well then.' Before Carol was able to reach forward and hug her father, he continued, 'Of course there is the matter of the deposit.'

'Deposit?' A new knot of uncertainty tightened in Carol's stomach.

'Well, the deposit was sent through this morning after the offer was accepted. That's how it works. We pull out now, and we don't get it back. That's the law.' Dave spoke as if Carol was much younger than forty-eight.

'Daddy, I'm so sorry. Look, I'll go back to work and I'll pay you every penny, I promise.' She leaned towards her father. He looked uncertain and then Moira cleared her throat.

'Just a minute. That's all very well but that would still mean we'd have given that pair thousands of pounds for sweet Fanny Adams.'

Carol and Dave looked at her, not quite sure what her point was.

'Well, that can't happen.' Moira presented the palms of both hands to indicate how very obvious her stance was.

Carol thought for a moment. 'So we give them hundreds of thousands of euros to prevent us giving them a few thousand?'

'No.' Moira sounded as if she was training a pup. 'We give them all the money and we get a house. Walk away now and they get money out of our pocket *and* they keep the house.'

'So what should we do?' Dave asked. 'Carol here doesn't want the house.' Carol shut her eyes. She couldn't help but feel that this was all going to be her fault, even though buying the house had never been her idea.

Moira chewed her lip for a moment and then placed her hands on the table. She had a plan.

'We go ahead.' She glanced at Carol and her husband to make sure they were giving her the full attention she deserved. 'We buy the house and then we tart it up a bit, before we put it back on the market. No offence, love, but the state of the place. Even a lick of paint and I'd say we'll turn a profit. I mean look what me and your father have done with this place.' Moira proudly indicated the pine kitchen cabinets and the swollen sofas lurking beyond them.

Although Carol had her doubts about her parents' interior design acumen, she could see the germ of a good idea. She herself had lamented the awful photos of the abandoned rooms. She knew that the little front lawn had just been left to grow wild. Maybe they could flip the house and make a small profit. She had to admit the thought of how annoyed Killian would be if they made more on the sale than he had was very sweet indeed. She looked at her father. Dave was nodding as if he could see the good sense in his wife's suggestion when in reality he would have supported any idea that meant he didn't lose the deposit.

'I'd say that's not a bad plan at all,' he said and Moira gave him a tight smile. She knew it was a lot better than not bad.

'What about you, Carol?' he asked. 'Is that all right with you?'

'Yes, yes, fine by me. I'd like to give that little house another chance to shine – show it off at its best.' She thought about Declan lying in St Brendan's and his love for the house he had never wanted to part with.

Christmas crept up on them, unwanted but inescapable. A small tinsel tree appeared on the reception desk in St Brendan's and Dave brought home a box of the Christmas cups from Crottie's Cafés. None of it felt very festive.

'Yes, I'll be there.' It was Linda, Carol's sister, calling from Edinburgh. 'She wore me down and I ran out of excuses. Still, at least Brian isn't coming!'

Carol laughed. 'Those children. Jesus, they're monsters. Even Mammy wasn't sorry to hear they're going to Cashel this year.'

'Are you sending presents for them?'

'No. I don't know. I might send a few selection boxes or something. They're coming down with stuff.' Carol began to think of the other presents she needed to buy. 'Don't get me anything and then I won't bother with you either. Deal?'

'God yeah.'

'What's Rhonda doing?' Carol tried to sound casual but she could tell from Linda's slight hesitation that she had failed.

'Friends. She has to work anyway. So.' The sisters' conversation spluttered to a halt.

'Look, I'll see you in a few days then,' Carol said brightly.

'Weather willing – the plane might not take off.'

'Don't even joke about it. I need help. I've been here for weeks.

They're driving me nuts. You forget what they're like twenty-four seven.'

'Not me!' Linda chuckled down the line. 'I was the one who told you not to do it.'

'I know, I know. I suppose I thought something would happen. I didn't want to think that I'd failed Declan so badly.'

A pause.

'How is he?' Linda asked nervously, neither sister comfortable discussing their relationships.

'Not good. They have him on some new medication and he's half asleep all the time.'

'Have you not asked the—'

'We'll talk about it when I see you.' Carol didn't want to relive it all again now.

The one bright spot on the Christmas horizon was that Craig was coming home. Carol suspected that Moira had shamed him into it or maybe even paid for his flight, but she didn't care. It had been years since they had spent a Christmas together. He usually made some sort of excuse about work or friends but Carol knew it was really to do with Declan and the other children. She got the impression that his absence suited Declan so she had never forced the issue. Now that she found how happy the prospect of his return made her, she wished that she had. Carol couldn't have articulated it but the idea of being reunited with her own flesh and blood made her feel calmer, as if she was moored to something again, rather than being buffeted through the storm by Killian and Sally Barry.

'A real tree?' Carol was very surprised to find her parents trying to wedge a heavy-bottomed conifer in-between the kitchen dresser and the wall.

'I thought it would be nice for Craig,' Moira explained.

'Mammy. He'll be thirty in a few years. He's not a baby any more.'

'If you're coming home for Christmas, you expect Christmas.'

'Exactly,' Dave agreed as he hung another of the black and orange baubles, which all bore the Crottie Café logo, on the tree. The overall effect was so well meaning and yet so ugly that it made Carol smile.

Christmas Eve was unusually mild and the newly arrived Craig was standing with his mother on the bleak patio. They could see rain showers in the distance smeared against the far headland. They warmed their hands on tall mugs.

'Even the smell of it. Jesus.' Craig pulled a face.

'Shh, he'll hear you.' Carol looked over her shoulder. Her father was busy inside making two more of his undrinkable Christmas cappuccinos for Linda and Moira.

'It tastes like air freshener,' Craig decided.

'Come around here, we can pour them away.' Carol led her son around the side of the house, out of sight and away from the wind. Giggling together, they poured their drinks down a drain.

'Oh my God, I can still smell it.' Craig gave a pretend retch.

Carol was closer to happy than she'd been for more months than she could remember. Her boy was back. They had been a small but perfect team for so long after Alex had left, but then she had lost him to whatever he got up to in London. Of course, she understood the idea of out of sight out of mind, but it had been so sudden. She had felt such a closeness, right up until the moment they weren't any more. Carol tried not to feel hurt. He was just young and thought-less, the way all kids are, and yet, she couldn't help thinking about her own mother. If Moira was being evicted and her partner put in a care home, Carol, no matter what age she was, would probably have called her at the very least. Maybe it was a daughter thing and sons were different.

She studied his face. Every time Carol saw him there was less of the boy. The angle of his jaw had hardened, the stubble seemed darker, and the small wrinkles to the sides of his eyes were per-manent now. She wanted to ask him everything, what he ate, who he spoke to, was he going on dates, but she knew better than to pry. The boy she had known so well was now a man closed off from her. He seemed happy and looked healthy, so Carol had no reason to suspect dark secrets, yet it was the not knowing that ate away at her. When he had gone to London first, Carol had bombarded him with texts and phone calls. She knew she was irritating him and forcing him to retreat from her, but she couldn't help herself. Now that she had finally learned how to be around him, she feared it was too late and the distance between them was permanent.

She risked giving him a hug and he not only accepted it but hugged her back.

'It's so nice to have you home,' Carol whispered into his hair.

Craig pulled away. 'Nice to be back.' He grinned and Carol won-dered, not for the first time, how it was possible that this man was single. 'Weird, though, all of us back here at Granny and Grandad's.'

'Yes. Not ideal, but I'll be back in Stable Row soon. Well, at least for a bit, before we sell again.'

'When do you think?'

'God knows. Solicitors shall speak unto solicitors. Hopefully end of January. You still happy in your flat?'

'Yeah. Love it. Shall we head back in?'

Thou shalt not pry.

After all the preparations and Moira ticking furiously at endless lists, Christmas Day itself seemed oddly stiff. Carol wondered if it might have been better if Brian and his brood had come after all. There was something uncomfortable about her parents sharing their dining table with three, they must assume, single adults. She remembered the Christmases of her childhood and when Craig had been a little boy. The sort of pure excitement and joy that no adult could ever feel. It seemed such a pity that along with a sore back, age seemed to remove your ability to feel delight.

Unwanted presents were opened. The expression on Craig's face when he tore back the paper to reveal a sweater from his grandparents made Carol wonder if it would even make it as far as the airport. She herself got slippers so ugly that she presumed her mother had bought them and then decided who to inflict them on. Linda feigned gratitude when she opened some suspicious-looking bathroom products from a brand no one had heard of.

Dave was folding wrapping paper to store away for next year and Moira was crashing around the kitchen, clearly a little unfocused after two glasses of Baileys. Carol got up to help.

'Sit down, Mammy, I'll put those away.' She took Moira's elbow and steered her to the nearest sofa.

'Right. Right. Dave, does Craig need a drink? Craig needs a drink.'

Her husband looked up.

'Another drop, Craig?'

'No thanks. I'm grand.' His wine glass was almost full.

'Moira?'

She held her small glass aloft. 'Maybe just a wee one. Baileys. We might as well use it – it only goes off, you know.'

Everyone did know. This information was part of the ritual of Christmas, along with *there's nothing on that television* and how Moira would be perfectly happy to sit down and just eat the stuffing. In the Crottie household these three facts were as traditional as the wise men.

The drink was fetched and the group settled down. Carol wondered how long it would be before she could announce that she was going to bed without causing offence. She glanced at Moira. The way she was slurping her Baileys suggested that she would be asleep in her chair shortly. Another Christmas over.

Linda leaned across the arm of her chair and spoke to Carol.

'Does Declan know that it's Christmas?'

Carol stared at her sister. Why would she ask such a question?

'I'm not sure. I don't think so, no.' She felt unwanted emotion tugging at her chin. Tears weren't far away. Moira had put down her drink and was glaring at Linda.

'Tell me this, Linda, how's your friend Rhonda getting on?' Her voice was just a little too loud.

Linda gave an audible gasp and turned to Carol.

'She's fine.' Linda folded her arms and sat back in her chair.

Carol looked at her mother innocently returning to her drink. She had no idea how Moira knew about Rhonda. She really was a marvel, but more than that, Carol felt protected by her. She might be nearly fifty but her mother was still her defender, and Carol had to admit, in a world where nothing seemed to be going her way, that felt good.

Time moved differently in the weeks after Christmas. With the visitors gone, hours slipped by unmarked as Carol sat in her parents' bungalow stabbing her phone or trying to find her place on a page of a book that had drifted away from her. Even her daily visits to St Brendan's did little to alleviate the monotony. It was comforting to sit with Declan but it was hardly what Carol would have called stimulating. She knew that she should be asking her old school for her job back or applying for other teaching posts but how could she make plans when there was so much about her future life that was unknowable? Carol no longer recognised herself. When had she become this passive lump that just allowed things to happen to her? She resolved to shake off her inertia. She would get up and do something. She would. Tomorrow.

Her mother had given up trying to engage her with trips into town or a late-afternoon stroll down to the pier. Dave just glanced at her occasionally to confirm that the situation was unchanged before he got on with whatever he was doing. When Carol considered the past, it seemed stranger still. Living in Stable Row, watching Declan every minute of the day had only been a few weeks earlier but now it seemed like fiction, a story she told herself and others about how she used to live. How could she have been so attentive and needed when even the simplest task now threatened to overwhelm her? The small pile of laundry in the corner of her room appeared to be insurmountable.

The days were peppered with guilt. Declan. How was she supposed to feel? She had loved him once, she was certain of that, but that wasn't what she felt now; or, if it was still something you could call love, it was so wrapped up in a desire to protect and please him that it seemed closer to what she had felt for Craig when he was a baby, not the reciprocated love between adults. Often when she thought about Declan sitting alone in the care home, her eyes filled with tears and she wanted to be with him, to hold him and reassure him, but when she was being brutally honest with herself, the number of times she allowed herself to consider his plight seemed to be dwindling by the day. She worried about herself. Was she becoming cold and heartless or was this what defeat felt like? The thing she had focused all her energy on was keeping Declan in his home. That battle had been lost and it wasn't clear what role she could play in his life now.

She took Eimear's advice and didn't confront the children, nor did she try to play them off against each other. She sent very plain and unemotional emails to them both asking about the wisdom of increasing their father's medication. Apart from saying she missed him and how she felt he might benefit from being more alert, she avoided any reference to emotion or even her relationship with their father over the last decade. She checked her inbox regularly, well, almost obsessively – what else had she to do? – but neither Killian nor Sally replied. She waited a couple of days and then wrote again, in a similar vein, but in this email adding her concern that time was of the essence. This too went unanswered.

Then time suddenly concertinaed, and everything seemed to be moving at a dizzying speed. After all the inertia, things were being asked of Carol.

'So that's it done.' Her father was speaking. 'We exchange in the morning. Funds should reach them before lunch, so you can get the keys from Reid's anytime tomorrow afternoon.'

'Me?' Carol didn't sound keen, not only because she wasn't sure she was ready to announce herself as the new owner of number seven, but also because it was an actual responsibility and that in itself seemed overwhelming.

'Us!' Moira announced. She suddenly looked ten years younger. 'Their faces when they see us come in and get the keys!'

'What? The kids won't be there, will they?' Carol was alarmed.

'No, no,' her father reassured her, 'but your man in Reid's will tell them soon enough.' Both he and his wife chuckled like cartoon villains delighted with their cunning plan. Carol wondered why she still felt so uneasy about this whole idea.

'I have to be up in Cork, so good luck to the two of you. Let the makeover begin!' Dave attempted an American accent on the last phrase, leading Carol to assume he was quoting some home improvement show from the States that she wasn't familiar with.

'I can't wait to get my hands on the place.' Moira wasn't clapping her hands together, but she might as well have been. 'Just a lick of paint, nothing major. We just want to turn a profit.'

Carol couldn't help but feel she was clambering on board a runaway train fuelled by fabric swatches and paint samples.

'Number seven?' The young man behind the desk seemed uncertain. 'Seven Stable Row? We've been dealing with a—'

'C. C. Holdings,' Moira interrupted impatiently and then brandished a contract. 'That's us.' She made eye contact with the two other estate agents slouched in front of their computer screens, daring them to challenge her claim. Carol was trying unsuccessfully to crouch unseen behind her mother.

'A Mr Crawford should have called to let you know we would be collecting the keys.' Carol was astonished at the tone of her mother's voice. It had risen an octave and her vowels were squeezed into rodent-like squeaks.

The hapless estate agent examined various bits of paper but clearly wasn't finding such a note.

'Oh, sorry.' It was the young blonde woman in the high-collared blouse. 'He did, yeah. He called. You were out at lunch, Phil. Sorry. I've got his number here . . .' She began to sift through several mounds of paper like a prospector panning for gold.

'That's all right, Ger. No need.' He stood. 'Right, all sorted.'

Moira gave a magnanimous smile and a slight nod of her head to suggest to the young man that they should both be happy she wasn't being forced to take this matter any further.

He held out a folder.

'Here's the homeowner's pack.' With his other hand he picked up a set of keys. Carol had to turn away. They were hers.

'Thank you very much. A pleasure.' Moira was now all smiles.

'Couple of bits to go over . . .' The young man licked his lips. He was clearly hoping that things weren't going to revert to the frostiness of a moment ago.

'Yes?' Moira said, the temperature falling rapidly.

'It's just because you haven't viewed the property. Some of the sash windows have been painted shut but that should be an easy fix. What else?' He checked his notes. 'They left some rugs. They weren't actually included in the sale but you're welcome to them.'

'Thank you.' Moira was growing impatient.

'Oh, yes, and the owners turned the electricity off at the mains. I'm not sure why. Maybe worried about the bill?' He shrugged. 'So when you go up there you might need a stepladder to reach the box.'

Carol hadn't known how apprehensive she felt about going to Stable Row until she experienced the sheer size of her relief at the suggestion of this delay.

'Not a problem,' Moira said tartly. 'I have kitchen steps in the car.' The *obviously* was silent.

Carol rolled her eyes, partly amused at the ludicrousness of her mother but also grudgingly impressed by her resourcefulness.

Back in the car, waiting for the traffic lights in the square, Carol gave in and asked her mother, 'Why have you steps in the car?'

'Just in case,' her mother replied airily.

'In case of what?'

Without missing a beat, Moira said, 'This.' The logic was clear to her, if to no one else.

'Right.'

'I packed a few other things too. Tape measure. Your father's tools. You know, to make a start.'

'Today?' Carol felt emotional enough at the idea of just setting foot in her old home. She really didn't think she was ready to begin home improvements.

'What do I always say, Carol?'

Her daughter couldn't begin to guess. There were so very many things her mother said. Not giving her any more time to think of an answer, Moira declared, 'The sooner you start, the sooner you finish!'

Carol didn't enjoy the drive up Barrack Hill. A strange sense of foreboding crept over her, as if they were heading towards an accident. She half expected to see number seven engulfed in flames or collapsed in a pile of rubble when they turned into Stable Row. But all at once, there it was. Nothing changed. The street as it had always been. The sky a pale blue, a scattering of early crocuses on the verge of grass. Picture postcard perfect. The only difference Carol could see was that the sold sign that had previously been outside number six was now tied to the gate of number seven. Moira parked a little further down the street. Mrs Buttimer, the well-meaning widow from number one, was walking Margo, her ancient West Highland terrier, along the communal strip of grass that ran opposite the houses.

'You're back!' the old lady called when she saw Carol. It sounded as if Mrs Buttimer had been expecting her. Did she think Carol had just been away on holiday? Surely not. Mrs Buttimer made it her business to know everyone else's.

'Yes,' Carol replied, hoping the old lady could hear the full stop in her voice.

'The new couple at number six will be pleased. They've been trying to get hold of you.'

'Really?' Carol had never met her new neighbours.

'Something to do with the drains, I think. Good girl!' Mrs Buttimer was distracted by Margo, her once white coat now various shades of nicotine yellow.

Moira appeared from the other side of the car, kitchen steps under one arm, a blue metal toolbox in the other.

'Right. Let's go.' This was a woman with things to do. Carol trailed after her mother, aware of Mrs Buttimer's eyes following them along the street. It wouldn't be long till the word was out.

The keys felt both familiar and strange in her hand and she thought of Declan as she walked towards number seven. The gate was swinging open. Declan wouldn't have liked that. It always annoyed him when the postman didn't close it. This was Declan's castle and even though it had been Carol's home she felt as if she and her mother were trespassing, unwelcome invaders to be fought back.

'Could they not have run a mower over the grass?' Moira sighed as they went down the path. 'Forget about selling the house, just out of respect for their father.'

Carol agreed but didn't feel like provoking a litany of Killian and Sally's shortcomings just now.

Both women smelled it at the same time. Moira sniffed the air like a hunting dog.

'What in God's name is that?'

The scent was as unpleasant as it was strong.

Carol wrinkled her face. 'Some sort of plumbing thing. It must be. Maybe it isn't as bad inside.' She reached forward and opened the door.

'Holy Christ,' Moira protested. 'It's worse!' she added, in case Carol hadn't noticed. She dropped her short ladder and toolbox on the floor and, wrapping an arm around her mouth and nose, ventured forwards towards the kitchen. Carol followed, trying not to breathe and seriously concerned that she might be sick.

Moira opened the fridge and pushed her face forward.

'No. Not this. I mean it stinks, but it isn't the main problem.' She reached out and turned on the tap. Just the noise of the water splashing onto the sink and down the drain seemed to make things slightly more bearable.

Before Carol had a chance to consider what to do next her mother called out, 'Bathroom!' and began heading upstairs. Carol followed. At the top of the house, Moira turned on more taps and flushed the toilet. She turned to her daughter.

'This isn't it, is it?'

Carol took a few breaths. 'No, I don't think so.'

Moira was thinking. 'It's not as bad up here, is it?'

The stench of decay was still overpowering but Carol had to admit that it was marginally better than it had been on the ground floor.

'It could be the basement?'

Moira glared at her daughter as if she had been withholding valuable information.

'This house has a basement? What? I never knew that!'

Carol was on the landing where she had struggled with Declan.

'It's just a little storage area. We keep – kept – the washing machine down there.'

Moira nodded, clearly satisfied. 'Sewers. That'll be it. Lead the way.'

Carol made her way down the stairs. As they made their descent the smell became overpowering once more. It was as if it had a physical presence. A fetid stench that she could feel on her skin. Carol opened what looked like a cupboard to the left of the kitchen door. She tried the light switch, but nothing happened.

'Of course – no electricity. Why would they turn it off? I'd say that caused all of this.'

'It must have. I mean I've never smelled anything like this before.'

Moira had retrieved the kitchen steps from the hallway.

'Where's the box?'

Carol pointed to the wall above the kitchen door.

In a matter of moments, Moira had climbed the steps, flicked the switch and folded the ladder again. Carol was reminded of the Mario Brothers.

Moira tried the light switch and a dim glow came from below.

Carol stepped onto the narrow stairs and then it really hit her.

'Fuck. Oh my God, this is it.' She turned back to her mother. 'I'm not sure I can.'

Moira jabbed her head forward.

'Jesus that is rank. Wait a second, love.'

She went to the toolbox and opened it; lying on top were some neatly folded tea towels.

Carol observed as her mother took the tea towels into the kitchen and placed them under the running tap. When she came back, she handed one to Carol as she wrapped the other around the lower half of her own face.

'This works for smoke inhalation.' Moira's voice was muffled by the damp fabric.

Carol obediently wrapped the dripping towel around her own face. She wondered what obscure Sky channel her mother must have been watching to learn these survival skills. One careful step at a time, they both ventured downwards.

Immediately they could see a shallow pool of water spreading across the worn lino of the small basement area.

'Where's that coming from?' Moira asked.

Carol pointed across the cramped space.

'That wall. Look – it's all damp at the bottom.'

It was true. A dark stain marked the base of the wall like a tiny ghostly mountain range.

'What's behind that wall?'

Carol thought for a moment. 'I don't know. Nothing?'

Moira shook her head. 'No. I'd say there is. Sure that's the front half of the house.'

Looking up the stairs and then back down into the basement, Carol realised her mother was right. The spaces didn't tally. She took the last few steps down and walked gingerly over to the stained wall. The water was only an inch or two deep. She could feel Moira right behind her.

'The water's clear. I don't think it's sewage.'

'Great,' Carol replied in a dry monotone.

She tapped the wall with her knuckles; it sounded hollow. She turned and looked at her mother. Moira also knocked on the wall.

'That's just plasterboard. A flimsy little partition. Was this always here?'

'As far as I know.' Carol could feel a nausea overtaking her as the smell made its way through the damp towel. 'Mammy. I need some air. I'm going up.' She headed straight for the front door and stood on the small overgrown patch of lawn, taking in deep gulps of air that now seemed mountain fresh compared to the basement stench. A moment later, her mother appeared at the front door.

'I'm going back down, love.' She was brandishing a hammer from the toolbox.

'Mammy,' Carol called weakly in an attempt to stop her mother from causing actual damage to the house, but it was too late. Moira was gone.

Carol sat on the grass, wondering who she should call. It was all very well that her mother was playing with a hammer downstairs but clearly she would need someone to actually fix this problem. Did plumbers do drains or was that someone else? What did Dyno-Rod do? This was precisely the sort of thing that Declan had been so good at. Even her father had got rusty over the years, just leaving everything to various people from the office to sort out with maintenance contractors. Carol leaned back on the grass, allowing the nervy anticipation of what was going to happen next wash over her.

Her thoughts were interrupted by Moira.

'Carol, love. Come and look at this.'

She sounded breathless and Carol resolved to stop her doing any more, even though it was clear how much she was enjoying it. By the time Carol got up and went inside, her mother had disappeared into the basement again.

'There's no other door to this?' Moira was standing in front of a hole the size of a modest television screen.

Carol was struggling with the rancid air. She pressed her damp tea towel tighter to her face.

'No. Not that I know of.'

'Look at this,' her mother instructed.

Carol peered through the hole. She could see some shapes and a small orange glow.

'Hang on.' She got out her phone and switched on the torch function. The light revealed a large chest freezer rusted at the corners and along its bottom edge. The motor sounded as if it was working harder than it should be. To the right of the freezer was an ancient water-stained sink with two taps perched high on the wall above it.

'Did you know that was in there?' Moira asked with a hint of accusation.

'No! Of course not. How could I?'

'You're *sure* this wall was always here?'

Carol suddenly doubted herself. 'I think so. *No* – it was here.'

'Right.' Moira began knocking the plasterboard with the hammer to increase the size of the hole. Carol grabbed her arm.

'Mammy, stop it.'

Moira wrenched her arm free angrily. 'Why?'

Carol was edging away back towards the stairs and air she could breathe. 'Because we need to call people. People who can fix this.'

'What are you on about? The freezer's back on, we can mop this up' – she pointed at the floor – 'and it'll be grand.'

'But what about whatever is in that freezer . . .' Carol's voice trailed away. Clearly there was nothing to be said that would dissuade Moira from her mission.

'Exactly.' She gave her daughter a meaningful look as she attacked the thin stud wall once more. A piece of pale wood was revealed and then, lower down, another part of the frame.

'Hold this.' Moira held out the hammer, and Carol found herself stepping forward to take it as her mother put her leg over the lower piece of wood and squeezed through the hole.

'Mammy, be careful.'

Moira was standing at one end of the freezer, her hand on the lid.

'Turn your head, pet. This will be the worst, I'd say.' But Carol couldn't turn away. What had thawed and rotted in this freezer she knew nothing about?

Moira gave a little grunt, and then another as she tried the lid.

'Fuck. It's locked.'

Grey and bubbling slowly, the water reminded Sally of the pot she sometimes used to boil up her old dish cloths.

'You get in that? Is it safe?' She sounded dubious.

Killian was all business. 'Colin has done all the pH tests and what have you. He loves all that shit. The water is perfect. We just need to buy some other thing, a clarifier or something, I don't know.' He walked away from the hot tub, literally trying to distance himself from it. If it was a disaster, he was going to make sure it was Colin's failure and not his.

A bottle of cava was sitting with three glasses on the wooden table outside the back door.

'Do you think we need to wait for Colin?' Killian asked, even as he was lifting the bottle.

'Well, he's your husband. We probably should.' Sally was still very unclear about how much of a celebration this should be.

'Fuck it. It's our house, not his.' And with that, the cork popped violently. The bubbles spilled over the glasses till Killian decided there was enough liquid in each. He handed one to Sally.

'Cheers! The money is in the bank.'

Sally clinked her glass gently and, not meeting her brother's gaze, muttered her cheers.

'Sit down.' Killian indicated one of the chairs set apart from the table. He watched his sister as she sat. In so many ways she was still just an awkward teenager. The way she used her hair to shield her face, how her limbs never seemed settled or comfortable. Sally was nearly thirty but seemed to have no apparent interest in adulthood. As far as Killian knew, she did the morning shift at the hospital and then headed back to her odd rented cottage behind the cattle mart. She grew vegetables – she sometimes brought a bag over for him and Colin – but he was unaware of anything resembling a social life. He didn't think she had ever had a boyfriend.

She seemed lost in thought.

'You OK?' he asked, sitting down beside her.

She raised her head. 'Yeah. I mean this feels a bit weird, to be honest.' She lifted her flute.

'Ah, don't worry about her—'

'It's not Carol I'm worried about,' she interrupted her brother. 'Well, a bit I suppose, but no, it's Daddy. Us here drinking and Da where he is.'

Killian put his glass on the table. 'Sally, it's all awful, of course it is, but that ship has sailed. Daddy has left the building.' He leaned towards her, his elbows on his knees. After a moment, Sally spoke.

'Do you really believe that, Killian, or is it just what you have to think to feel all right?' Her voice was even, unaccusatory; she just wanted to know.

Her brother sat up straight and picked up his glass again.

'I do. Why? Don't you? I mean we took him off the heavy drugs and he's no better.'

Sally bit a tag of dried skin off her thumb. This was clearly difficult for her. She spent her life avoiding anything close to confrontation, so the idea of disagreeing with her brother felt very uncomfortable.

'I don't know. Sometimes. But no. When I sit with him now, I still think it's Daddy, our daddy. You know, I speak, or tell him something, and then when he looks at me, he may not answer or use the words you'd expect, but in his eyes . . . I don't know how to say it right, but I feel like he sees me. I'm not just some girl sitting there giving him Polo mints, I'm his blood and he—' Tears sprang into her eyes and she covered her face with her hands. Killian wished Colin was back. He was much better in situations like this. He sighed. He supposed he ought to do something so he leaned over and squeezed Sally's shoulder. 'You're all right. You're grand,' he said in what he hoped was a soothing voice. His sister rubbed at her eyes and nose with the sleeves of her cardigan.

'Do you want a bit of kitchen roll or something?'

Sally shook her head. The worst seemed to have passed so Killian removed his arm.

'I do know what you mean,' he told his sister, even though what he meant was that he could imagine her experience sitting with their father was how she described it. For him, that was never what he felt. 'No one wants it to be this way, but what else were we to do? We could have ended up just waiting for your one Carol to die so we could get the house. She's not even fifty. We'd have been waiting decades.'

'I know, I know,' Sally said, her voice still a little breathy following her tears. She drained her glass.

'More?'

'Please.' She held out her glass and Killian tilted the bottle carefully.

'Started without me, I see!' It was Colin coming around the side of the house.

'Sally wouldn't wait. I begged her but she had a fierce thirst.'

'Not true!' Sally laughed. Killian was struck by how rare it was to see her face lit up by a smile. She looked not unattractive. If only she would do something about her hair.

'Here you go.' Killian handed a full glass to his husband.

'Sorry I'm a bit late. We couldn't set the alarm.' He sat down heavily. 'Cheers all!' He raised his flute before drinking. 'Oh, I needed that.'

'Did you get it fixed?' Killian asked.

'Yeah. Cath had left the small toilet window open.'

'Oh, I see,' Killian said, as if he understood more than what Colin had actually said.

'Yup. Morning sickness.'

'Colin!' Killian reprimanded his husband and Sally realised that she was being excluded from something.

'Oh!' It dawned on her. 'Morning sickness. Is Cath having a baby?'

Killian and Colin looked at each other.

'Are you going to tell your sister our news?'

Sally looked from one to the other. 'News?'

Killian smirked and put his drink back on the table.

'Top secret. Not for public consumption but yes, Cath is having a baby.' He glanced at Colin and took his hand. 'She's having our baby.' The two looked at Sally with the wide, bright smiles of the truly blessed. As if on cue, a neighbour's child began to cry and somewhere in the distance the mindless chimes of an ice-cream van could be heard.

Afterwards, Sally would ask herself why she had reacted in

the way that she had. Why couldn't she have just returned the smiles, voiced an insincere congratulations and raised a toast to her brother's happiness? This was his news. A happy plan hatched between the two men and Cath. It was a situation fully contained within their world, so why did she feel as if she was being attacked so personally by their news? She remembered how she had stood up from the table, knocking her glass over. The repeated 'No, no, no' angry and loud. She had fled the garden as if they were chasing her with sticks, instead of their worried cries of 'Sally, Sally, are you OK? Sally, sit down! Please, Sally. We didn't mean to upset you.' She could see their stricken faces, concerned and slightly horrified. Even as she was flailing her way back to her car, a part of her was aware of how mad she must seem, but she had no choice. Her reaction had been chemical. Unfiltered. Basic.

Later that night she phoned Killian to apologise. She tried to make light of it.

'I don't know. It was just the shock, I think. And the cava – I hadn't eaten. I'm so sorry. Please apologise to Colin for me. It's wonderful news. I'm thrilled for you. Thrilled!' But even if she was now able to say the words, it wasn't what she felt. Her outrage from the afternoon still pulsed inside her, violent and unwelcome. Did she feel judged by her brother or was it simply jealousy? She wasn't sure. Before that afternoon she had never thought she was that desperate for a child, but Killian's big smug face had triggered something. Maybe it was just that she wanted something, anything, when he seemed to have everything. The husband, the house, the lack of guilt. Was that it? The absence of any sort of conscience when they had spoken that afternoon? It just seemed so twisted and wrong to Sally that Killian was to become a father when he showed so little love for his own. The sense of unfairness that had knocked her so badly wasn't because she didn't have a baby, but because her brother didn't deserve one.

Moira and Carol were perched on the front steps of number seven having an unlikely picnic. A travel blanket protected them from the cold stone and hot tea was being poured from a flask, both produced from the car by Moira.

'You are a marvel, Mammy,' Carol said, truly impressed by everything her mother had managed that afternoon.

Moira shrugged. 'Well, I knew there was nothing in the house. I'm only sorry I didn't bring some biscuits. I'd say my blood sugar is very low. You'll have to drive, love. I'd be afraid I'd fall asleep at the wheel.'

Carol looked at her mother. It was easy to forget this powerhouse of a woman was almost eighty.

'I'll make dinner tonight. You could have a nap.'

'Done already,' Moira declared, implying her daughter was very foolish to have thought otherwise. 'Just needs to go in the oven.'

While this efficiency irritated Carol, it was also a relief that she wouldn't have to cook a meal when they got back. She was actually quite tired herself. This much activity after all her empty days was surprisingly taxing.

'Hello!' A youngish man, maybe mid-thirties, prematurely grey, was at the gate. He gave an embarrassed wave. 'Fintan Walsh,' he said, pointing at himself. 'We're the new people in number six.' He turned his finger to indicate the house next door.

Carol stood. 'Hello. Carol. This is my mother.'

Moira gave him one of her polite smiles but clearly this new arrival did not warrant the effort involved in getting up.

Fintan made his way down the path. 'Are you the new owners?'

Carol considered how to answer that question but opted for a simple 'Yes.'

'Great. Great.' Fintan pawed at the ground like a performing horse – or perhaps he had stepped in something. 'We were trying to get hold of you through Reid's, but . . .' He raised his hands skywards to indicate how futile those attempts had been.

'Oh right. I see.'

'It's just there's, you can sort of smell it there now yourself, an odour or something.'

Carol held up her right hand to stop him. 'We've actually found the source of the problem.'

'All sorted!' Moira called from the steps, interrupting her daughter. 'A sewer. Simple fix. The smell will be all gone very soon. Must have been awful for you but all sorted now.' She gifted Fintan another one of her adequate smiles and knocked her plastic cup against the stone steps before screwing it back onto the flask.

Fintan gave a small chuckle and mimed fanning himself. 'Thank God for that! It was fairly intense.'

'Fixed.' Moira was clearly keen to move the conversation on.

'So is that you moved in?' He tried to peer into the darkened hallway for signs of furniture or boxes.

'No,' Carol replied. 'We have a little work to do on the place first. Nothing major, don't worry.'

'Oh I know, I know. We're putting in planning for a kitchen–diner at the back. They're actually quite pokey houses when you get in, aren't they?'

Carol felt personally insulted, which she knew was foolish.

'We must get on. Lovely to meet you. I'm sure we'll see you around.'

'And you. And you,' he repeated a little louder to Moira, still perched on the step. She gave him another cursory wave and smile – any words might delay his departure.

With no reason to stay, Fintan left.

The two women watched him go and then waited for his footsteps on the other side of the hedge followed by the sound of the door to number six opening and shutting. Moira leaned back slightly, looking up at her daughter accusingly, and asked in little more than a whisper, 'Were you going to tell him about that freezer?'

'Well, yes. It seemed a lot more straightforward than telling him some story about sewers. Any of the neighbours knows there were no workmen up here today – old Mrs Buttimer is like our very own CCTV camera, so who was fixing sewers? Why not just tell him the truth?'

Moira's mouth hinged open and shut a couple of times, then she reached out to grab her daughter's sleeve and pulled her back down to her level.

'Carol.' She looked into her daughter's eyes. 'What do you think is in that old freezer down there?'

Carol shrugged, though she could see that her mother was implying something.

'I don't know. Some old meat? A few bags of chops?'

Moira looked at the ground as if distracted by an insect or a crack in the stone.

'Did you not see the baskets down there?' She looked up.

'What? What baskets?' Carol was confused.

Moira shook her head, disappointed but not surprised by her daughter's poor powers of observation.

'The wire baskets from the freezer were on the floor. You know, the top-layer baskets?'

Carol nodded. She could vaguely remember the configuration of her mother's freezer that lived at the back of the garage.

'So, it would be a fair guess, I'd say,' Moira continued, 'that there wasn't room for them in the freezer.' She widened her eyes. Again, Carol knew that something was being communicated but exactly what remained unclear.

'And?' she asked uncertainly.

'Carol, there's something big in that freezer. Large. Trust me, love, a bag of chops wouldn't stink up the whole street.' Her voice remained low and earnest.

Carol was becoming impatient. Her mother seemed to have a morbid interest in the forgotten contents of an old freezer.

'Well, Daddy can just get someone to open it up and then we'll know what's in there. It's probably just a side of beef or something. The main thing is the stink is cured.'

'Carol Crottie, you are not to tell your father about this. Not yet.'

'Oh for God's sake Mammy, why not?'

Moira hesitated, not wanting to criticise her husband, even to one of their children.

'Well, he's a bit keen on calling the guards, if you know what I mean.'

Carol had had enough. She stood.

'Look, Mammy, what are you talking about, why would we be calling the guards?' Her voice was slightly raised with frustration.

With surprising agility Moira got up and led her daughter back into the hallway. She slammed the door behind them.

'Jesus Christ, girl, why do you think anyone would wall up a freezer?'

Carol struggled to think of a reason. 'Too heavy to move? I don't know.'

'And since when did home improvements include making rooms smaller. Think!'

Carol just stared at her mother, who was clearly very agitated about something.

'Only one thing makes sense.' Moira had her face very close to her daughter's now. 'There's a body in that freezer.'

'What? Don't be ridiculous, Mammy!'

'Carol, that freezer has a body in it and I'd bet good money that it belongs to Joan Barry!'

'Mammy, stop it!' Carol pushed herself away from her mother. This was too much. 'That's just crazy talk. I mean, thanks for your help today, but that is madness. You can't be saying things like that.'

'Oh Carol, for a grown woman you can be an awful innocent. A woman goes missing and a big freezer gets hidden away. It doesn't take Hercule . . . whatshisname to work it out.' She tilted her head to one side to see if she was getting through to her daughter.

For a terrible moment Carol found herself giving credence to her mother's story. 'No!' She slapped her hand against the wall. Moira gave a little jump. 'You've got me all confused. I can't think straight, but I know there must be a thousand reasons for that freezer to be down there. A human body? Declan's wife? No, Mammy, that is just ludicrous. Nonsense. Look, let's just get out of here.'

She swung open the door and bent down to retrieve the blanket and the flask. Behind her she could hear the clank of Moira picking up the toolbox. They walked in silence back to the car.

'Remember you're driving.' Moira's voice sounded uncharacteristically sheepish, even contrite.

'I know.' Carol walked around to the driver's side, already feeling guilty that she had snapped at her mother.

Neither of them spoke as the car left Stable Row and edged its way down Twomey's Lane onto the Back Quay. Carol resisted the urge to switch on the radio. She felt that if the silence got awkward enough her mother might actually apologise for being so fanciful.

They had been driving for almost twenty minutes when Moira cleared her throat.

'Carol?'

'Yes, Mammy.'

'I'm going to get that thing open and then you'll see who's right.' Moira sounded defiant, and slightly indignant. Carol glanced at her mother. Moira was sitting up, rigid, her lips tight, her eyes fixed on the road ahead, as if she imagined she was the one driving the car.

It was nearly nine thirty and Sally was still lying in bed. She hadn't even managed to make breakfast. The sound of her mobile phone had woken her at seven and then she heard herself telling Brid, her second in command at the hospital, that she was ill and wouldn't be in. She explained about using the carrots in the blue cardboard box first, and sorting through all the use-by dates on the little yoghurts they put on the breakfast trays. Sally knew that Brid believed her feigned illness, and why wouldn't she? Sally was not a woman to mess anyone around.

As she lay on her side, the pillow hot beneath her face, she wondered if the hospital might send her flowers later in the day. Probably not. She'd need to be really ill for that, maybe recovering from an operation. She turned to find a cooler patch of pillowcase and shut her eyes. It came as a surprise to Sally to find how glad she was not to be at work. Now she was here at home in her bed, she struggled to imagine a morning in the future when she would be happy to be boiling cauldrons of water and setting timers. If she never did another inventory in the walk-in freezer she would be perfectly content. Of course she felt guilty about Brid and the others. She had heard the stress in her voice on the phone, but Sally wasn't delusional. She knew that she was easily replaced. Was that what she wanted? Not setting the alarm had been a genuine mistake, she was fairly certain of that, but had there been some unspoken, subconscious desire to not go to work?

Sally thought about her brother. Perhaps she was taking a leaf from his book and discovering the power of being a selfish prick, or was it as simple as the money coming from number seven giving her the freedom for the first time in her life, to not have to go to work? She threw back the duvet and sat on the edge of the bed. Killian. The very idea of him cast a shadow over her like a hangover. She didn't think he was a fully fledged bully, yet he had managed to manipulate her into bending to his will their whole lives. She didn't really blame him for it. Sally had been an eager foot soldier. As young as she had been when their mother had left them, she could still remember how Killian had tried to protect her. Their father had either been out searching or at home locked away in what they continued to call Mammy and Daddy's room. Killian was the one who had made sure breakfast was on the table, went through her timetable to see she had the right textbooks, replaced the toothpaste. If Sally had come to believe that her brother knew best, it was because he had. But that was then.

Yesterday had been the conclusion of a lengthy conversation Sally had been having with herself. She had struggled to go along with Killian's decisions about the house and their father's care but hearing about the baby had crystalised her thoughts. Yes, her brother knew best but only when it came to himself. Killian was now only interested in how things affected him. Sally didn't think that was necessarily a bad thing, unless you happened to not be Killian, and she was not. She had to find a way to untether her life from her brother's. He had to see that she wasn't just an appendage, a buy-one-get-one-free deal.

Padding across the floor carpeted with her discarded clothes, she came downstairs into the kitchen, where her laptop sat on the cluttered table. Carol was on her mind. This would be her first act of independence. She would email Carol Crottie and try to make peace with her. Sally still couldn't forgive Carol and her father for how they had behaved, but it was Killian who had demonised Carol. In his mind there seemed to be no fate too grim for her. Sally wanted Carol to know that while she supported selling the house, she also sympathised with her. Clearly Carol did care for their father and watching his decline must have been awful. As she sat poised at the keyboard she wondered for a moment if this might be the start of she and Carol becoming friends again. If it was her father who had got in the way before, well, he could no longer interfere. Sally wondered what their friendship might look like without a pile of books between them.

Before she could type a word, she heard the cheerful ping of a new message on Facebook. It was from Bindy, just wondering how she was doing. Sally hesitated for a moment but then started typing her reply. Much easier to chat with Bindy than broker a peace deal with Carol Crottie. Sally quickly gave her the headlines: the house was sold, and she was trying to make things better with Carol. She didn't mention Killian and his baby news. That seemed too much to share before she really knew how she felt about it herself. What if Bindy judged her for not thinking it was unqualified happy news?

Wow! Good for you, Sally. You're a much better person than I am. I don't think I'd ever want to see her again.

Sally almost purred reading the reply from Bindy. She was a good person. Offering up an olive branch to Carol really was a beautiful gesture.

I just think there has been so much anger and sadness. Now the house is gone we can just focus on Daddy. By the way, I'm not so wonderful – I couldn't be bothered to go to work today!!!

Enjoy it, girl! You've got your house money now! Do you know the people who bought it?

No. A developer I think. End of an era. So many memories! Do your parents still live where you grew up?

Yes! My bedroom is like a shrine. Seriously, it's like the Anne Frank museum!

Sounds lovely!! I must go and email Carol. What should I say to her?

Hideous. I don't know. If I were you I'd meet her for a coffee or just go and see her. I know that sounds worse than writing an email, but it's easier in the long run and she can't ignore you the way she might do with a message. What do you think?

Christ! I'd be afraid she might stab me! I'll think about it. You not working today?

Mm. Sally, I'm AT work! Lmao!!! Laters. B xxx

Don't work too hard – as if!!!! Xxxxx

Sally leaned back in the chair and stared at the blank screen. The kettle. She'd make herself a tea and then decide what she should do.

Moira had a great deal on her mind and most of it concerned the subject of death. She was standing at the ironing board in her kitchen. She had her back to the large window, trying to ignore the heavy rain from the Atlantic that was hammering at the glass. Moira leaned into the iron as it eased its way along the sleeve of one of Dave's shirts. She felt she did her best thinking at the ironing board.

It was a body in the freezer, of that she had no doubt. Carol just didn't want to consider the possibility that she loved a killer. Even if Declan wasn't a murderer, he certainly knew that there was a corpse in his basement. While Moira didn't consider herself an actual expert in criminal law, she was fairly sure that must be some sort of crime. That was the reason she hadn't wanted to involve Dave. Maybe it was all his years dealing with health inspectors and audits for his business but he had developed a very rigid approach to rules, compared to how he had been as a younger man. Back then it had been very different. Moira could remember sitting in the back of their first café, after hours, not long after they'd been married – certainly before the children, anyway – changing the 'best before' labels on unsold sandwiches. Back then, Dave did whatever was necessary. Now he seemed to have trouble embracing areas that seemed a little greyer than black or white. Moira still saw life differently. Often watching the news, she found herself having a twinge of sympathy for the person huddled under a blanket being ushered in or out of court. When someone killed another person she assumed they must have had a very good reason. Something or someone must have driven them to it. Of course, there were monsters in the world and murder was wrong in principle, she accepted that, but Moira felt the motive, the circumstances, should have some influence on both the crime and the punishment. She couldn't just unleash the guards on Declan, especially now that he was in that care home, unable to explain or defend himself.

Moira slipped the pressed shirt onto a hanger and hung it from a low rail under the kitchen island. Then she grabbed another shirt from the basket and stretched it across the board. A body. A whole adult frozen stiff. Would herself and Carol be able to dispose of that? Moira sighed. Even if they could, she didn't trust her daughter not to get hysterical and tell someone, or run to the police even if it meant the worst for Declan.

If the body turned out to be Joan Barry, and it probably was, then in all likelihood Declan was a killer. At this stage no one would ever know why. A fight gone wrong, a crime of passion, an affair exposed – it didn't really matter. Unless Joan Barry's corpse was dressed in a Nazi uniform or something worse, then Moira would go to the guards at once. No need to tell them that she had delayed her visit in order to be sure of the crime and the culprit. It was her house now, her basement, her freezer. She had every right to poke around a bit if she so wished. It wasn't as if she had stumbled upon a freshly bleeding body on the stairs and not reported it. This was what they called them on that television show. What was the phrase? Then she remembered. A cold case. She chuckled to herself. Cold? This case was freezing.

How would Carol cope? Moira feared the worst. If her daughter was this upset because her boyfriend had lost his marbles, Moira dreaded to think how she'd react when she discovered that he was a murderer. In fairness it was terrible to think of sharing your life, your bed with a cold-blooded killer. Maybe there was the slim possibility that Carol might decide to look on the bright side, and just be happy to be out of the relationship without suffering any physical harm herself, but somehow Moira doubted that.

The doorbell rang. Moira glanced at the window. Whoever it was would be soaked. She placed the iron carefully on the granite worktop of the island where it could do no harm and headed out to the hall.

She didn't recognise the young woman at the door, her hair smeared across her face by the rain, her glasses like two shower doors.

'Hello, awful day isn't it?' Moira hardly stuck her nose out the door.

'Hello. I was wondering, is Carol in?'

'Carol? No, I'm afraid she's out.' Moira was instantly suspicious. What did this person want with Carol?

'Oh. Right.' The young woman seemed deflated.

'Am I any use to you? I'm her mother.'

'Hello. No. I was hoping to talk to her myself. We've met before, haven't we? Down in Stable Row. I'm Sally Barry. Declan's daughter.'

Moira bristled. What fresh humiliation did this girl intend to visit upon Carol?

'Well, she's not here and I don't know when she'll be back, so if you'll excuse me . . .' She began to close the front door, but Sally put out her hand to stop her.

'I'm here to apologise. I wanted to talk because it, well, it's all such a mess.'

Moira couldn't help feeling a twinge of sympathy for the rain-soaked visitor. She seemed so young to be making decisions about healthcare or property deals. Moira decided the girl was sincere. It would be good for Carol to speak to her, and besides, Moira had some questions of her own she wanted to ask. Maybe she could find out some more about the basement partition.

'Will you come in and wait?'

Sally's expression changed. It was like watching the sun emerge from behind clouds.

'Thank you. Thank you so much, Mrs Crottie.'

'Please. Moira!' her hostess called as she led her into the bungalow and out of the driving rain.

'Some view!' Sally exclaimed as they walked into the kitchen area.

'You should see it on a fine day.' Moira pulled a chair away from the table. 'You'll sit down.'

'Thanks.' Sally did as she was told.

'Can I get you a towel or anything? You're soaked.'

'No. I'm grand, thanks.'

'Cup of tea?'

'No. I won't. Thanks though, all the same.'

'You're sure?' Moira pointed towards the kettle. 'It's no bother.'

'Certain. Thanks.'

'Right.' Moira took a seat on the other side of the table and a silence descended on the couple. The rain hammered at the windows and an occasional howl of wind could be heard whipping around the house.

Moira studied her damp visitor. A funny-looking little thing, she was busying herself pulling strands of her rain-flattened hair behind her ears. Her shoulders were hunched and her head bowed. She didn't look very brave and yet she must be, either that or stupid, to think she'd get a warm welcome in this house.

'Sorry about the state of the place. I was just catching up with a bit of ironing.'

Sally looked up and noticed the ironing board for the first time. If Mrs Crottie thought this room was in a 'state' she should see how Sally had left her cottage.

'Don't let me stop you.'

'No, no. I was due a break.'

Sally allowed her head to bend forward once more.

Moira's mind returned to the only thing she could think about. Did this girl know about the hidden freezer? No. How could she? If either she or her brother had had any suspicions about the basement room, they would never have put it up for sale. Moira remembered Carol telling her how Declan had insisted he never wanted Stable Row to be sold. Not exactly evidence, but in Moira's mind, it wasn't looking good for Declan.

Later that evening Moira would ask herself why she had said what she had. Was she really just searching for a subject the girl might have some interest in or had Moira been trying to stir up trouble? She wasn't sure but the next words out of her mouth were, 'Good news about selling Stable Row.'

It certainly provoked a reaction. Sally's head sprang towards Moira as if the older woman had caught her doing something she shouldn't.

'Oh. You heard about that.'

'Yes.' Moira was enjoying herself. The thrill of the fisherman feeling a tug on the line.

'End of an era,' Sally said uncertainly.

'You got a good price too, I'd say.' Moira knew she should stop. This was cruel and unnecessary. The girl was losing a game she wasn't even aware she was playing.

Sally squirmed in her seat. She evidently didn't want to talk about money.

'Do you think Carol will be much longer?'

'No. Not long,' Moira said brightly. 'She's just popped into Stable Row.' This was a lie. Carol was in fact getting her hair cut but Moira was impatient to deliver her news.

'Right,' Sally said flatly, her unease increasing. Moira was looking at her intently. Sally shifted in her seat.

Moira, worried her prey might leave, went in for the kill.

'Oh. Didn't you know?' The hint of a smirk played at the corners of her mouth.

'Sorry. Know what?'

Moira took a deep breath. 'Well, that Carol owns number seven. Carol bought the house.'

Sally tried to stay calm. She hoped her face wasn't betraying her confusion. How could this be true? Killian would never have sold number seven to Carol without mentioning it. Moira was smiling broadly now. Did Mrs Crottie think this was funny or was she playing some sort of joke on her? Without deciding to, she stood.

'I'm going to go.' She looked in the direction of the front door.

'Are you sure? Carol won't be much longer.' Moira couldn't stop smiling. She imagined Sally rushing off to tell the brother her news.

'Yes. I . . .' Sally hesitated, unsure if she needed an excuse to leave. No. This woman was not being kind. She didn't fully understand what had just happened but she knew she was being taken for a fool. 'Thank you, but I must go.' She hurried towards the front door. Moira fussed behind her. 'Well, I'll be sure to let Carol know that you called.'

The door opened and Sally was running through the rain towards her car.

'Bye now!' Moira waved, feeling the first hint of guilt, as she watched Sally struggling to get out of the rain into her car. Was Moira's little bit of fun going to get her in trouble? No. There was nothing the Barrys could do now. They had played their last hand. The game was over.

Colin checked the amount of gin he had just poured into his glass, and added another generous splash. This was not an evening for restraint. Behind him he could hear Killian pacing the floor. Colin had hoped he might have tired himself out by now but there seemed to be no respite.

'It makes no sense. What are they up to? They must be up to something.'

Colin knew better than to mistake this monologue for conversation. It was his job to listen and nod and then when he judged the timing to be just right, offer something that might help to defuse the situation. He dribbled a small amount of tonic into his glass.

'It must have something to do with Daddy. Do you think they've come up with some scheme to get him out of St Brendan's? Is there some legal loophole we didn't see?'

Colin sipped his drink and picked at an uneven thread in his trousers. He suddenly became aware that Killian had stopped pacing. Colin looked up to find his husband staring at him. Clearly he wanted some sort of answer but Colin hadn't really been listening.

'You've got the money so I don't see how it matters who owns the place now. It's weird, I'll grant you, but you just have to try and forget about it.'

'But what if it's about Daddy? Is it a way of her getting her claws back into him?' Killian started pacing again. 'Maybe Sally got the wrong end of the stick. And what the fuck was she even doing out at Crottie's?' He stopped and held out his empty glass. 'Can I get a refill, please?'

Colin wondered why it wouldn't have been easier for Killian to get a fresh drink himself since he was already standing up, but, saying nothing, eased himself out of his chair.

Killian rested one arm on the fireplace. 'I googled the company and there's no mention of Crottie anywhere.'

'Well, there you go. Maybe you shouldn't be getting all worked up about something Sally says. Have you called Reid's?'

'Left a message.'

'OK. So, drink this and try to relax until you know something for sure.' Colin handed Killian his drink.

'Have we no limes?'

Colin gave his husband a look to suggest that he was pushing his luck.

'Cucumber's grand. Thanks.'

The two men sat on either side of the empty fireplace. Colin met his husband's eyes. 'Cheers.' They lightly clinked their glasses.

'Right, Killian, are you ready for my news now? Well, our news.' Colin was smiling.

'Sorry. I'm useless. The news. Your news. Yes. What is it?'

Colin arched his eyebrows to suggest there might be something Killian was forgetting. 'What day is it today?'

'Wednesday,' Killian replied uncertainly. Clearly he had forgotten something but nothing came to mind.

'And what was happening this Wednesday?'

Killian shrugged. 'I give up.'

Colin gave a dramatic sigh. 'Cath?'

'Cath?' Killian repeated the name, but then the clouds of his memory parted. 'Oh fuck. The scan! The scan was today. How was it?'

They were both laughing with excitement now.

'Great. Cath and the baby are both doing great.' He reached into his jacket pocket and held a small piece of paper against his chest. Killian gasped.

'Is that it? Is that the baby?'

'Do you want to see?' Colin teased.

'Yes. Yes please.'

Colin was surprised and relieved to see tears rolling down Killian's face. Surely this was proof that he shared his joy.

'The state of me!' Killian laughed, wiping his eyes.

Colin slipped from his chair and knelt down, kissing his husband's wet cheeks. He slowly turned the piece of paper so that Killian could see the blurry printed image.

'There you go. That's her. That's our little baby girl.'

The only light in Sally's cottage came from the screen of her laptop. She sat hunched before it, still wearing her coat. Her fingers were drumming out a long message to her internet friend Bindy. She wasn't currently online, which meant Sally could type an uninterrupted monologue about her strange and upsetting day. It was the longest message she had ever sent Bindy. Normally they just left a one-sentence greeting if the other wasn't online and waited till they were both at their computers to chat. Sally felt she couldn't wait.

She had tried to tell Killian what had happened, but of course he had immediately made it about himself and began to rant down the phone about how he had been betrayed and how he was going to sue the estate agent. It had been a mistake to think her brother might have sympathised with her, paused for even a moment to consider how awkward and humiliating it had been for her.

Describing everything for Bindy in her message was completely different. Sally took centre stage in this version of the story and she was able to list her grievances against old Mrs Crottie and Killian equally without fear of repercussions. As she pressed send, Sally wondered how Bindy might react. She would be sympathetic but there could hardly be any practical advice. Sally closed her laptop. It didn't matter. She already felt infinitely better than she had when she'd got home. She was just wondering what might still be edible in the fridge when she heard a light knocking at the front door.

Sally rarely got visitors and as she took the few steps to the door she considered who it might be. A neighbour with some problem; a Jehovah's Witness; the survivor of a car crash seeking help? She turned on the light in the hallway and opened the door. Her visitor was so unexpected that it took Sally a moment to recognise her. Carol Crottie, clutching her coat against the rain, was standing on the doorstep.

'Hello,' Sally said automatically.

'I wasn't sure anyone was in.' Carol nodded towards the gloom of the interior.

'I just got in,' Sally lied. 'What can I do for you?' She still had some of the fire from her message to Bindy.

'I just wanted to say sorry, to explain.'

Sally felt Carol was trying to trick her. Why would she be here speaking in a soft voice of concern?

'Oh yes?'

'Sally, Mammy told me what happened. I don't know what she was playing at. Sorry.'

'So, is it true?'

'What? That we've bought number seven? Yes, we have.'

Sally wanted to slam the door in Carol's face.

The noise of a car driving slowly past distracted them. They turned to see its headlights cutting a wedge through the darkness, the air etched with the heavy rain. Sally hoped it wasn't anyone she knew. For a moment she considered asking Carol inside, but then she remembered the state the house was in. It wasn't fit for any visitor, but especially not this one.

'It's a long story,' Carol continued. 'Daddy thought it was a good idea—'

'Why?' Sally interrupted. 'Why would you go behind our backs and buy our family home?' She could feel her heartbeat increase and her voice bristled with the indignation of the wronged.

'Whoa, there.' Carol held her hands up defensively. 'Sally, I don't want to fight with you. We've known each other a long time.'

'We have. I was a child when you came into that house and stole my father. A child.' It was frightening to finally tell the truth but it also felt liberating.

Carol stared at Sally for a moment and then turned her head away, looking into the rain that shone in the reflection of the hall light.

'Is that really what you think happened?' she asked quietly.

'Well, isn't it?'

Carol wiped the sheen of raindrops off her face.

'Jesus, Sally. And now, here?' She waved one hand to indicate the night and the weather but she meant much more. It was Declan alone in his room, Killian and Sally evicting her, all the unnecessary cruelty that had gone on. 'This is when you tell me? Now that your father can't explain? Can't defend himself? Can't defend me?' Her arms dropped to her sides. She spoke slowly and deliberately. 'What sort of person do you take me for?' Carol looked into Sally's eyes. 'What kind of monster have you decided I am?' A small shake of her head. 'We never wanted to hurt you. We were trying to protect you.'

There was something about that phrase. A childhood memory that Sally couldn't quite place. What she could remember was the horrible feeling of being alone in her bedroom, feeling abandoned and rejected by Miss Crottie, the same Miss Crottie who was now trying to tell her that she cared.

'Well, you didn't do a very good job of it, did you?' Sally spat.

Carol took a step back onto the narrow path. 'And so this – turfing me out, selling the house, telling me all this now – this is what? Some sort of revenge?'

Sally didn't speak.

Carol began to leave but after a couple of steps she turned.

'Instead of trying to hurt me, you might want to spend some time with your father. You wanted your daddy back, well, now you have him, so the least you could do is spend some fucking time with him.'

Carol's coat flapped behind her as she disappeared into the night. Sally raised a hand. She felt she should call out, stop her from leaving like this, but she couldn't imagine what she could say to make this better.

Whatever relief she had felt telling Carol the truth had gone. Now she just had an uneasy feeling. A nagging that there was something she didn't know, or something she was choosing to ignore. Sally saw the lights of another car approaching and gently shut the front door.

Ballytoor looked nauseous. The whole town had the sickly pallor of the terminally ill. The grey of the sky bled into the buildings, which in turn seeped into the wet streets and the drab sludge of the river churning its way under the bridge towards the roadworks on the Cork roundabout. The bright postcards of Ballytoor that sat in the racks hanging from the door of Cassidy's the newsagent did not look like this. The heavy downpours of the day before had been replaced by a sticky mist of rain. As Moira scuttled away from Carol down Stable Row the red round of her umbrella looked like a bullet-hole in the landscape.

Carol sighed as she locked the car and walked slowly after her mother. She didn't want to be here. The confrontation with Sally the night before had left her feeling tense and anxious. For Declan's sake as well as her own she wanted to fix this. It was her job to try to be the adult. The mature, objective side of Carol, as much as it wanted to cast Killian and Sally as simple villains, understood they were just reacting – albeit overreacting – to ancient hurts.

Carol tried to talk about it all with her parents but her father had invented some unconvincing reason for having to be in the office. He gave his tell-tale splutter before he announced he had to be off. Moira hadn't even looked up from her iPad. She just pursed her lips and announced, 'Busy busy,' in a flat tone that said *goodbye* and *I don't believe you* at the same time. Moira had an impressive alternative vocabulary that it had taken Carol years to decipher. A few minutes later when Moira said, 'It's a surprise,' in reply to Carol asking her why she needed to go to Stable Row that morning, she understood her mother was really saying, 'If I tell you, you'll just try to stop me.'

The drive into town had been the mother-and-daughter version of silent. No actual conversation but still Moira kept up her little monologue.

'So many cars parked outside that house always.'

'Would they ever resurface this road.'

'Not a day that woman doesn't have washing out.' Finishing with a 'No sign of Mrs Buttimer today,' as Carol found a parking spot at the end of the street.

Moira was waiting for Carol at the door.

'Keys!' she called and held out her hand like a surgeon to a nurse in the operating theatre.

'Will you tell me now? What is this about?' asked Carol as she handed over her keys.

Moira gave a little grunt as she opened the door and then looked back at Carol. With raised eyebrows she used her 'stating the obvious' voice to say, 'The freezer.'

Carol groaned. She should have known that something was up when Moira had stopped talking about the basement and what it might hold.

Moira rustled around in her handbag and then proudly held aloft a large hairpin. '*Voilà!*'

'And what are you going to do with that?' Carol asked, knowing what the answer would be.

'This is how we're going to unlock that freezer.' Moira seemed very pleased with herself. There was clearly something else she wanted to tell her daughter, and Carol reluctantly took the bait.

'How? How are you going to do that?'

Moira tried and failed to suppress a smirk.

'I googled it, didn't I? Watched a video on YouTube. Turns out it's no bother.' She inclined her head with a showman-like flourish and headed towards the small door that led down to the basement. Carol, like an unwilling volunteer from the audience, shuffled after her.

Downstairs, now that the worst of the smell had gone, both women were able to examine the room properly. Carol saw the baskets from the freezer piled in a corner, but she also noticed for the first time how rough the edge between the partition wall and the ceiling was. Obviously, it had been put up in a hurry. A couple of scouring pads sat curled and dry on the edge of the sink that had been hidden for so many years.

Carol's irritation with her mother was quickly being replaced by nervousness. What if her mother was right? No. It wasn't possible. This was going to be like those deep-sea explorers opening a long-lost treasure chest only to find sand and fish bones. Wasn't it? She became aware of how dry her mouth was and swallowed hard.

'Hold that.' Moira handed her daughter her handbag and hoisted up her skirt so her leg could clear the lower strut of the rough hole she had made. With a grunt she was through and now stood beside the freezer. She bent down and peered at the rusted lock. 'Have you got one of those lights on your phone, love?' she called over her shoulder.

'Yes. Hang on.' Carol slipped the handbag over her arm and then retrieved the phone from her pocket. She stabbed at it till the torch function sparked into life. 'Here,' she said, holding it through the hole for her mother.

'You keep it. Hold it steady,' Moira instructed. The hairpin trembled in her hand like a tiny divining rod as she pushed it into the lock. She twisted it sharply but it slipped away in failure.

'Hold that light steady,' she snapped at her daughter. 'And you need to get closer altogether.' She tapped the wooden bar to encourage Carol through the hole. Reluctantly she did as she was told, struggling with the handbag and the torch as she squeezed through the opening.

Once both women were together in the tiny forgotten room, the atmosphere changed. Although the air seemed cooler, it was still infused with the putrid smell of decay. Carol could hear her own breathing in a way that unnerved her. Moira stood up straight and rolled her shoulders. She was an athlete going for gold. Her hand approached the lock once more. To Carol it seemed steadier. The hairpin was pinched and placed. A quick twist and then the unmistakable sound of a lock clicking. Both women froze.

'There,' Moira said. Her hushed voice sounded more apprehensive than triumphant. There was no going back now. She looked at Carol. Her eyes shone in the light from the phone. 'Do you want to stand back, love? We don't know how bad this might be.'

Now that the moment had arrived, Carol wanted to do much more than stand back. She wanted to flee the building. Why had she ever believed this freezer might only contain a few leftover chicken bits? Everything about this partition and the secrets it contained was now undeniably sinister. She croaked a small 'No.'

Moira nodded and put both hands on the lid of the freezer. As she pushed forward, the lid slowly rose up. The women peered in and then the light in the freezer suddenly flashed brightly, illuminating the contents. Carol let out a high-pitched yelp and Moira dropped the lid with a heavy thud, plunging them into semi-darkness.

'Oh my God. Oh dear God,' Moira panted.

Carol inched away. 'What was that?' she whispered as if a secret could still be kept.

'The question is, *who* was that?' Moira replied, leaning on the lid as if the freezer's contents might try to escape.

Although she had only seen the body for a second, Carol had a vivid image of mottled greys and dark pinks. There had been feet, that was certain; and eyes, there had been eyes – or rather, two murky shadows beneath the shroud of frost. She found that she was shaking, and her breathing was a series of short shudders. Moira hugged her but she too was in need of comfort. The excitement she had felt mere moments before had evaporated. Now there was just a sense of horror. This wasn't just her proving a point or solving a mystery. Somebody had died and now they were going to have to do something about it.

Wearing a heavy anorak over his pyjamas, Dave was outside picking leaves and stray strands of seaweed off the wall of windows. He tiptoed his way over the remaining puddles, careful to keep his slippers dry. He was placing the debris into a black bin bag that trailed behind him like a deflated balloon. The storm was over and a wide blue sky arced over the bay. Moira and Carol sat watching him from the kitchen table as they had breakfast. He waved and they waved back.

The day before had ended abruptly when Carol had been violently sick. Just as her mother had been comforting her in the little space beside the freezer, Carol had suddenly pushed her away and then turned her head, vomiting in hot splashy waves onto the dusty lino. Moira had steered her still retching daughter up the stairs and sat her on the front step to get some air. The dampness of the misty rain had felt soothing. Moira had imagined she would open the freezer again and have a better look at its contents, but she was secretly relieved that she now had an excuse to leave any more investigations till another day. She was beginning to think that she might have to involve her husband after all.

Looking out of the window this morning, as Dave picked his way down the path peeling fronds from the glass, he seemed so innocent. He was a good man, a moral man. She loved him and she liked to think there were no secrets in their marriage. Still, overnight, doubts had begun to pester her. When Carol had first mentioned Declan Barry, the way Dave had claimed he didn't really know him. Was that true? Moira was certain she could recall Declan Barry calling at the house. They'd been in the Chamber of Commerce together, she knew they had played golf – and then nothing. Had something happened? Moira kept returning to the way Dave had come up with the idea of buying Stable Row. It wasn't like him to throw money around. Not like him at all. Had he a reason for not letting strangers get hold of the house? Moira felt she might be losing her grip on the whole situation. Maybe she was just tired, but she knew she couldn't allow the secret of the freezer to get out. It was too soon to say whom it might entangle.

'He'd want to involve the guards. You know he would,' Moira told her daughter when Carol had asked once more about telling her father about the freezer contents.

Carol wrinkled her forehead. 'But he'd be right? I mean, we're going to have to tell the guards at some point, aren't we?'

Moira picked at a patch of dry skin on her scalp.

'I suppose so, yes.' She paused, trying to gather her thoughts. What could she tell her daughter to appease her?

'It's just . . .' she glanced out at Dave, to reassure herself that he couldn't hear them speaking '. . . well, it's just that we know so little. Why is the body there? Who is it? Was Declan hiding it? Could it be something to do with Killian? We just don't know enough. Once we involve the police, well there's no going back then, is there?'

'Oh Christ, Mammy. It's all such a mess. It can't be Declan. It just can't. There has to be another story behind it.'

'Maybe.' Moira sounded doubtful. She understood her daughter's reluctance to believe Declan was a killer but it was hard to imagine a scenario where he wasn't responsible for the body in his freezer in his basement.

'But you know that if we tell anyone now, Declan's going to get the blame and there's no way for him to defend himself or explain. Is that what you want?'

'No. Of course not.'

'And what about you? Don't think there'll be any walking away from this for you. You'll be up to your neck in it.'

The two women looked at each other across the table. Somehow this whole situation had become their problem and no one else could help.

'So what are we going to do next? We can't just leave it down there.'

Moira ran her tongue over her front teeth. 'Well for now we can, can't we? Then I'd say we go back and have a better look. You never know, you might recognise them.'

'Recognise them? Jesus, Mammy, you saw it.'

Moira nodded thoughtfully. 'Yes. It was a bit meaty all right – and the problem is we can't defrost it again to get a better look.'

'Well, at least we know it's not Joan,' Carol said as if she was going through a list.

'Do we?'

'Mammy. The feet. They weren't women's feet.'

Moira gave a small shrug. 'You don't know what happens to a body after being in that freezer and who knows, maybe Joan Barry had very large feet?'

'Mammy!' Carol objected.

'Some women do!' her mother insisted.

Carol knew better than to pursue the point, so she let it go.

Their conversation was interrupted by Dave coming into the room. He brought a draught of cold air in with him.

'All done. Must have been some wind. The little picnic table was turned over.'

'Was it?' Moira struggled to sound interested.

'I'll have a shave and head off. I thought I'd have a look at Stable Row. We should be making a start.'

Carol almost spat out her tea and in panic turned to see how her mother was reacting, before realising that she must try to compose herself. She hoped her father hadn't noticed. On the other side of the table Moira appeared completely nonchalant. She stood up, reaching for the cups.

'Oh, I forgot to tell you. You can't.'

Dave turned back from the corridor. 'What? Why not?'

'Myself and Carol tried to pop in yesterday and the key broke in the lock. So annoying.'

Dave exhaled sharply. He clearly believed that the women in his life had done something very stupid and that this broken key was in some way their fault.

'And were you ever going to tell someone?'

'Dave Crottie, who do you think you're married to? I did of course. The locksmith couldn't get out yesterday; I told him it wasn't an emergency, so he's coming out this afternoon. He's going to ring here with a time.' Moira sounded breezy and untroubled. Carol thought about herself trying to tell this lie and how she would have immediately betrayed them both with stammering and contradictions. Her mother really was an impressive woman.

Dave looked thoughtful for a moment, now that his plans were being forced to change.

'I suppose I'll just go up to Cork then. I haven't been into the office in a few days.'

Moira brought the cups across to the sink.

'OK love, we'll see you tonight.'

Dave padded away towards the bedroom.

Moira snapped her head around to Carol and leaned forward.

'Right. We have to decide what to do and quick,' she hissed.

Carol gave an impotent shrug of her shoulders. She had no idea how to proceed. Surely now that they had run out of time, there was no other option but to go to the police? Carol couldn't imagine what else her mother might suggest. Anything else would just mean that when the guards finally did become involved then Carol and her mother would be the ones in trouble with the law. She might want to protect Declan but she wanted to safeguard herself more.

Moira was staring at the ceiling and chewing her lip. Clearly, she was still trying to conjure up options that didn't involve law enforcement.

'How can I get more time?' Moira whispered, more to herself than to Carol. 'More time,' she repeated.

Her daughter knew that no response was expected or required so she just stood awkwardly by the table waiting for Moira to come up with something.

'Right. Right.' A plan was clearly being hatched. 'I didn't know that room was down there, so I would bet my life your father doesn't either.' Moira looked to her daughter for agreement.

Carol hesitated. 'Would he not have seen a floor plan?'

'No. Not at all.' Moira dismissed her daughter's concern. 'We just put in the offer. We didn't go near any floor plans. Sure, if we had I'd have known about the basement room.'

'But he'll see the door now that he's looking around the place.' Carol couldn't see how any of this would help them.

'He will, he will,' her mother agreed. 'But, it won't open.' A smile. It seemed she had achieved a victory of sorts.

'Mammy, I'm fairly sure there's no lock on that little door and even if there is, we don't have the key.'

Moira shook her head. 'Then we'll have to close it another way.'

'But how are the two of us meant to do that?'

'We'll google it!' Moira snapped, running out of patience with her daughter's objections. 'You go and get ready if you're coming. We'll wait for your father to head off and then we'll go.' A wave of the hand to dismiss her daughter and then Moira turned back to the sink, busying herself with the dishes as if she was being watched.

Less than an hour later, Mrs Buttimer and her West Highland terrier were on patrol on the green verge opposite the houses on Stable Row when they saw Carol Crottie drive by with her mother perched in the passenger seat. Mrs Buttimer had thought the Walsh lad from number six had been confused when he'd described the new owner of number seven. Carol Crottie was the person moving out. However, it was then confirmed that he'd been correct. The Crotties were the new owners. It was all very peculiar. Mrs Buttimer didn't like it. There had been enough changes on the street and the last thing she wanted was builders' vans and the noise and the dust.

The old woman stood and watched as Carol tried to squeeze into a parking space further along. She tutted when the doors opened and the two women got out of the car. It was hardly what one might call parked. The back of the vehicle was still sticking right out into the street. Mrs Buttimer doubted that a delivery truck would be able to get past. She decided to retreat inside and keep watch from the front-room window.

'It'll have to do,' Carol was telling her mother. 'You're the one in a rush.'

'All right. All right.' Moira had more pressing concerns than her daughter's inability to parallel park. She hurried along the pavement towards the gate of number seven with Carol just behind her.

Moira stopped abruptly. Carol almost bumped into her. 'What's—' she began to ask but then she saw what had caused her mother's sudden halt. The door to number seven was standing wide open.

'Why do you think—' Carol began to whisper into her mother's ear, but Moira silenced her question by raising her left hand. She began to walk slowly down the path, careful not to let her heels make any noise on the paving stones. Carol had the feeling that they were on a mission behind enemy lines. They had reached the doorstep and Moira was just deciding if she should go in or not when a figure appeared at the door.

'Jesus. You gave me a fright!' It was Dave. 'What are ye doing here?'

Carol instinctively looked to her mother. What *were* they doing here?

'The locksmith called. I just came in to check on things,' Moira explained, her voice steady and calm. Carol vowed never to believe anything her mother said again.

'But that's the thing. There was no problem with the lock or the key. I just came up to check it out and there was no broken key.' Dave tapped the lock on the front door.

Without hesitating for a second, Moira explained, 'That's right. The locksmith was able to get the broken piece out with some tool. He just called to say that we didn't need a new lock and there was just a call-out fee.'

'Right. That's something anyway.' Dave already seemed to have moved on from the subject of locks. He stepped back into the hall and pushed the door open wider to encourage Moira and Carol in. 'The house looks good, I'd say. No need spending mad money. Bit of paint. Do you think we should sand the floors?' He was peering down, assessing the potential. Carol looked over his shoulder. The basement door was still closed. She wondered if her mother had noticed but of course she had.

Moira walked towards the stairs. 'Maybe this floor and the living room, but no need to do the bedrooms.'

'Stairs?' Dave ran his foot along the bottom step. 'They'd come up nice, don't you think?'

'What are the floorboards like upstairs?' Moira casually led her husband towards the first floor, away from the small unseen door. It did just look like a cupboard. No wonder she'd never noticed it when she'd visited her daughter.

Carol watched them go and wondered if there was something she was supposed to be doing while her mother distracted Dave. She couldn't think of anything, so she opened the door into the small dining room and stood in the hall shifting her weight from foot to foot, anxious to usher her father out as quickly as she could.

From above came the hollow sounds of her parents walking around the living room. Moira's voice echoed indistinctly through the floor. The sun had come out and was streaming through the open front door. It was hard to imagine what lay hidden in the basement. What was even harder for Carol to accept was that the body had been lurking down there for the entire time she had lived in this house. How was it possible not to sense something so dark and horrible when it was that close? But then she had to wonder – could she have lived with a killer for all those years and never suspected anything? No. Until someone proved otherwise, she still refused to believe that Declan was capable of harming another person, never mind killing them.

'Well, look, Carol isn't busy,' Moira was getting louder as she and

Dave came back down the stairs, 'so why don't you let her sort out times with your guys? They'll need to measure up and figure out how much paint to order. All white?' They were in the hall now. 'What do you think, Carol? Everything white?'

Carol struggled to adjust her thoughts to considering paint colours.

'Mm. White? Yes, or maybe . . . I don't know . . . maybe something a bit warmer?' She hoped she was saying the right thing.

'We'll look at some paint charts and decide. It needs to be neutral, isn't that what they say on all those programmes?' Moira had kept walking and now all three of them were standing outside.

'I'll just close up,' Moira said as she double-locked the door. Dave watched with a puzzled expression. 'I thought you broke your key in the lock?' he asked.

'I'd a spare at home,' she replied without missing a beat. Carol suppressed a smile.

What was the point of the television? Why have it on when the volume was so low no one could possibly hear it, so that all the picture did was jerk your attention away from the person you'd actually come to visit. It was obvious Declan wasn't interested in seeing some march through Dublin. His chin was on his chest and his breathing had the soft rumble of sleep.

When Sally had arrived at St Brendan's half an hour earlier, he had been awake. She had taken comfort in the way he had smiled at her when she peered around his door. He didn't use her name until she said it herself, but his face suggested he knew who she was. He had asked her questions, but whenever she mentioned someone else, such as Killian, then her father would ask the same questions about them. Sally had tried to navigate her way through a small chat. She had learned the sort of subjects that Declan felt comfortable with. Sleep, food, the weather; it was like going through the repeated phrases of a language lesson.

Soon Declan had tired himself out and his head had nodded forward, the folds of flesh concertinaed under his chin. Sally didn't mind, in fact she preferred it when her father slept. She liked being able to deliver little monologues to him with no expectation of a response. It reminded Sally of her imaginary friend from childhood and the way she used to explain everything to them because for some reason her invisible pal, Belle, had been from France and didn't understand the ways of Ballytoor.

It astonished Sally how quickly she had become accustomed to this version of her father. She could remember the man from when she was much younger, imposing and strict, but who had he been in the lead-up to this? Sally really hadn't spent any significant amount of time with Declan after she'd left home. She was fairly sure it had been the same for Killian. Only Carol knew who Declan had been before he began to fade away.

Today Sally was telling her father about not going to work. She had now phoned in sick three days in a row. If anyone had asked her the week before if she enjoyed her job she would have had no hesitation in telling them, without really thinking about it, that she did. Now she wasn't sure. The money from the sale of the house had changed things. Without the immediate pressing financial need to go to work, Sally thought about her job differently. She had a growing suspicion that she was never going to go back. Obviously, she would need to earn money, but maybe this was the moment for her to think again. This might be the first time in her life when she didn't just settle. Sally had begun to wonder what it would be like not to describe everything in her life as 'fine'. What if even just one thing in her life was great?

'Oh, I'm sorry. I'll come back.'

It was Carol taking a step back out of Declan's room.

Sally immediately stood. 'No. No, I was just going. He's having a rest.'

Carol leaned forward towards the door. 'Are you sure?'

'Of course. Of course.' Sally began to gather her coat from the chair and reached for her handbag.

'I normally come earlier,' Carol explained.

Sally went to leave but Carol put a hand on her arm.

'The other night – I'm sorry.'

Sally was happy that Carol had brought up the evening on the doorstep.

'No, I'm sorry too.' She glanced towards her father. 'This is a lot. I don't know why I said those things.'

'Because you meant them,' Carol said. A beat, and then, 'He, your father, is my world.' Sally nodded and Carol continued, 'But sometimes I forget that everything else, all the rest, that keeps going. Just because Declan is like this doesn't mean that you're not angry.'

Sally wasn't sure how she felt. This kindness was so unexpected. 'And I should try to remember that you get hurt too. For so long I thought you were the winner and I was the loser,' she said.

'Oh, Sally.' Carol pulled her into an embrace, and Sally allowed the scent of Carol's familiar perfume to transport her back to the kitchen table in Stable Row, when this woman had meant so much to her.

'We'll talk more.'

'Yes,' Sally agreed.

'But maybe not on the doorstep in the rain,' Carol said with a laugh.

'It's a deal.' Sally stepped out towards the corridor. 'He was on good form earlier.' She gave Carol a smile and then turned and walked away.

With Sally gone, Carol went about her normal routine. She draped her coat on the back of the chair and put her bag down. Then she crossed to the bed and stroked Declan's face gently before kissing him on his forehead. As she did all of this she whispered her hellos and asked the sleeping Declan about his day. She wiped a small trail of saliva from the corner of his mouth.

Carol edged the high-backed chair closer to the bed so she could easily hold Declan's hand or rub his arm. From her bag she pulled out an old leather-bound book. Recently she had begun to read to Declan. He seemed to like it and Carol enjoyed the way her voice flowed uninterrupted, giving the room a sense of life that her stilted one-sided conversations didn't. She had found a book on the history of Ballytoor in the local library. It was dry going, but she knew things would pick up when she got to the section on the garrison and hopefully the building of Stable Row.

Just as she was about to start her reading she became aware of the television. The low, indistinct sound of a weatherman was going to irritate her. Carol looked around for the remote control but couldn't find it. Putting her book down, she examined the television, which was perched high on the wall above Declan's bed. There was no obvious button to press to switch it off. Carol gave a sigh of frustration and left in search of the nurses' station to see if they had a spare remote or knew where Declan's was. Halfway down the corridor she bumped into the only male nurse at St Brendan's. Carol liked him. He was young, with a shock of red hair and a thick Kerry accent. She explained her problem.

'Come on and we'll have a look,' he said, leading Carol to a small area surrounded by a high counter where the nurses gathered and kept files on the patients. He lifted some papers and folders on the desk and opened a couple of drawers.

'No sign of one. Sorry.'

'Why do they get moved?'

The nurse shrugged. 'You wouldn't know. It might be in the bed with him, did you have a look?'

'No, but Declan would never touch it – I don't think so anyway.'

'Come with me.' He waved her further down the corridor. 'We'll borrow the one out of Maggie's room and see if that works.'

Carol followed. 'Won't she miss it?'

'Miss it?' The nurse laughed. 'She wouldn't miss the whole telly! She's even more far gone than your fella.'

Carol knew he meant no harm, but it felt so dismissive. As if all these old people, with their lives behind them, were now interchangeable.

She waited just inside the door of Maggie's room. The light was dimmer than in Declan's, just a small lamp throwing a pool of light across the bed where the shape of a body could scarcely be seen in the folds of the blankets.

'She's a lovely little thing. No bother,' said the nurse as he took the TV remote from the bedside table. He handed it to Carol.

'See how you get on with that. Any problems, just give me a

shout.' He smiled and walked away, leaving Carol standing in Maggie's doorway. She hesitated. Had the door been closed or open? She decided to leave it slightly ajar.

Returning to Declan's room, she was surprised to find someone standing by his bed. They had their back to Carol and were bent to get a better look at Declan's face. They didn't appear to be a doctor or nurse, dressed as they were in a long padded coat with a small fur collar. Carol cleared her throat and said, 'Hello?'

The woman turned. Carol noticed an instant reaction in her face. A strange expression that came and went in a moment. Was she simply surprised by Carol's presence or had she recognised her? Carol didn't think so and yet there was something vaguely familiar about the mysterious visitor.

'Sorry. The nurse downstairs just gave me the room number and I came up.' Her voice was soft and seemed to have a hint of a British accent.

Carol presumed there had been some mistake at reception.

'This is room 107. Declan Barry. Is that who you were looking for?'

The woman looked at Carol for just long enough to unsettle her and then said, 'Yes, yes it is. I'm his wife, Joan Barry.'

Sally wasn't sure what to say. She had met Cath before, so she couldn't just fill the silence with a 'nice to meet you'. Her first instinct had been to offer congratulations, but was that appropriate? Yes, she was going to have a baby, but then she was just going to give it away to Killian and Colin. After a beat, all she could come up with was, 'You look well.'

Cath smiled and nodded.

'Thanks. Feeling OK now. It wasn't too great there for a while.'

'No. We had fierce morning sickness, didn't we?' Colin was pouring cups of tea at the breakfast bar. Cath giggled her agreement. Sally was fairly sure that if she was in Cath's position she would have punched Colin, or at the very least pointed out that *we* had done nothing at all.

'Where's Killian?' Sally asked. He had been the one to text her, asking her to come over.

'Apologies. He's on his way. He lost track of time – you know what's he's like. You don't take sugar, do you?

Sally leaned forward to take her cup of tea. 'No thanks. This is perfect.' She wasn't sure if she had imagined it but she thought Cath had reacted slightly at the mention of Killian's name. Not for the first time, she asked herself what on earth this woman Cath was getting out of the arrangement. If you wanted to have a baby, surely you'd want to keep it? Unless they were going to be some modern trio of parents. Sally had no idea how that might work and no inclination to ask.

'Did Killian show you the scan?' Colin was asking.

'No.'

'Oh, would you like to see it?' His voice had gone up an octave as if he was about to unveil a tiny unicorn.

Sally knew that this wasn't really a question and if it was, the only possible response was yes.

'Yes please,' she said with a great deal more enthusiasm than she felt. Cath folded her hands in her lap and composed her face into what Sally thought Cath might imagine to be a saint-like expression. This was her moment.

Colin held out a blurry image. Sally thought she knew what she was looking at, even though the head did seem strangely large. Again she struggled to come up with an appropriate response. She settled on 'That's amazing!' because no matter what you thought about the unborn child, the technology that delivered the image was very impressive.

'Thank you,' Cath purred, with just the hint of a blush. 'I can't wait to meet her.'

Sally felt something shift, and her emotions were untethered for a moment. She couldn't explain why knowing the sex should make this whole scenario harder for her to deal with, but there was no denying that it did.

'A little girl?' There was a croak in her voice and she feared that she might not be able to control herself. She stood abruptly.

'Will I put the kettle on?' she asked, turning her back on Colin and Cath and heading towards the sink.

'We haven't finished the tea we have, Sally,' Colin objected.

'Right. Sorry. Of course.' She turned and leaned against the kitchen counter. She felt a little better away from the two excited parents and their blurry trophy.

The door swung open and Killian staggered in, weighed down by shopping bags. Colin rushed forward to help him.

'Jesus, Killian, there are only the four of us!'

Killian dumped the bags on the breakfast bar and looked up with a wide grin.

'Sally! You came.'

'You invited me. I said I would.' She was instantly irritated, and then annoyed with herself for allowing her brother to aggravate her so easily.

After their mother had left, they had been so close. When had things changed? After Carol came on the scene? No. She could remember them sharing their disapproval of that, the way they both always called her Miss Crottie or the Grotty one. Oddly, Sally thought the rift had happened when Killian had come out about his sexuality. No one had been especially surprised or shocked and Sally was certain that even subconsciously she hadn't felt any disapproval. There had been gay guys at college and she had loved spending time on the periphery of their circle, listening to them gossip about all the sex they were having while she wasn't having any. With Killian it was different. He used his sexuality to set himself apart. As if he believed that Sally was no longer capable of understanding anything he might be experiencing. His new life going out in Cork and trips to London and Mykonos made Sally feel as if she had been left behind. She was just a leftover from his previous life. The final shutter had come down on their relationship when Colin had come along. At that point Killian seemed completely consumed with his lover, then their new house, followed by the awful wedding and now this pretend baby.

'Buck's Fizz, anyone?' Killian was holding a cold bottle of cava.

Sally found herself replying, 'Yes please,' and it was the only sincere thing she had uttered all day.

A click and a sliver of light.

'Carol? Are you up?'

Moira's shadow loomed large in the doorway.

Carol turned on her bedside lamp. 'Yes, Mammy.'

Moira quickly closed the door and scuttled forward to sit on the edge of the bed.

'So, what happened?' Moira's eyes seemed to be bulging out of her head.

'What about Daddy?'

'Fast asleep in front of the telly. I'll wake him to go to bed.'

When Carol had got home from St Brendan's she had tried to get her mother alone but Dave never seemed to be out of earshot. She had managed to whisper to her mother while he went to the toilet, 'I know for certain it isn't Joan Barry in the freezer.'

Moira had quickly pulled her daughter further into the kitchen.

'What?'

'She's alive. She's here.'

'What?' Moira repeated, urgent and hoarse. 'How do you know?'

'I met her!'

Moira opened her mouth to let forth a torrent of questions but then Dave was back in the room, asking about the timer of the central heating and if anyone had been 'messing with it'.

As soon as she could after dinner Carol had crept away to her room. She knew that Moira wouldn't be far behind. And here she was like a hungry dog that had been promised treats.

'So, where did you meet her? Did you just bump into her or what?' Moira leaned forward encouragingly.

Carol pulled herself up to rest her back against the pillows.

'No. She was in St Brendan's. I came into Declan's room and there she was.'

'And did she know who you were?'

'She did. It all seemed . . .' Carol searched for the right word. 'Relaxed. Like, normal between us.'

'And where has she been? What happened?' Moira was looking for the meat on the bones of this story.

'Well, she lives in Wiltshire – Salisbury, she said. Works as a legal secretary. No more kids. Still single.'

'Still married, more like,' Moira muttered. Her eyes turned to the wall for a moment while she gathered her thoughts.

Carol knew that nothing she had to report was going to satisfy her mother. Apart from Joan's sudden reappearance there was nothing even vaguely dramatic or noteworthy about the woman or their meeting earlier that evening. No voices had been raised, no revelations had been made. Joan had asked a few questions about Declan, and Carol had answered without editing herself. She felt oddly at ease talking about him with this stranger. Joan knew a version of Declan that she never would. The young father, the man starting a business. If any of his memories washed up on the shores of his consciousness, it seemed far more likely that they would be from when he lived with Joan. He might be the great love of Carol's life, but she had only known him for a fraction of his years and for some of that time he had already been slipping away.

Of course, Carol had questions, but standing in the hushed still of the nursing home with the steady rasp of Declan's breath marking the passage of time, it hadn't seemed like the place to quiz this woman. It was Joan who had volunteered where she lived and what she did for a living. She seemed open and unguarded. It was Carol who had bristled when Joan had touched the small pile of CDs on the side table and casually observed, 'Still likes Leonard Cohen, I see.'

'Yes.' Carol felt like a mistress. She had to remind herself that it wasn't Declan who had left.

It was only as Joan was leaving, after she had told Carol that she would let her spend some time alone with Declan, that she had casually asked Carol not to mention seeing her to Killian or Sally. Carol had readily agreed. There was no need for Joan to explain further, but she did: she wasn't sure if she would see them; it wasn't that she didn't want to, but she was worried that she would upset them and that was the last thing she wanted, especially when they were dealing with their father.

'Don't tell the children?' Moira whispered urgently. This was more like it. 'So, she *is* still hiding something, isn't she?'

'I suppose so.' Carol shrugged. It was hard to summon the energy to argue with her mother.

'And you didn't ask her anything at all about why she left?' Moira was incredulous that her daughter hadn't even attempted to get more information.

'I told you. It just didn't seem right. She was with Declan for years and she was seeing him lying in that place. She had enough to deal with, without me digging around for gossip.' Carol hoped that this might stop her mother nagging, but no.

'Gossip?' Moira's voice was indignant. 'Have you forgotten about the dead body we have in her old basement?'

Carol slumped down in her bed.

'Oh Mammy! I can't, not tonight. Look, I've got her number now and we said we'd meet up for coffee tomorrow. It'll be easier to talk in the Koffie House, I'm sure.'

Moira stood. The look on her face suggested that she had a plan.

'Not the Koffie House. No.' She paused. 'Stable Row. Tell her to meet you at Stable Row. You'll soon find out if she has something to hide.'

Before Carol could reply, they heard Dave's sleepy voice echoing through the house.

'Moira?'

'Coming, love!' she called and slipped from the room.

White cars were rental. Sally was sure someone had told her that, especially new ones, and this car was gleaming. Why would a rental car be parked outside her cottage? Sally's was the only house on this stretch of the lane. Not many cars drove past at all, but it was even rarer to see anybody parked.

How long had it been there? Sally wasn't sure. She had only noticed the roof of the car peeking above the hedge when she had been making her breakfast. Then when it hadn't moved, she had sneaked out the back door and down the moss-covered path that led to the unused washing line. Cutting through the wet grass, she was able to get a better view through a gap in the hedgerow. A small fog of exhaust fumes floated at the back of the car, so clearly it hadn't been abandoned. Bending forward, Sally tried to see the driver. Was it someone she knew?

A small head was protruding above the back of the driver's seat. Definitely a woman and Sally would have said older. The figure didn't appear to be looking around, just staring straight ahead. Maybe they were on the phone?

Sally padded back to the house and tried to forget about the car. This was the day she had told herself she was going to resign from work. She had no idea what she was going to do next but these few days off had given her the gift of clarity. She didn't want to still be working in the same place in six months' time, so why not leave now? Even if she just ended up stirring huge pots in another industrial kitchen then at least it would be a new one with fresh faces and different things to irritate and bore her. She might even prefer it.

Sally had never quit a job before. As a student she had left a few part-time positions but that just involved never going back. This was different. After this many years Sally assumed that there had to be some formality to it. She knew she wasn't going to do it in person. The thought of bumping into Brid was too much. She would text her when the deed was done. Sally didn't want Brid trying to talk her out of her decision or guilt tripping her into staying. Did she need to write an actual physical letter or would an email do? Given that the only stationery she possessed was a box of notelets with cartoons of French poodles on them, Sally decided that an email would suffice. She sat and opened her laptop.

Before she approached her email she made the rounds of her usual websites. Not really engaging with what was on the screen, she checked the news and then scrolled through Facebook for longer than she had intended. No new messages, not even from Bindy. Sally knew that she shouldn't allow herself to be disappointed, but she was. It had been a while since she had heard from her. Not since her horrible day with old Mrs Crottie. Should she be worried? Maybe she would send her a quick message. No. The email. She had to write her email. She had just typed in the address when she remembered the car. Was it still there?

Half standing from her chair she could see that it was. The white roof hadn't moved. Very uncharacteristically, Sally had a sudden urge to confront the driver. She had a right to know what she was doing parked outside her cottage for so long. She had to admit that it was also a way to delay her resignation for just a while longer. Grabbing a discarded sweater from the kitchen counter, she headed out, hastily pulling it over her head.

At her gate Sally hesitated. She was suddenly aware of how alone she was. How could she confront anyone? She told herself that she would give the driver just a moment or two more to drive away. Nothing. Just the soft purr of the idling engine. Sally gave her arms a slight shake. She could do this. Surely a polite 'Can I help you?' wasn't too aggressive? She opened the small wooden gate and stepped out into the road.

A sudden engine roar made Sally jump backwards, and the white car sped away, spraying a rattle of loose gravel against the gate. A flock of indignant crows burst noisily up into the sky. Sally found she was panting. What had just happened? Was it something to do with her or just a coincidence that it had all played out in front of her home? She wasn't sure how or why, but she suspected that it must have something to do with Killian. She would call him and ask . . . after she had written her email.

She really should come down to this spot more often. She wasn't sure why she didn't. For some reason, even when they were growing up, they had never been encouraged to explore the long narrow piece of the garden that sloped down to the sea. Perhaps it was because her father had never learned to swim. For Dave, the sea would always remain something to admire rather than engage with. Their play area had been on the far side of the house, a flat patch with a swing set and a small hut where they stored games and played shops or hospitals.

Carol's feet were cold in the wet spongy moss that covered the slope below the concrete slabs of the patio and above the long ridges of rocks and pebbles that led down to the sea. She knew she would have to change her shoes when she went back inside but she didn't care. This moment was worth it. The wind blowing a light mist against her face and the sea slapping lazily against the rocks. Some birds on the hunt for food were diving into the waves further out. Carol chided herself for not knowing what sort of birds they were. She resolved to look them up when she got back inside. Her brother Brian had been the one for nature. His bird books were still on the shelves in his old bedroom.

'Carol!' Her name was carried by the breeze. She turned to see her mother, fully wrapped against the weather, standing on the patio.

She was waving. Clearly she wanted something. Carol started walking back up the slope.

'We should be making a move!' her mother called.

Carol's good mood immediately evaporated. Why was Moira saying 'we'? Carol had made the arrangement to meet up with Joan Barry, and it didn't include her mother tagging along as if it was some sort of mature playdate.

Back on the patio, when Carol tried to insist that she would be going alone, Moira quickly wore her down.

'You won't get anywhere. I can just hear you coming back here with no more to tell me. I have it all worked out. You do all your Declan chat and then I'll ask a few questions about the house, casual like.'

Carol didn't think this sounded like her mother's style.

'Like what? Did you leave a body in the freezer?'

Indignant, Moira glared at her daughter.

'Not at all. I thought I'd talk about raising little ones in that house and washing nappies.'

Carol shrugged.

'Washing,' Moira repeated. 'Washing machine. Basement. And, well, then it's almost as if she's brought the subject up herself.'

Carol folded her arms. 'And you're sure that's how it's going to go?'

Moira was heading back to the house. 'Well, something like that. Now hurry up. We don't want to be late for her.'

Carol followed her mother. Clearly, she would not be making this trip solo.

Once more, the car journey was Moira's version of silent. To-day's monologue included notes on hedge-cutting, a loose dog that should have been killed by now, and a house on a dangerous bend that she would hate to live in. Carol felt an unsettling mixture of irritation and nerves by the time they arrived at Stable Row for the meeting.

No sign of Mrs Buttimer, but the high-pitched shrieks of children at play echoed from the garden of number two. Carol and Moira were standing on the doorstep of number seven, searching her handbag for keys – 'You should have had it out, ready,' Moira scolded her daughter – when the door abruptly opened itself.

Moira gave a little yelp of surprise and shock and Carol instinctively stepped back. She had the urge to run.

Inside the house stood a smiling Dave and beside him a garda in full uniform. Why was there a policeman in the hallway? Moira and Carol willed each other to remain calm.

'Dave!' Moira said, as brightly as she could. 'You never said you were coming up?'

'Moira, Carol, this is Sergeant Draper. Sergeant, my wife and youngest daughter.'

The policeman touched his cap and gave a small cough in greeting. Carol was too frightened to risk speech, but of course her mother managed: 'Nice to meet you.' The women only wanted the answer to the question 'What is a guard doing here?' but feared that actually asking might hasten their fate.

All at once Moira stabbed a finger into the air in front of her. 'Haven't we met before, Sergeant? I'd swear I know you.'

The guard smiled and looked at Dave before answering. 'Well, I've been stationed in Ballytoor for a fair few years. You've probably seen me around.'

'No. That's not it, no,' Moira said with the air of a woman who was not in the habit of noticing policemen.

'Would it be the Chamber of Commerce?' Dave suggested. 'You probably met at one of those dinners. That's going back a bit now though.'

Moira's face paled. 'You know, I think that might be it. Well, nice to meet you again.' She took half a step back from the door, her mind frantically trying to calculate what this new information meant.

'I asked the sergeant up to have a look at the locks and that. I was a bit worried with the place being empty.'

The guard nodded his confirmation.

'Very wise, love,' Moira said.

Dave stepped back from the door. 'Are you coming in?'

'We are of course,' Moira began, but then stopped and turned to Carol. 'Oh love, I forgot something in the car, would you ever get it for me.' She hooked her daughter's arm and led her towards the gate. As they walked she put her lips to Carol's ear. 'Stop Joan Barry.' Carol gave her mother a wordless look, seeking some clarification. Moira whispered close. 'Take her somewhere, anywhere – she can't walk in here with your man. She'll run for the hills.' Then, separating herself slightly from Carol, she said, loud enough for the men to hear:

'If you can't find it, you could always pop down town. Do you mind?'

'Not at all!' Carol waved and hurried back to the street. She thought she could hear a car.

Moira returned to the front door, where Dave and the sergeant were looking at her with puzzled expressions. She ignored them.

Moira had long ago learned the wisdom of never explaining and never apologising.

'The house has good bones, wouldn't you say, Sergeant?'

He moved back to allow Moira into the narrow hall.

'Oh it does, in fairness – good bones all right, Mrs Crottie.' His voice had a Kerry lilt and somehow that made Moira feel better about the whole situation.

From the lack of reaction in the Koffie House, it seemed that no one remembered Joan Barry. Behind the counter Noor was her usual gleaming self. Her smooth, waxy face framed by the colourful bandana that was casually tied to hold back her hair. She beamed at each customer with her wide, even-toothed smile that looked designed for biting into apples. Noor seemed to have forgotten all about Carol being a tragic figure as she urged her to buy pastries to go with the coffee.

'The appleflap is just from the oven, ladies!' Her eyes were the glassy blue of a shop mannequin. There was something about them that unsettled Carol.

'I don't think so. Joan?' Joan shook her head. 'No thanks. Just the coffee.'

'Oh, sweet enough is it, ladies?' A slightly mannish laugh without any further eye contact.

Joan and Carol settled themselves at a small table wedged between the cold drinks fridge and the stairs leading down to the toilets.

'Very cosmopolitan. All new since my day,' Joan said, looking at the abstract paintings, each sporting an optimistic price tag.

'Good coffee. The town needed it.'

'And you must know your coffee, being a Crottie. You are that Crottie, aren't you?'

Carol suddenly felt very self-conscious. It was strange to be sitting with this stranger who seemed to know things about her.

'Yes. Daddy hates it that I come in here.' She smiled, hoping to appear more relaxed than she felt.

Carol explained to Joan that the floors were being sanded in number seven so that was why they had walked down the hill to have a coffee. Now that they were sitting across from each other at the table, Carol felt the weight of Moira's expectations.

'So do you think you'll see the kids on this trip?' That didn't sound too intrusive, Carol thought.

Joan stirred her coffee for a moment.

'I don't know. I mean I want to, of course.' Her eyes met Carol's, to see if she believed her.

'Of course.'

'The truth is I drove out to Sally's this morning but I couldn't get out of the car. It just seemed too sudden, too dramatic. Do you know what I mean?'

Carol nodded. 'Yes, though to be fair, she probably wasn't there. She works mornings.'

'Oh, she was there. I saw a young woman come to the gate, it must have been her. I panicked. Drove off. Stupid, I know.'

They both took a sip of their coffee.

'What about Killian? Have you seen him at all?'

Joan studied the painting above their table for a moment.

'You have children, don't you, Carol?'

'Yes. A son. Craig. He's over in London.'

'Right. A son. Well, I don't know if you'd agree, but somehow I worry about the boy less. I suppose he was older when I left, not quite eleven but he seemed more than that. Strong. I knew he could cope. It was Sally that I felt most guilty about. She was so little. Tiny.'

Carol could see tears filling Joan's eyes.

'Well they've both turned out fine. They're well. Very well.'

She felt like an awful person as she placed her hand on Joan's to comfort her, when she knew she would be telling her mother all of this in an hour.

'So what people in Ballytoor have you kept in touch with over the years?' Carol kept her voice low, aware of the other tables.

'No one really. I . . .' Joan didn't look up from the table. 'I just left.'

Carol thought about her reply for a moment.

'Oh, I see. It's just that you didn't seem very surprised that I owned Stable Row when I texted you.'

A fraction of a second before Joan looked up. Her gaze was steady. 'I never knew you moved out.'

Carol gave a perfectly agreeable 'Right. Of course.' But inwardly she was asking herself questions. How did Joan know that she had ever moved in, and who had told her where Sally lived, or that Declan was in a home?

What followed was careful and polite. Joan asked questions about Declan's condition. She was sensitive and understanding. Carol got the feeling she was genuinely interested, not just fishing for information. Joan shook her head with disapproval when Carol told her a sanitised version of Killian bullying her out of Stable Row, but stopped short of actually saying anything. They talked more in generalities than specifics. Joan told Carol about a partner in the law practice where she worked and how they had developed a similar condition to Declan. It wasn't anything very personal or revealing but to Carol it seemed like Joan's way of telling her that she understood.

Talking about Declan with someone who had known him, loved him at some point, felt comforting. It brought him back for a moment, made the life they had shared real because here was someone else who had experienced similar things. It was oddly intimate to be sitting next to someone who knew about the trick to opening the bathroom window or Declan's hatred of rice. Carol knew that she was talking too much. Her mother would be furious if she didn't come home with some new information. Spurred on by this thought of the inevitable interrogation she would face later, she risked a question.

'I hope you don't mind me asking, but I've always wondered why you left?'

Joan's mouth gave a momentary twitch.

'Did Declan never tell you?' There was something in the way she asked the question that gave Carol the impression this was the question Joan had come here to ask. This was what she needed to know. Clearly there was still a secret that needed protecting.

'No. He didn't. He rarely talked about you. I mean, not in a bad way,' she quickly clarified, 'just in the way I didn't often mention my ex-husband. You know.'

'I do. I do.' Joan drank the last of her coffee. Carol sensed that she might be about to leave. She couldn't let her get away so easily.

'So what was it? Why did you leave?'

'It was a lot of things. Too much for now, I think.' She buttoned her coat as she stood. Carol found herself reaching out to take hold of the other woman's arm.

'One thing. Isn't there one thing, one reason, you could tell me about now?'

Joan sat down again and studied Carol's face.

'Is there something specific you'd like to ask me? If there is, please ask it.'

Carol's heart drummed in her chest. This was the moment. The chance to ask her about the freezer. A swarm of options filled Carol's head – 'Do you . . .' 'Did you . . .' 'Was there . . .' 'Has it . . .' – but the words she found herself actually saying were:

'No. I just wondered, that's all. It was a big decision.'

'It was,' Joan said in little more than a whisper and then, as she stood up again, a little louder, 'It was.'

'And why come back now? Is it just a coincidence or did someone tell you about Declan?' Carol was finally hitting her stride. Moira would have been proud.

Joan looked left and right as if seeking her escape route.

'So many questions. I'm not very . . . you're making me very uncomfortable.' She stepped away from the table and added, 'We'll speak again. Thanks for the coffee.' Then she was gone. Carol stared towards the door. What was her story?

From behind the counter Noor called, 'Bye now. Come again!'

The whole building seemed to have moods. Some days the corridors of St Brendan's echoed with scattered giggles or snippets of songs learned long ago. People happy to spend time with the memories they could find. At other times there was a feeling of loss and anxiety. A wailing that could not be comforted, a question with no answer yelled over and over again. Only Declan appeared to be impervious to the mood of St Brendan's. When he was awake, his eyes focused on the television screen, or, if he had visitors, he might glance at them, as if he was checking they were still there.

Killian preferred it when his father was asleep. Then he got to feel like the dutiful son, nodding to the nurses as he made his way through the hallways, but once in his father's room, he could while away half an hour scrolling through his phone without feeling guilty. If he found Declan awake, as he had on this occasion, he felt compelled to try to make some sort of conversation.

Today he had brought props but by the time he was sitting in the tall chair by his father's bed he had thought better of the idea. He touched the breast pocket of his coat. The scan of his daughter was held there. Killian had brought it with him thinking that it might be a kind thing to do, perhaps even meaningful, to share this image of Declan's first grandchild. Now here in the room, with his father just grunting the phrase 'some fella' at the television screen, the idea of getting the scan out seemed at best maudlin and at worst, cruel. Killian himself found it difficult to imagine that the grey blurry kidney bean with limbs was going to be an actual child, so how on earth could he expect Declan to understand what he was being shown?

Killian glanced at the time. He'd only been here ten minutes. Clearly Declan wouldn't mind if he left, but Killian always felt the unspoken judgement of the nurses if he didn't at least manage half an hour. He knew it was stupid – what did it matter what the staff thought? – but that was just the way he felt. He checked his phone. A text from Colin about dinner. Apparently they would be having chilli. Killian hated Colin's chilli. It was always watery and never quite spicy enough. He sighed and took out the picture of the scan to look at it himself. Why had he brought it? Had he hoped that if his father reacted to it then he might find some emotional connection to the blurry image? Killian saw the way that Colin looked at the scan. It was as if the picture itself glowed, the way it lit up Colin's face. Why didn't Killian feel like that?

Sometimes he could imagine an actual baby daughter making him happy. On the floor with toys, the child gurgling with laughter, Colin taking pictures. Killian could imagine that Christmas with a daughter would be special, maybe trips to the seaside, but every day, all the meals, the talking in stupid voices, those things didn't appeal in any way. He also found himself bristling every time Colin commented about something in the house, a wine glass on the coffee table, candles by the hearth, 'Oh, we won't be having that when baby comes.' It felt to Killian less like a welcome visitor and more like a home invasion where his presence in his own house was going to be chipped away.

He could never have voiced these doubts – well, not to Colin. His husband seemed so sure about the *rightness* of this child, and certainly Killian agreed it did seem like the *right* thing to do, but what for? When you really thought about it, for all the things he would be losing when this child arrived, what was he getting in return? It wasn't even as if they were doing a lovely thing and adopting some desperate waif who needed all the things they could provide. Killian and Colin had conjured this child from thin air, where nothing had existed previously. If they hadn't made it then it wouldn't need anything. What if this little girl wasn't grateful to be alive? What if she resented Killian and Colin for forcing her into existence?

Maybe it didn't help that Killian's experience of a child–parent relationship was now reduced to this bare room. Was Declan glad he was a father now? That seemed very unlikely, and his mother had clearly answered the question of how much she was enjoying parenthood when she exited their lives all those years ago. Would the grey kidney bean one day be in a room like this, trying to rearrange Killian's pillows? What on earth was the point? Why was Colin so inexplicably overjoyed by the thought of it all? Killian slumped down in his chair. In this room it was very hard to see who was benefiting from this family bond.

Later, when he got home, Colin dashed out to the hall where Killian was taking off his coat.

'Did you show him?'

'I did, yes.'

Colin bit his bottom lip. 'And? What did he say? Did he under-stand?'

Killian slid his scarf onto a wall hook. 'You know, I think he kind of did. It was lovely. Beautiful really.'

He allowed Colin to hug him and kiss his neck.

Surrounded by boxes, their conversation was going in circles. Moira picked over every word that Joan had said to Carol.

'That was her asking you to ask her!' She threw up her hands in frustration. Carol felt attacked.

'I don't know why I didn't ask her! You weren't there. Yes, she has secrets, but I'm not sure if the freezer is one of them.'

'Oh, Carol, cop yourself on. It's her freezer, she disappeared and now the house is sold she suddenly comes back? You do the sums.' Moira sat heavily on one of the boxes that they had moved into Linda's room. They'd told Dave it was to make Carol's bedroom a bit more comfortable but really it was just an excuse to be alone and out of his earshot.

'But why come back? If you'd hidden a body you wouldn't want to be around when it was found. It makes no sense.'

Moira chewed her lips. It was irritating for her to admit, but Carol had a point. If you'd got away with something for so many years there was no reason to reappear at the exact moment your crime was going to be unearthed.

'Is it something to do with you? Did she know you had bought Stable Row?'

Carol gripped a handful of her hair as if she might try to rip it out. 'I told you already. She said she didn't, but it's hard to know what she does and doesn't know. Someone in Ballytoor is talking to her, that's for sure.'

Moira stood and tried to pace but there was so little room she was basically turning in small circles like a figure on a music box.

'Well, one thing's for sure. Now the guards are sniffing around the house, we have to do something with the body.'

'What? Like tell the police about it? Like we should have done the second we found it?' Carol looked up into her mother's face, appealing for some agreement. She continued, 'This doesn't have to be so messy. Who cares about Joan Barry? We'll tell the guards and then they can do what they like. We didn't kill anyone so we aren't going to be the ones getting in trouble.' She folded her arms, her point made.

'You know what will happen then. Joan will fly the coop and then your precious Declan will end his days being branded a murderer!'

While Moira believed this to be true, she still couldn't fully explain to Carol her fear that Dave was somehow involved. Why had that guard been at the house? It made no sense. Sergeant Draper must have known Declan Barry too. Was he involved somehow? Moira hated having these doubts about her husband but try as she might, she couldn't dismiss them. Moira had no answers. Unless she dealt with what was in that basement, she couldn't see how this could end well for any of the Crotties. Moira had found the body and now it felt like hers and she wasn't ready to hand over their mystery yet.

Feeling slightly dizzy, Moira sat again.

'I want to meet Joan Barry.'

Carol didn't say anything. She knew that no matter how much she thought this was a bad idea and no matter how much she fought it, the meeting was bound to take place.

'Why, Mammy?'

'So that I can ask her myself what she knows about the frozen person in her basement!' Moira barked, annoyed that her daughter even needed to ask.

'What if she won't tell you anything? Maybe she really doesn't know anything about it. What then?'

'Then we think again. But mark my words, that woman knows something. You said it yourself, she has secrets.'

The car was back. Sally had no idea how long it had been there. Now that she no longer had to get ready for work she had developed a habit of staying up late and then sleeping till nine or even ten. She felt guilty stretching her limbs under the duvet as the morning sun filled her bedroom, but not enough to stop. The white roof of the car had caught her eye as she came down the stairs and spied it through the clear glass above the front door.

Killian had denied all knowledge of the car when Sally had asked him, but afterwards she realised that really didn't mean very much. Her brother was an excellent and frequent liar. If he didn't want her to know something about the mysterious white car then he wasn't going to blurt everything out just because she asked him.

Wearing her new morning uniform of yesterday's T-shirt and some sweatpants, Sally crouched at the kitchen table, busy with her phone. Now she didn't have to go to the hospital, social media had become her full-time occupation. Just going through her Instagram feed could take hours. She no longer just saw and liked photos but had begun to go deeper. Often she clicked through to find the other people who had liked or commented. What did their lives look like? Who did they know? It was utterly pointless, she was aware of that, but she found that she was good at recognising the faces or even the interiors that she had spotted in other feeds. It might be stupid, but she couldn't deny the satisfaction of making unexpected connections. It made her feel involved somehow, not just a voyeur. This morning she was scrolling through reels. Attractive people doing simple dances, while their clothes magically changed. She couldn't explain it but she felt like she was dancing too. Sally became aware that she was smiling, and she didn't know why or for how long she had been doing it.

A knock on the door brought her back to her kitchen. The car. It must be the woman from the car. Sally walked slowly into the tiny hallway. She wouldn't have said she was nervous exactly, but she did feel apprehensive. This was not the way good news was delivered. Sally hesitated but then another series of knocks drummed at the door.

Sally only partly opened the door and peered around. The woman was older. Short hair, but layered in a way that made it look expensive. Clearly the visitor on the doorstep was nervous. Sally might even have described her as frightened. This made Sally relax slightly. Whatever this was about, it was someone else's drama.

'Hello.'

'Sally?'

'Yes.'

The visitor's face became softer, a smile tugged at her lips, but she said nothing, just gazed at Sally expectantly.

'Can I . . . what is it?'

The visitor shook her head. 'Sorry. It's just that I thought maybe you might recognise me.'

As the woman said this, Sally had an odd sensation. There was something familiar about this person on the doorstep. Did she know her? How had they met? Was it someone from work? No, that wasn't it. This face was from longer ago. Different hair? No, it was more than that.

The woman put her hand up to the doorframe and leaned in.

'It's me, Sally. Joan. Your mammy.' She began to raise her other arm as if expecting an embrace.

There seemed to be no air. Sally felt as if her lungs were being squeezed empty. She just let out a strangled cry and slammed the door shut. She fell backwards and stumbled into her kitchen. Her mother? The woman at the door wanted to be her mother? Sally's mother had left and never come back to see her, not even once. All the times she had longed to have her mammy with her. The nights she had imagined her sitting on the edge of her bed, stroking her hair as she fell asleep. The hugs she had yearned for when Darragh Whelan had changed his mind and brought that little slut Susannah to the school dance, and her after telling everyone that she was going with him. The shopping trips for dresses, watching the girls from her class clacking through the rails with their mothers while she had to try things on to show her brother. Why the fuck would she want to see that woman now? She slumped down onto her heels and hugged her knees, letting out a low howl. She was shaking and could feel an anger growing inside her. She imagined throwing the front door open and battering that woman till she fell to the ground.

Through the glass of the front door Sally could see the dark shadow of her mother. It moved away and then came closer. She seemed to be crouching down. What was she waiting for? Why didn't she just leave? Another series of knocks.

'Sally?' Her voice sounded hurt and surprised. Really? Sally wondered how her mother had imagined this reunion might go. Had she thought Sally would react like one of those dogs she saw on the internet, losing their mind when their soldier owner came back from the war?

She pressed herself back against the wall and felt a little calmer. Her sobs subsided. The shadow was moving around as if deciding where to go next. More knocking, softer this time.

'Sally, love. I'm sorry. I know this is a shock. I just wanted to talk.'

This time the shadow stayed where it was. Sally didn't know what to do. This was the woman she had wanted to see, longed to see. It made sense to let her in, but this was also the woman who had hurt her, abandoned her. Why should she allow her to do it all again?

Inching her way up the wall, she wiped her face dry. She walked to the door, imagining she might say something, safe behind its protection. But what? Sally reached forward and opened the door, letting it swing inwards. She immediately scuttled back. Joan stood on the doorstep with her legs braced and her hands held out low. It struck Sally that they were both as frightened as each other.

'Sally. I'm sorry. I didn't know the best way to do this. I'm sorry to upset you.' Joan's voice was hushed and coaxing. Sally knew she was studying her, trying to guess what she might do next.

Sally struggled to control her breathing and little unwanted tremors were pulsing through her body. She raised her head and took a good look at the visitor on the doorstep. 'Why are you here?' Her voice was brittle. Suspicious.

'I promised your father I'd never come back, but then I heard what had happened to him.'

Sally put a hand over her face and turned her head sharply towards the kitchen. Then she spoke again, very quietly.

'Was it Daddy who made you leave?'

'Oh no, pet. No. Look, this is a lot, I know.' Joan paused, then asked, 'Can I come in?'

Sally didn't answer, but she broke away, darting into the kitchen. Joan decided to take this as an invitation and stepped into the hallway to follow her. She paused before closing the door behind her.

In the kitchen Sally was leaning against the edge of the sink. She was aware of the woman being in the house with her, but she kept her back turned. Looking down, she saw her stained sweatpants and her bare feet. This was not how she had ever imagined this reunion, and she had dreamed of it so many times. Almost as a reflex to the presence of another person, she found herself asking, 'Do you want tea?'

Joan was framed in the doorway. 'That would be nice. Yes please.'

Sally filled the kettle. 'There's no milk.'

'That's fine,' Joan lied. 'Can I sit?'

'Sure.' Sally waved a hand in the general direction of the small table. Joan pulled out a chair, removed the magazines piled on the seat and sat down.

'Give them to me.' Sally took the magazines and placed them on top of assorted junk mail and flyers on the kitchen counter.

Once the mugs of tea were poured, the two women sat opposite each other. Sally studied Joan. She had always imagined that when her mother returned she would look dishevelled and drawn, having escaped the place where she had been held captive. This woman looked groomed and well cared for. A cold and uncertain silence descended.

'So why did you leave us, then?' Sally was surprised to find that after the initial shock, an artificial sense of normality seemed to be taking over. Chairs, table, tea – she felt calm, or at least the involuntary shivers had stopped. This woman had a lot of explaining to do, questions to answer. Normally in any awkward situation, or emotional confrontation, it was Sally who apologised. It didn't usually matter if she was in the wrong, it was just her way of trying to make things better, but not this morning, not after all the . . . everything.

Her mother took a moment to lock eyes with her, and now Sally could see the woman in the photos she had treasured for so many years, looking out from this lined face.

'It wasn't your father's fault. I want you to know that.'

'But you said he was the reason you never came back. Killian said he shouted at you. He said you screamed at each other.'

'Really?' Joan sounded surprised. 'That's not how I remember things.'

Sally eyed her mother suspiciously. 'Why would Killian tell me that if it wasn't true?'

Joan thought for a moment. 'He was young, I suppose. I mean it's not like we never had rows – maybe that was all he could remember?'

'Then why leave us?'

'Oh Sally, please just know that I never wanted to leave you. I've thought about you so much.' Joan reached out and held Sally's hands. She didn't pull away. Her mother's hands felt good – warm and strong.

'But you did. You did leave us. I just want to know why.' Sally's voice had softened.

'Something happened. Something . . .' Joan wiped away a tear. 'Something terrible, and I couldn't stay.'

Sally tried to speak but her mother stopped her. 'And maybe one day I can tell you what happened but not now, not today. But please, please believe me, if I had thought for a second there was another way, I would never have left you. It was for you, you and Killian that I had to leave.'

'But Mammy!' Sally's face was flushed and she pulled her hands away.

'I know, love. I know. It's no answer but maybe one day I can tell you and you'll understand.' Joan tried to take Sally's hands again but her daughter stood up and retreated to the sink.

'I'm not a little girl. Not any more. What can't you tell me? What? Did you have some sort of breakdown like Uncle Cathal, is that it?'

Joan gasped. 'No! No, that wasn't it.' She tried to recompose herself. 'Oh Sally, I never stopped loving you.' She got up from the table and went to her daughter. The tears were flowing freely now. 'I've loved you every minute of every day.' She tried to give Sally a hug but she resisted, pushing herself free.

'You left me! I needed my mammy, and you left me.' Sally was crying too now. She waved her hands wildly. 'My life is fucked and you fucked it! It's not fair. I don't know why you left and I don't know why you've come back!' Her voice was loud, the words jumbled through her tears.

'But I'm back. That's the important thing.' Joan wrapped her arms around her daughter again and this time Sally allowed it. 'I'm back. Your mammy's back.'

They had failed to park on Stable Row. Even after Carol had looped up Twomey's Lane and around twice, there was not a space to be found. Eventually Carol had conceded defeat and parked on the Back Quay. The sound of Moira sucking her teeth made it very clear that somehow she blamed Carol for having to walk up the hill to Stable Row.

'Do you not have stickers?'

'No, Mammy, we don't.'

'Ridiculous,' Moira continued as if her daughter hadn't spoken. 'You should be able to park outside your own house. Who do those cars belong to?'

'I don't know.' Carol was trying to remain calm and not snap at her mother. This afternoon was stressful enough without Moira blaming her for the failures of town planning.

'Well, they don't live on Stable Row, that's for sure and certain. Those big SV what have yous – ridiculous. No need for them. No need in the wide world to be driving them on our little roads. This country is not made for them. Ridiculous.'

As they neared Stable Row halfway up the hill, Moira was becoming breathless. Carol hoped that might turn off the tap of words.

They were just about to head down towards number seven when they practically bumped into a figure heading in the opposite direction. It was Sergeant Draper from the day before.

'Oh, ladies! Sorry, sorry. I'll just arrest myself for dangerous walking!' His wide face glowed with pleasure at his little joke.

'Sergeant.' Moira held one hand on her chest, trying to catch her breath. 'Nice to see you again.'

'I was just checking on your house, like the boss man asked.' He pointed a thumb back over his shoulder at number seven.

'Thank you,' Carol managed to utter, despite her fright at encountering the police again so soon.

'Tell me this, Sergeant,' Moira said with a tight smile, 'is the crime rate in Ballytoor so high that we should be worried? It seems a bit over the top.'

'Well now, Mrs Crottie, define crime.' The sergeant paused as if he was really expecting Moira to expound on her philosophy of rule-breaking, but then he continued, 'I mean, it would just be young lads, you know yourself. I've seen it. Leave a property empty and they'll get in. For nothing. Just sport like, but the damage is done. Windows smashed, messing around, you just don't need it. We had it out at Glenville. You know it, that estate they never finished.'

'I do.' Moira did.

'Awful. Sinks broke – the lot. Pure devilment. If they see the uniform around they might think twice, you know yourself.'

Moira nodded. 'True. True. Well, thank you very much.'

'Yes, thanks,' Carol chimed in.

'Tell Mr Crottie I was asking for him,' the sergeant called as he walked away.

'I will. I will,' Moira said, loud enough for the policeman to hear, and then under her breath, 'I could kill your father.'

Before Carol could say anything they were confronted by Mrs Buttimer and her grubby dog Margo, who was straining on her leash to be somewhere more interesting. Cursory greetings were exchanged and then the old lady asked if Carol had moved back in to number seven.

'Not yet, no. Just going to give the place a bit of a freshen up.'

Moira squeezed her daughter's arm. Obviously, she felt that even this was too much information to share.

'Well, we must be off.' Moira made to steer Carol on but Mrs Buttimer turned to block the narrow path.

'Did you have a break-in at number seven?'

'No, no break-in,' Moira said breezily and tried to move her daughter past. Mrs Buttimer only backed up a couple of inches.

'It's just that the guards have been seen up here twice now. Twice,' she repeated for emphasis. 'This has never been that sort of street. You understand.'

Moira dropped her daughter's arm and fixed Mrs Buttimer with a stern stare. Carol cringed in anticipation.

'What exactly are you accusing us of?' Moira wanted to know.

Mrs Buttimer tilted her head back slightly, unused as she was to being challenged.

'Well, nothing. Nothing really. I was just commenting.'

'Do you think we're selling drugs up here, is that it?'

'No. Of course not, Mrs Crottie.' Mrs Buttimer was clearly rapidly regretting ever bringing up the subject of the police.

'A brothel, maybe? Are you calling my Carol a prostitute?'

'Mammy!' Carol objected while Mrs Buttimer spluttered, 'Really, Mrs Crottie, that is too much. I was just saying—'

Moira interrupted her. 'Well I'm just saying that maybe you should spend more time minding your own business.'

Mrs Buttimer was stunned into silence. Her jaw hinged open and shut.

Moira took Carol's arm. 'And while you're at it, you might want to wash that dog of yours. This isn't that sort of street.' With that she stepped into the road and walked on. Carol could feel her face burning with a combination of shame and pride.

'That was too much, Mammy. She didn't deserve that.'

'You're probably right,' her mother said with a hint of contrition. 'But your father wasn't here to shout at so she was the next best thing.' She shrugged to indicate that the anger she had felt was spent.

Once inside number seven they stood in the hallway, awaiting the arrival of Joan Barry. Moira checked her watch. Carol kicked at the narrow door to the basement.

'We still haven't got this closed up.'

Moira walked into the small front room to look out of the window.

'No point yet if we're bringing Mrs Barry down there,' she called back to her daughter.

'Don't call her that, Mammy.'

'Why? Isn't it her name? If Declan had ever bothered to make you Mrs Barry we wouldn't be in this mess.'

Carol clenched her jaw. She hated it when her mother was like this, clearly spoiling for a fight. It was difficult for her not to say something to defend Declan but Carol knew that was what her mother wanted, and she would just end up more upset.

Carol felt her phone twitch to life in her pocket. She looked at the screen.

'It's a text from Joan.'

'And?' Moira asked.

'*Apologies. Something has come up. Not sure when I go home. Soon I think. Jx*'

Carol looked at her mother, awaiting her response.

'Oh for God's sake.' Moira slapped the wall. 'Well, that's it. Clearly it's her secret.'

'We don't know that for sure, Mammy.'

'That's twice now she hasn't shown up. She's scared of something!' Moira prodded the air to make her point.

'No, Mammy. She did come the last time. It was us that sent her away. We still have no idea if she knows anything about the basement.'

Moira dismissed her daughter's objections.

'Well, be that as it may, we can't wait any more. We have to move that body.'

Carol was astonished at how matter-of-fact her mother sounded.

'What? You aren't going to find out who it is? What happened to telling the police?'

'It's pure luck no one has seen the inside of that freezer yet. I don't see how we can wait.'

'But we don't need someone to find it, Mammy. We could just tell them it's there.'

Moira bowed her head and then looked back at her daughter.

'Really? You still think we can report this and everything will be over? Carol, this will drag on for months. Declan will be accused of all sorts, and somehow, I just feel it in my bones, we are going to get the blame for something.'

'Yes, Mammy. Hiding a dead body!' Carol's voice was almost a shriek of frustration.

'Well, no one will ever know we hid a body if we get rid of it.'

Carol's nostrils flared and she pushed her shoulders back.

'Maybe this time I'm not going to listen to you. It's my boyfriend, my house. Maybe I'll just go to the guards myself and put a stop to this madness.' The effort of standing up to her mother winded her. She gave a series of little pants.

Moira gave her one of her looks, cool and measured with just a hint of scorn.

'Carol Crottie, you know full well that you are not going to do that.' A single eyebrow arched to punctuate the end of the sentence.

Carol's shoulders collapsed. Her mother was right. That wasn't going to happen. Doing what her mother told her was so deeply ingrained in her, she was powerless to fight it. When she was a little girl, it had meant she was well behaved and obedient, but now, as an adult, what did it make her? She didn't really want to know.

'OK. OK.' Carol walked slowly across the room and stood beside her mother at the window. 'You keep talking about getting rid of this body. How on earth are the two of us going to do that? Lift a freezer between us?'

Moira rolled her eyes. 'We'd take it out of the freezer, of course.'

'Even then we're going to need help. We can't ask Daddy to do it.'

Moira scratched at a rough patch of paint on the window frame.

'I know someone,' she said quietly.

Carol tried to imagine who her mother might be referring to, but she drew a blank.

'Who? Someone you'd trust to get involved in this?'

'He owes me. He has a small trawler. Fishes off the pier in Stranach.'

'Wait a minute.' Carol scrutinised her mother. 'Have you already planned all of this? Is this what you were always going to do?' She turned away and then quickly back to her mother. 'Christ, Mammy. Have you told this fisherman friend of yours all about this?' She was making herself panic at the thought of more people knowing their secret.

'No. Of course not. But, well, you have to admit a drop in the ocean is a lot easier than digging a big hole.' Moira gave her daughter a look, daring her to disagree.

Carol leaned back against the wall. Could it be that her mother was right again?

Things were moving in the garden. In the darkness Sally couldn't actually see them but as she stood at her bedroom window looking down she could sense them. Nothing frightening. Sally imagined a hedgehog snuffling around the few dead pot plants she had at the back door. Maybe a fox was walking across the fields, his nose to the breeze. She supposed they were out there every night, but she had never thought about them before, never felt part of all the life that must be teeming around her little cottage all the time.

She doubted that she would be able to sleep. Her mind was racing, reliving everything that had happened that day. Sally turned away from the window and realised that it wasn't just the outside world that was transformed. Her little bedroom that she would have described as sad or cramped now seemed cosy and inviting. She sat on the bed and wondered if her mother was thinking about her too.

The knock at the door. The crying in the kitchen. Already it felt as if it had happened days ago rather than a few hours earlier. So much had happened since. Sally watched the day unfold in her mind's eye.

They had sat downstairs and talked for over an hour. Sally told her mother about what it had been like without her, how Killian had looked after her. She skirted around the arrival of Carol into their lives and then described college and how she had quit her job. Joan sat opposite her and listened. No, she had done more than that.

Talking to her had given Sally a feeling she had never experienced before. On the rare occasions that she had shared her problems with the girls at college or even Killian, it had always felt as if she was being indulged or tolerated. With Joan it was different. Her attention was complete. She leaned forward, hungry for every detail. Sally felt as if she mattered, and it was a wonderful feeling. One, she realised, she had been missing ever since her mother had left. No wonder she had been so hungry for the crumbs of care Carol had shown on those Thursday nights. It wasn't enough, though. How could it be? While Sally spoke, small flashes of anger still sparked inside her. As wonderful as the moment was, she had not forgiven, could not forgive this woman for all that she had deprived her of.

Joan, in turn, spoke about her own life. Sally guessed she was probably downplaying things so as not to give the impression she had ever enjoyed her time away from Ballytoor. She described her flat on the top floor of a house on the outskirts of Salisbury. She told stories about the people she worked with in the solicitor's office. Eventually Sally plucked up the courage to ask her if she had a new family and felt foolish at the relief that coursed through her when Joan revealed that she had never met anyone else and that Sally and Killian were her only children.

'Have you seen Killian yet?' Sally asked.

'No. Not yet.'

Sally struggled not to cry again when she heard that. The thought of being her mother's first choice, not Killian, made her feel special, like a winner. Her tears splashed onto the tabletop and she wiped them away. Almost at once, though, another spark of anger flared. She thought of all the ways this woman could have made her feel special over the years, if she hadn't chosen to go away and leave Sally behind. She would have grown up to be an entirely different person – a better person, Sally couldn't help feeling.

'Who told you I lived here? How did you know about Daddy and the house?'

Joan traced her upper lip with the tip of her tongue.

'I saw the house for sale online. I check on Ballytoor all the time. Sad, really, but thank God for the internet. For years there I had no idea what was going on.' She offered her daughter a weak smile.

There was a moment's silence while Sally decided if she believed her mother or not.

'Did you think Daddy was dead?'

'No. Yes. Well, at first.' Joan seemed flustered. 'I thought he might be but then his name never showed up on the death notices website.'

'RIP.IE?'

'That's the one.'

Perhaps it was the mention of websites that caused a sudden shift in Sally's mind, but all at once she recalled why Salisbury had rung a little bell when she'd heard it mentioned. She pushed her chair back across the floor with a dry squeak.

'Are you on Facebook?' She studied her mother's face for any clues.

Joan refused to meet her gaze, looking around the room. She shifted in her chair, and then bowed her head.

'Yes.' It was the voice of someone who knew that the game was up.

Sally knew the answer to the question before she asked it.

'Are you my friend Bindy?'

Joan didn't speak, just nodded her head.

Sally leaped from the table, knocking over her chair. Another betrayal, but at the same time, it did mean her mother had been thinking about her, had perhaps cared all along.

'Why pretend? Why wouldn't you just tell me who you were?'

Joan stood to face her daughter.

'I never meant to message you. Not at first. I just searched for you and there you were. Oh Sally, you've no idea. When I saw your picture . . .' A hand went to her trembling chin, trying to control her emotions. 'When I sent the friend request I just wanted to see your life. You know what it's like on there, photos of parties, holidays, whatever, but you never posted anything for me to see.'

'Because I don't go to parties. I don't go on holiday,' Sally said, her voice flat, with no hint of self-pity.

'It was torture, Sally. I had so many questions and suddenly you were in reach. I know I shouldn't have messaged you but I needed answers. Can you forgive me?'

Sally was struck by the phrase. This was the first mention her newly returned mother had made of forgiveness. It put a little shard of flint into her heart and the mood chilled.

'Forgive you? For catfishing me? Or leaving me and breaking my heart and wrecking everything?' Sally found her voice getting louder as she finally unleashed her resentment. 'Jesus, I don't think it's as easy as that, it can't be. How is it up to me to make this all better? You come home, say sorry a few times and then I'm supposed to paint on a happy face and forgive you? No. I can't. I can't do that.' Sally pushed the pile of magazines from the counter onto the floor, where they landed with a series of heavy slaps. Not looking at her mother, she continued, 'I want you to suffer. I know that's not right but I want you to hurt. I need you to pay for what you did to me.' Her shoulders were hunched and heaving with her sobs.

Joan stepped over the pile of magazines and took hold of Sally's face, raising it to look at her.

'Oh darling, do you really think I didn't suffer? My heart broke too and every day away was agony for me. You've got to believe me.'

Sally took her mother's hands away from her face and held them.

'That was your choice. You didn't come back.'

'Sally, I've explained. I couldn't. I couldn't come back.'

'No, you haven't. You've explained nothing. If you can show up at my door now, why not years ago?'

Joan put a hand to her brow and leaned back.

'Oh if only I could talk to Declan, if only both of us could talk to you. I don't know what to say for the best. I'm trying to protect you. Always.'

'Have you seen Daddy?' Sally sounded surprised.

'Yes, I went to see him.'

'And?'

'He was sleeping. Carol came in.'

'Carol? Carol knows you're here?' This idea horrified Sally. Bad enough that Carol should lay claim to her father but now she had met her mother before Sally herself had even known she was back in Ballytoor.

'There wasn't a scene. It was all right. She explained how bad your father has got.'

'He has good days still,' Sally insisted.

'Really?' Joan looked doubtful. In reality, Sally was talking about the days her father felt like chatting. He seemed to know the names

205

of streets and shops when she told him about any changes in the town. Sally knew Killian disagreed, but she thought their father was not completely gone.

'Yes. Go and see him again. See him with me. He calls Carol Joan sometimes; he's called me Joan.'

'Oh dear God. I had no idea. Joan? He says my name?' Joan looked at Sally, horrified. 'Yes. All right. I'll see him so. I'll go again.'

Sally looked at her mother. She seemed older than when she had arrived, smaller somehow.

'And then will you tell me? Tell me why you left.'

Joan blew out her cheeks and exhaled loudly.

'Maybe. I don't know. Maybe.'

Stranach wasn't a fishing village, though that was what it had been once. Now it was just a T-junction on the coast road with a stone pier that curved out into the ocean like a question mark. Across the road were the faded remains of a pub and a shop, both long closed, and a scattering of bungalows and old cottages dotted along the hill above the pier. Two small trawlers with peeling paint bobbed and leaned against the high concrete wall rising up from the sea. Messy piles of lobster pots and nets were pooled along the walkway. The whole place seemed abandoned.

'He fishes here?' Carol sounded doubtful as she peered through the windscreen from where Moira had instructed her to park at the top of the slipway beside the entrance to the pier itself.

'Yes,' Moira snapped. 'Well, he doesn't any more. It's his son has the trawler now.'

'It doesn't look like those trawlers have been out for years.'

'Well, the son has a fondness for the drink. Bit of a waster really. Awful. Two little ones. I'd say he has his father's heart broken.'

Carol looked around, taking in the ridge of pines trees that had survived decades of ocean gales, their short green branches all pointing shoreward.

'So, what's the plan? Are you just going to stand at the end of the pier waiting for him like the French Lieutenant's woman?' Carol smiled at the image.

'No.' Moira sniffed. 'He has a house over there.'

'Which one?' her daughter asked, looking over her shoulder.

'The white one with the blue door,' Moira replied without making the effort to twist around to see it.

Carol spotted it straight away. A long, low cottage set back from the road behind a small orchard of some ancient stunted apple trees.

'No light on. I told you we should have phoned.'

Carol had not wanted to make this journey at all, but Moira had, as usual, prevailed.

A woman in a high-vis jacket walked by with a golden retriever pulling her along. She took a long look at the women sitting in the car and smiled, before giving an awkward wave with her free hand.

'She'll know us again.' It was the sort of thing Moira had said as a quip many times but now it took on an ominous gravity. What if the people walking along this road or driving past were no longer curious strangers but actual witnesses, who might be asked to describe what and whom they had seen?

'I'll go and knock on the door.' Moira pulled at the handle. Carol followed suit but her mother stopped her.

'No. You stay here. He won't be expecting you.'

'He's not expecting you, is he?' Carol felt as if she hadn't been paying attention properly.

'Stay here,' Moira repeated, ignoring her daughter's question, and slammed the door behind her. Carol watched her cross the road and then approach the blue door. She turned in her seat to get a better view.

A light came on in the glass above the wooden door and then it opened. It was a man, too old to be the son – this must be her mother's friend. Even from this distance Carol could see that his face was deeply tanned and lined. Grey curls framed his high forehead. He was smiling and then Moira followed him inside. The door closed.

Carol turned back in her seat and watched the grey clouds sitting heavily on the horizon. Rory Lynch. Why had her mother never mentioned him before? Who was he and how did Moira know him? It was clear that he was her friend in particular rather than someone both she and Dave knew. And why had her mother refused to phone him? Had Moira forgotten his number or did she think that if this Rory Lynch saw her name come up he wouldn't answer? From the smile on the old man's face when he'd opened the door, it didn't look like they had fallen out.

The minutes passed. Carol began to think about the conversation that might be going on in the cottage. She berated herself for not trying harder to stop her mother. The secret was being shared and now another person knew about the body in the basement. This was madness. It was bound to end badly for everyone. Would her mother end up in prison? Surely not; they hadn't killed anyone. But what Moira had planned next, moving the body, disposing of it, that had to be a crime. Carol had a strong urge to tell her father, because Moira was right, he would go straight to the police.

Her thoughts were interrupted by the car door being thrown open and a burst of cold air. Moira dropped into her seat, breathing heavily.

'You were gone for a fair while. What happened?'

Her mother stared straight ahead; the side of her face twitched as she chewed nervously at the inside of her cheek.

'He's in,' she said finally. There was something about the way

Moira uttered the words, a crisp smugness, that incensed Carol. She slapped both hands on the steering wheel.

'In? He's in? What the fuck are you talking about, Mammy? In what? Jesus, you're not getting the old gang back together for one last bank robbery.'

Carol's sudden eruption filled the car and took both the women by surprise. Moira turned and looked at her daughter, head bowed, her hair hanging forward, both hands gripping the wheel. When Moira spoke, she was calm and measured.

'Finished?'

Carol didn't reply.

'What I was trying to tell you is that he has agreed' – and then Moira slowed down, enunciating each word carefully – 'To. Help. You.' She waited for her meaning to sink in and then added, 'Now you better get going or your father will think we're dead.'

Carol started the engine, then felt she had to try one more time.

'Mammy, it's just that I want to know why we can't—'

'Carol!' Moira stopped her and now it was her voice that was raised. 'We've had this conversation and I don't intend to have it again. We have a plan now. It's simple and leaves no loose ends, so you can just get on with the rest of your life. This is all for you and it's going to be over very soon, so just drive.'

Moira pulled the seat belt down with a violent yank and clicked it into place. Carol knew that this was not the time to try to reason with her mother, so she eased the car off the gravel apron by the road and headed back towards Ballytoor.

They drove in silence, actual silence, without Moira's customary travel monologue. A light rain was being blown in from the sea and the steady swish of the windscreen wipers seemed to be restoring a sense of calm in the car. Finally, Carol risked another question.

'So tell me again, how do you know this Rory Lynch?'

Moira pulled the edge of her coat from under her thigh. 'I've known him for donkey's years.'

'You told me that, but how do you know him? Where did you meet?'

'We went to school together,' Moira replied quickly.

Carol glanced across at her mother.

'Mammy, you went to the convent.'

'Ah, you know what I mean. We were at school at the same time. He was up in the Christian Brothers.'

Carol considered this for a moment. 'So, longer than you've known Daddy then?'

'I suppose so, yes.' Moira sounded vague.

They drove on for a while with only the slow arc of the wipers breaking the silence. Eventually, as the road turned away from the sea, taking them up and over to the other side of the headland, Carol spoke.

'He certainly seemed very happy to see you.'

'Did he?'

'Yes.'

Another stretch of silence and then,

'Mammy?'

'Yes.'

'Was Rory Lynch your boyfriend?'

'No he was not,' Moira replied at once, but Carol thought she caught the flicker of a smile on her mother's face.

As they drove along, a suspicion began to grow in Carol's mind. She felt slightly sick. How was it possible that this situation could be made even worse? Carol had the very unwelcome thought that her mother might be having an affair with Rory Lynch.

She lowered her window and let the sharp breeze wash across her face.

Something had changed. Killian was parked outside the house, but found that he had no desire to go in. The lights were on in the front room and he could see Colin moving about. The flicker of a candle being lit. Killian could almost hear the Spotify jazz piano playlist from where he sat. Colin loved to set a scene. The fuss if Killian dared to sit in a room with the overhead lights on, rather than the selection of lamps that Colin had placed strategically around the room. He wouldn't say anything, of course, just patrol the room clicking each switch until finally he turned off the central ceiling light. Sometimes he would mutter a 'that's better' under his breath. Colin had a way of saying the word *ambience* that made Killian want to harm someone or something. It sounded like a small child struggling to say ambulance. It was remarkable to Killian how often his husband had occasion to say the word *ambience*.

Sitting with his father in St Brendan's wasn't pleasant, he certainly didn't look forward to it, but it gave him time to think in a way that he hadn't done in years, maybe never. When did a normal person get to just sit in silence pondering the past and the future? The world seemed to conspire against anybody doing that. Music, television, phone calls, texts, emails, were they all just a way of fooling yourself that you were busy, living with a sense of purpose, or was it all just a noisy distraction?

Killian did not consider himself a thinker, and certainly not what might be called a deep thinker. When he sat in his father's room, most of his thoughts were occupied by trying to figure out how not to end up in a room like this one day. But beyond that, if it was inevitable that sooner or later he was to be a mound draped in a faded candlewick bedspread, what sort of life did he want to have lived?

He had been happy. Perhaps that was overstating it, but he had certainly not been unhappy. Coasting seemed fine. Killian had lived his life with goals, but equally with a slight detachment. Somewhere in the back of his mind, he held on to an undisclosed plan B. The idea of actually marrying Colin had made him uneasy. He could hear doors being closed, escape routes being blocked off. Killian would never have told anyone, but he didn't really understand all the fuss about gay marriage. Of course, it was nice to know that the nation didn't hate all the homosexuals any more, but wasn't there a way the country could have expressed this that didn't involve him having to get married? In the end it had felt like a shotgun wedding, with all their straight friends who had voted yes pressing their fingers against the trigger.

Why was the baby different? He had been in favour of it. He could remember being excited, clinking champagne flutes, and imagining all the precious moments he would enjoy and share as a father, but now the thought of the baby just made him feel anxious and defeated. It was the forever of it. He felt like he was buying an enormous expensive yacht that would require endless upkeep, when he didn't know how to sail and had no desire to learn. This child wasn't going to be an addition, it was going to consume him, become his whole life. Killian did not want that.

Colin was in the kitchen now. Killian could see his shadow through the open doorway. He glanced at his phone, surprised that Colin hadn't texted yet. He was late. The idea of heading inside, his husband's dry little kiss, the newly acquired habit of a cucumber slice in his gin and tonic, the wittering about Cath or childproofing the house pinned him to his seat. What was wrong with lemon, why childproof the fucking house now when it was too late? The child was already on its way.

He wanted to blame Colin for it all, say that he had bullied him into these choices, steered him into this life cul-de-sac, but it wasn't true. Killian had thought he wanted this, but something had happened. He wasn't sure what. Was it his father? Jesus, was it the hot tub full of grey water lurking outside the back door? All he knew was that he wanted to start again. He wanted . . . what, what did he want? He pulled at his tie. What he really wanted was to be his mother. To disappear. To vanish. The thought of her and what she had done suddenly made him feel calm. Is this what she had felt? Had his mother sat outside Stable Row one night, watching the shadows of her husband and children move across the windows, and decided that she never wanted to see them again? He felt like he was looking at one of those magic eye pictures, the image suddenly coming into focus. This thing he had never understood finally made sense. No one had forced his mother away, it wasn't his father's fault, she had simply chosen plan B.

Killian didn't have a plan, but he started the engine and inched the car away from Brook Drive and back through the cloned streets of Castle Heights.

Joan Barry wasn't a big drinker – well, hardly a drinker at all – but on this night she was making an exception. It had been a long day and as much as she wanted to turn on her heels and disappear again, she knew it wasn't over yet.

After she'd finally left Sally, poor Sally, she had driven back into Ballytoor and found Killian's house. Sally had given her the number and made her promise to go and see him. It touched Joan, the way Sally clearly still cared for her brother even though they were obviously no longer close. Sitting in the car, Joan wondered how she herself felt about Killian, really felt. So many years had passed, years when she had tried not to feel, numbing herself against the pain of separation, denying the hope of this moment ever happening, so now that she was actually about to be reunited with her son, along with the excitement and fear there was also a kind of detachment. Her reunion with Sally had taught her not to plan or assume how things might go. Killian had been older. Did that mean he might be more forgiving or even angrier than Sally? There was only one way to find out.

In the event, it was all an anti-climax. Killian wasn't there. It was the husband Colin who opened the door. Friendly enough, he had made a great show of insisting that she come in and wait, but Joan, mostly due to cowardice, had declined. She told herself it was a sign as well as a reprieve. This was not the time. Colin had seemed distracted by whatever was cooking in the kitchen, but he rushed around gathering a pen and paper so that Joan could leave her number for Killian. Joan hated the part of herself that was silently assessing Colin, judging him. He seemed so ordinary, commonplace. She had imagined that the boy she remembered would have wanted sparks and charisma in his life. Had her son really grown into the man who loved this person? Maybe it was a gay thing and besides, no one knew what made a relationship work. Her life certainly hadn't turned out the way she'd planned. She wrote her number down and said goodbye to Colin, who awkwardly tried to kiss her on the cheek.

At the bottom of the hill was a large SuperValu with a car park, new since her day. Joan stopped and grabbed a couple of sandwiches, along with a bottle of red wine. She didn't know anything about wine but it was Italian, and the price was in double digits, so how bad could it be? Now she sat on the edge of the sagging double bed in her bed and breakfast, cradling a toothbrush mug full of her vino, and actually, it was very nice. Maybe she was just imagining it, but Joan thought she could feel it seeping through her body like someone was loosening the strings of a puppet.

It was dark outside and all she really wanted to do was go to sleep, but just a few sips of the wine had made her braver, or maybe foolish; she was going to bite the bullet. She wasn't stupid. She knew Carol knew. The way she wanted to meet her up at Stable Row, even though Carol had steered her away for some reason. Joan had intended to meet them earlier in the afternoon, but then she couldn't leave Sally, and certainly couldn't have explained where she was going.

Joan sat back against the headboard, which hit the wall with a muffled thud. Sally. All the questions that Joan couldn't answer, some because she didn't think her daughter should have to deal with long-hidden secrets, others because Joan found that she didn't really know herself. Simple, obvious questions like why she had never come back seemed much harder to answer now that she was trying to justify her actions to someone other than herself. Before her return, Joan would have said it was the deal she had made with Declan, and initially that was true, but why the 'never' part? It wasn't as if she hadn't wanted to come back. She had asked Declan but he always told her it would be too dangerous, too painful for the children, but here she was walking around Ballytoor, and the sky hadn't fallen. She sipped her wine. The sky hadn't fallen *yet* might be closer to the truth.

Had it been Declan? Maybe he had grown to prefer life without her, or had the whole plan been a convenient way to get rid of her? Joan remembered what Sally had said about the shouting. Had they been unhappy? She had never thought so. They'd been a youngish couple with two kids and a business to run. She couldn't remember ever thinking about the concept of unhappiness. They were just getting through the days. Maybe she had lost sight of her marriage in the midst of everything, and then after what happened, their relationship, whatever it was they had, had seemed like the least of their worries. Then what bonded them was the very thing that was keeping them apart. If only she was able to ask Declan. What did any of it matter now anyway? The past had happened and nothing was going to change where she had ended up. She caught sight of herself in the mirror on the dressing table. Her face was chequered with the shadows from the rattan lampshade. It looked unexpectedly exotic. Maybe this was the moment she could start charting a different future for herself. It seemed she didn't need to hide any more. The situation wasn't exactly ideal but at least, for the first time in a long time, Joan felt that she had choices.

Draining the mug of wine, she picked up her phone and found Carol's last message. Joan began to type.

Dave checked his phone, which was sitting on the coffee table. Nothing. He heard the ping of a message alert again.

'Carol! Your phone.'

''Kay,' his daughter called from somewhere in the house. Then he heard the gentle squeak of her trainers on the remaining patch of polished wood that surrounded the kitchen.

Dave took his eyes away from the TV screen to glance at Carol.

'It just beeped,' he informed her.

Carol picked up her phone from the side table and studied the screen. Dave looked at her.

'Everything all right, pet?'

Carol's whole head sprang up from the phone as if she had forgotten there was anyone else in the room. A smile snapped into place.

'Yes. Yes, it's just Craig. He's off to Greece for the weekend.'

'Ah, love. I know it's hard. But he's a grown man now. He'll be grand.'

'I know. I know. Silly, but I can't help it.' Carol was inching away and the moment her father's eyes returned to the television screen, she bolted for the corridor.

'Mammy? Where are you?'

There was the sound of flushing and then a muffled voice. 'Just coming.'

Carol got to the bathroom door just as her mother was opening it. Moira found herself being pushed back and then Carol shut the door behind them with a click.

'In the name of Jesus, what's got into you?' Moira protested.

In response Carol held up her phone but then her face creased into a look of disgust.

'What's got into you more like? Is that you? Are you all right?' She fanned the air with her free hand.

Moira was indignant. 'It's my nerves. Everything's going straight through me. And the wind . . . Honest to God, if it wasn't for the noise of the electric carving knife they'd have heard my farts in Ballytoor.'

'Mammy!' Carol hated it when her mother spoke like this. It was as if she didn't know her.

Moira rolled her eyes. 'Well, what is it? Why are we trapped in here with my business?'

'Joan. She's texted again.'

'And? What does she want?'

'She wants to meet up. She wants to see me tonight. What should we do?'

Moira looked at her daughter impatiently, as if she were wondering how she had raised this girl.

'Well, if you want to know anything about freezer man I'd say yes. You don't know how long she's going to be here. She might be off tomorrow for all you know.'

Carol nodded. That made sense.

'Where? Where should we meet her? It's nearly nine now.'

Moira weighed up their options as she spoke. 'Not here with his lordship inside. We could meet in the pub – no, we'd be seen and

221

word would get back to himself. I mean, I would say Stable Row, but that Buttimer one will still be sniffing around at this time of night, asking questions. Where is Joan Barry staying?'

'I'm not sure. Some B & B she said, but she can't want to meet there because in the text she says, "Tell me where". It's up to us.'

Moira put the lid down on the toilet and sat – 'It helps me think,' she explained. Suddenly her face brightened.

'Now, hear me out,' she began. 'What about St Brendan's?'

'What?'

'Think about it. We can tell his nibs that's where we're going without being caught in a lie, and if anyone spots us they won't think it's odd.'

Carol considered her mother's suggestion for a moment. 'But where in St Brendan's? Do you mean in Declan's room?'

Moira gave an apologetic shrug. 'Yes? I mean, that's where you met her before.'

Carol felt defeated. She knew that Moira's idea was far from perfect but, unable to think of anywhere better, she agreed.

'All right. Half an hour should get us there at this time of night. Will I say you're coming?' Carol asked, knowing that her mother would be.

'Up to you.' Moira stood and straightened the waistband of her slacks. Carol unlocked the door.

'Let's get out of this smell hole.'

'You never know, when Declan sees the two of you he might snap out of it and spill the beans about all of it!' Moira gave a rasping chuckle.

'Not funny, Mammy. Not funny.'

Joan checked her face in the rear-view mirror. Not as bad as she had imagined; in fact, she might have even said better than usual. She supposed it was having a few days away from staring at a computer screen for hours on end. She switched off the engine and the world went dark. There were a few outdoor lights dotted around the car park of St Brendan's, but the shrubs had overwhelmed them, leaving nothing more than a gentle green glow.

Visiting hours were over but Carol had assured her that they would be allowed in. Nonetheless, she was not going to attempt it by herself. She waited for Carol to arrive. Her phone was lying on the passenger seat, its screen dark as the night. No messages. She prodded the phone to check the time. She'd only been waiting for a few minutes. It felt longer. How much was she going to tell Carol? She didn't need to know everything, that was for certain. The fact that the police weren't involved yet told Joan that Carol was trying to protect Declan. That was fine with her, because that meant she was protected as well.

Eventually she saw two long wedges of light coming through the trees that lined the avenue from the gates. The car pulled into the visitors' car park and its lights were extinguished. A woman, Carol, stepped out but then a second woman emerged from the car. Joan peered through the darkness. The other woman was older. Had

Carol brought her mother to this meeting? What on earth for? It made Joan want to drive off again. There was something so petty about it. Did they think there was some advantage in outnumbering her? It made Joan pause. Was this meeting not about the basement? Did they need her to sign divorce papers? Something to do with Declan's will? She shrugged off her reservations and gathered her handbag.

Joan was just about to get out of the car when her mobile rang. It was an Irish number. Who could that be ringing at this hour? Then it came to her: Killian. He must have returned home and got the message. She hesitated. She really ought to answer it but now was not the time. She couldn't just say hello and tell him that she'd call him back. She let the call go to voicemail. Tomorrow would be better. She'd know more after talking to Carol and her uninvited mother.

There was no one at the reception desk so Joan just made her way to Declan's room. The building seemed empty apart from the snatches of tinny television soundtracks that drifted through the halls. As she got closer to Declan's room she could hear voices. Women, but also a man. Was Declan awake? Would he know her? She found her heart was beating fast. Joan gave a timid knock on the door and peered into the room.

The two women standing by the bed turned. Carol smiled. Just a look from the mother that wasn't exactly hostile, but could certainly not be described as friendly.

'Joan. Hello again. Come in.' Carol moved aside to make room by the bed. Declan was propped up on pillows, holding a glass.

Joan stepped forward and held out her hand to the older woman. 'Hello. Joan, Joan Barry.'

After the briefest of pauses she shook it. 'Moira. I'm Carol's mother.'

'Nice to meet you,' Joan said and in response got something approaching a smile and a curt nod.

'Joan.' It was Declan and he was looking at her. His gaze made her feel like a ghost. Did he really know it was her or was he just repeating the name that the others had said? Moira looked at Carol with raised eyebrows.

'Declan.' Joan touched his arm. The dry warmth of his pyjama sleeve sent a cold shiver of memory through her. 'Nice to see you. How are you doing?'

'Can't complain. Can't complain.'

His reply conveyed neither shock nor surprise at the sudden reappearance of his first wife

It was clear that seeing Joan again hadn't prompted some sort of breakthrough for Declan. She was not the human key that could unlock his memory.

'You're enjoying your drink?' Joan spoke to him, her voice slightly raised. He lifted his glass.

'Just a drop of . . .' His eyes moved away from them and the tip of his tongue peeked pink and wet from his lips. He had lost the word.

'Drop of whiskey, isn't it, Declan?' Carol said helpfully.

'They don't mind him having a bit at night. Helps him sleep,' Moira explained in a conspiratorial way, which made Joan feel slightly awkward, with Declan lying in front of them.

'Are you finished there? I'll take that.' Carol put the empty glass on the bedside locker and then began rearranging the pillows.

'I'd say you're ready for a big sleep, aren't you?'

Wordlessly, Declan slid down under the cover and rolled over so that his back faced the visitors.

'Has he had his pills?' Moira asked.

'Yes, just before we got here. He'll be fast asleep in a second.'

The three women stared at the figure in the bed for a moment.

'You'll sit.' Moira indicated one of the high-backed chairs, and Joan sat down. Moira perched on the other one, while Carol pulled a small plastic chair across from the sink.

'Thanks for meeting us.' Carol smiled nervously.

'Not at all. I wanted to talk to you.'

'Great.'

Carol looked to her mother, hoping that she might get the ball rolling, but Moira didn't seem very sure of how to begin now they were all here.

Carol cleared her throat. 'You know we bought Stable Row, of course.' This seemed a neutral introduction.

'I did. You outbid me, in fact.' Joan gave an apologetic smile.

Carol couldn't hide her surprise. 'Really? You were planning to move back?'

Moira rolled her eyes but said nothing.

'No,' Joan said quietly. 'I knew that Declan wouldn't want to sell, so I was trying to help. It's great you bought it. I was so relieved.'

'And who is it you're still in touch with in Ballytoor?' Moira asked. It had been bothering her.

'My daughter. Sally.'

'Sally?' Again Carol didn't hide her surprise.

Joan shook her head. 'It was stupid. She didn't know she was talking to me. I found her Facebook and I suppose I catfished her. Is that what they call it?'

Moira looked at Carol, nonplussed.

'God. Does she know?' Carol asked.

'She does now, yeah.'

Declan rolled over in his sleep and the three women looked at him. Carol saw the man she loved. Joan saw a man who had managed to control her for far too long, and Moira still wasn't clear who she was looking at. Was he a murderer or not? She turned back to Joan, impatient for answers.

'What are your plans for Stable Row? Are you going to move back in?' Joan asked Carol, but it was Moira who answered.

'We had hoped to sell it, but we can't do that at the moment. Can we?' She gave Joan a meaningful look.

Joan hesitated. 'No, I'd say not. Not if we're talking about the same thing.'

Carol tensed. Was this the moment when they learned everything?

'The freezer in the basement?' Moira pressed.

'Yes.'

'The body in the freezer in the basement?'

Both Carol and Joan looked at the door. What if someone heard?

'Yes. You're right.' Joan bent forward, the unexpected relief of her secret being shared washing over her.

Carol and Moira glanced at each other. This was it. They felt that nervous satisfaction you might experience when the right key finally slid into a lock, or a reluctant car engine sparked into life.

'So, who is it?' Moira demanded.

Joan squirmed in her seat and pressed a fist against her mouth. 'I don't know how much to tell you. I don't want to get you involved in it all.'

'Involved?' Moira squawked, and then remembering to lower her voice, continued, 'We own the body, how much more involved can we be? Who is it?'

Joan winced. 'It's my brother.'

'What? The one who killed himself?' Carol was confused.

'Jesus wept, Carol. Sometimes I wonder how you're any relation of mine.' Moira rolled her eyes. 'Do you really think he committed suicide by climbing naked into a freezer and locking the lid?' She turned to Joan. 'Sorry about her.'

Carol felt seven years old again. She hated that her mother still felt she could humiliate and shame her, and she hated herself for being too embarrassed to say anything in front of Declan's wife.

'Go on.' Moira was keen to hear more.

'Go on?' Joan hesitated.

'Well, what happened? How did he end up dead in the basement?'

Joan looked at the two women sitting opposite her and the shape of Declan in the bed behind them. The room was dark, with just the glow of the lamp by the bed silhouetting them all. Far away there was the sound of voices, and a door being shut. Was this to be the moment? She took a deep breath. Yes, it was. The story she had never told. Joan Barry began to speak.

The arrangement had suited everyone. Declan had been short-staffed at the pharmacy and it made sense for Joan to fill in until he could find someone permanent. When her younger brother Cathal had finished his studies in Limerick, he didn't seem to have any pressing plans, so they had agreed he could live rent-free at Stable Row for a few months, so long as he picked the children up from school and watched them until Joan got home after work.

Sally and Killian were delighted. Walking to and from school with Uncle Cathal was an adventure. He told them stories about strange lands and allowed them to run across the street, when their mammy always insisted they walk. In the afternoon, they felt proud to hold his hand on the way home. With his long hair and his denim jacket covered in bright patches, he looked cooler than anyone else at the school gates, and he belonged to them. Sometimes he let them read comics in Cassidy's or made them bowls of cereal when they got home. 'Don't tell your mammy' became his catchphrase.

For a couple of months everything went smoothly. Joan and Declan were too busy to be annoyed by sharing their home with an extra adult. On Sundays, Cathal usually took the bus up to Cork to see friends and then it was the working week again. A couple of nights a week Joan allowed Cathal to cook dinner. She knew Declan didn't approve of the tuna noodle casserole or the big vats of chilli, but the children loved the student feasts their uncle made and Joan was so grateful not to come home and, almost before she had taken off her coat, start peeling spuds. Declan had asked a few times how long her brother was planning to stay, but until a new girl was hired to work in the pharmacy, Joan couldn't see why it mattered.

'This is Orla,' Declan announced one day a few weeks later. A small girl with dark hair stood shyly by his side. She had the sort of very pale skin with red blotches that looked as if it had just been boiled.

'Hello, Orla.' Joan shook the young girl's hand, formal but friendly.

'I'm giving Orla the job.'

Joan felt a little put out, though she couldn't have said why. There was no reason that Declan should have consulted her about the new girl, and yet just announcing it like this did seem like a slight.

'I wonder could you show her the ropes this afternoon, and then maybe stay around for a few hours tomorrow, just till Orla here feels confident enough to be left on her own?'

Orla looked at her new boss with ill-disguised horror. Declan laughed.

'Don't worry, I'll still be here. Any problems you can always ask me. That sound OK?'

'Yes.' The sound of her voice surprised Joan. Deeper and more confident than she had been expecting.

Orla proved to a be a quick learner. The till, the mysteries of the stockroom, the ledger with customer accounts, had all been explained that afternoon by Joan. The next morning Orla was doing everything by herself, only occasionally turning to Joan to check on something. By mid-morning it felt safe to leave her. Joan exchanged her white nylon coat for her anorak and happily headed home.

The house was empty when she got there. It felt luxurious to walk from room to room with nobody asking her for anything, no little hands grabbing at her clothes. Joan made herself a pot of tea and sat at the kitchen table. They had told Cathal about hiring Orla but later, when they were alone, Declan had asked, 'Does he realise that he needs to go now?'

'I'm sure he does,' Joan had replied when in fact she wasn't very sure at all. Cathal tended to need things spelled out. She would tell him this afternoon. Maybe they would do the school pick-up together. She was confident he wouldn't take the news too badly. He had always known the arrangement wasn't going to last forever and besides, he must be anxious to get back to his life. Joan wasn't sure what that was exactly, but it had to be more fun than looking after two small kids in Ballytoor.

It struck Joan that she had no idea how much luggage Cathal had with him. She assumed he had arrived with just a backpack but it had been Declan who had let him in and shown him to his makeshift sleeping area down in the basement. Joan had put some fresh towels on the little camp bed they had set up for Cathal, but she hadn't been down there since. She listened for a moment. The house was silent.

Joan only intended to have a quick glance but once she had made her way down the narrow staircase, her eye was caught by piles of books. What was Cathal reading? They seemed to be mostly novels and, judging by the names of the authors, books in translation. Joan hadn't heard of any of them. A sketchpad was lying open on the bed. She peeled back a couple of the large pages. Detailed pencil drawings of various doorways. Joan recognised the front door of number seven. She was quite impressed. They were good.

Beside the washing machine there was a neat stack of T-shirts and jeans and on the floor a messy pile of clothes that she assumed needed to be cleaned. A large canvas holdall bag sat tucked away to the side of the low camp bed. Joan didn't want to intrude or pry. She just wondered if the bag was empty, trying to figure out if all Cathal's belongings would fit in it. Not wanting to disturb it, she used a thumb and finger to pull back the top of the bag. No clothes, just a few bits of paper and old photos. Joan was about to stand up again when she spotted the corner of one of the pictures. It looked familiar. She slid it from the pile. Yes, it was Sally in the front garden, wearing her little green pinafore, surrounded by her dolls and teddys for a tea party. Joan had taken this photograph herself. What was Cathal doing with it? If he wanted to take it with him as a keepsake, why not just ask? Joan picked up the rest of the photos. More of Sally playing, blowing out her candles, family pictures that lived in the drawer of the hall table. Joan had planned to put them in an album but somehow there was always a task more pressing. Cathal must have known these weren't his to take. Then there were photographs that Joan didn't recognise. They were Polaroids, quite a few of them. Sally pulling funny faces. Sally dancing in her nightdress. This didn't feel right. Joan slowly sank down to sit on the bed. Sally standing on the stairs wearing nothing but her little seahorse knickers. In the bath. Joan's hand had begun to tremble. The last two Polaroids were of Sally, naked, lying on the bed where Joan now sat.

As she stood, her breath coming in hot tight gasps, still holding the photographs, not knowing what to do with them, she heard the front door open. She knew it was him.

'Cathal!' she screamed.

'Hi. Yeah. Where are you?' He sounded confused, but unconcerned.

'I'm down here.' What Joan was feeling went beyond anger. It was repulsion and the irresistible urge to protect her baby and punish the man who had done this to her.

In a moment, Cathal was standing before her. She saw his face register what she was holding. He took a step backwards but she grabbed the edge of his coat.

'What the fuck are these?'

'They're nothing. Just messing around.'

Somehow, hearing his voice trying to explain them away unleashed something in Joan. She dropped the photos and began pounding her fists against her brother.

'You are a monster. I can't believe I left you alone with my kids. A fucking monster!'

Cathal slid to his knees and raised his hands to try to shield himself from his sister's blows. Joan could hear him speaking, presumably trying to invent excuses, but she couldn't make out the words. He looked so pathetic crouched on the floor, but it wasn't enough. Joan knew her punches were too feeble. She wanted him to feel pain. She had to hurt him more than this.

Afterwards, she could never remember making the decision to do it, but her hand had shot out and grabbed the iron perched on the shelf above the washing machine. She raised it and then let it swing down onto Cathal's head. He let out a roar of pain. Yes, Joan thought, this was more like it. She lifted the iron again and this time the sharp corner at the base seemed to pop through the bone of Cathal's skull, like breaking into an Easter egg. He slumped forward and more blood than Joan had ever seen was suddenly pumping out of her brother across the floor. She dropped the iron on the bed and stared at the body on the floor.

'Cathal?' No response.

She pushed a foot against the top of his thigh. No reaction. Joan's hands hung by her side and her chest was heaving after the exertion of all the violence. With a sudden hunch of her shoulders, she darted to the stairs and at the top switched out the basement light and slammed the door behind her. She leaned against it, still panting. Thoughts swirled around her mind. What should she do? Before she even considered what to do about Cathal, she wanted to get Sally. She had to make sure no harm had come to her. But she couldn't bring the children back to this. Declan. He would know what to do. She called the pharmacy and Orla answered.

'Barry's Chemists. How can I help you?'

'Orla. Hello, it's Mrs Barry here.' Joan tried to control her breathing. 'Is Mr Barry around?'

'I'll just get him there now for you.'

Joan gripped the receiver tightly as she waited.

'Joan?' It was Declan's voice.

'You've got to come home.' She whispered the order urgently as if there might be someone listening outside the front door.

'What? Are you all right? What's after happening?'

'I'm fine. The kids are fine. But you have to come home now. Please. I can't explain on the phone.'

'Look, let me finish a few prescriptions and I'll be up.'

'No, Declan!' Her voice rose with panic. 'Now. You have to come home now. Please believe me. Now.'

'All right.' He gave a sigh of irritation. 'I'll be up in a few minutes.'

'Thank you,' Joan whispered into the receiver, but her husband had already hung up.

By the time Declan got back to Stable Row Joan appeared to be close to hysteria. She couldn't stop crying and nothing she said made sense. She had ended up crouched in a ball by the door to the kitchen. Declan knelt before her and gripped her arms, trying to calm her down. Slowly he began to piece together what she was saying. Cathal had been taking pictures of Sally, and Joan had hurt him, hurt him badly. He understood that Cathal was in the basement. He pulled his wife to her feet and opened the door to the stairs.

The scene that greeted him was much more horrific than he had imagined from what Joan had told him. He tried to shield her from it but then remembered that she had already seen it. Cathal lay slumped forward in a wide pool of dark blood. Not wanting to walk in it, Declan knelt down at its edge and leaned across to check the body for signs of life. There were none. He retrieved the photographs from where they lay in the blood. He stared in horror at the images he could still make out.

'Jesus Christ. And he was alone with the kids so much.' He turned to Joan. 'How could you not know this about your own brother?'

'What?' Joan said from where she sat at the bottom of the stairs, her face streaked with tears, her mouth laced with snot. 'How could I have known this? Christ, Declan, what are we going to do? I have to go and collect the kids soon.' She stood. Declan was just staring at Cathal's body. It didn't seem as if he was going to answer her.

'The guards?' she whispered.

'No. No.' He didn't look away from the corpse. 'You've killed someone. We can't go to the guards.'

'But the pictures . . .' She pointed weakly in the direction of the Polaroids.

'They're not an excuse for murder, Joan.'

'Murder? It was an accident.'

'You smashed a hole in his skull with an iron. This doesn't look like an accident.'

Joan let out a wail and slumped against the wall. Declan's shoulders tensed.

'You go. Go and collect the kids. I'll deal with this.'

Joan hesitated. 'Really? You can?' She was crying again.

'Just go.' She knew that voice. An angry outburst wasn't far away. She climbed the stairs, almost crawling upwards.

Her story told, the three women sat quietly. Then one by one they all turned to look at the man in the bed, bathed in the lamplight. His breathing was untroubled, while his pale eyelids gave an occasional twitch. This was a man enjoying pleasant dreams, unaware that his secrets, which were now lost even to him, had been revealed.

'But – I don't understand – why did you have to leave?' Carol had guessed so often at the reasons for Joan's departure, but she'd never imagined something like this.

Joan bowed her head, and when she looked up her eyes were filled with tears.

'Jesus. That's all I've been asking myself every second since I came back.'

'If you don't want to talk about it . . .' Carol said, reaching out a hand.

'No, no, you should hear this. This!' Joan gave a small laugh and threw her head back. 'Whatever this is. The truth, the real truth is that I don't really know. To start with I thought I understood. He was protecting me.' She nodded towards the bed. 'I should go and stay with his cousin in England. I ran. I had killed someone. I was terrified. But now I think it was him, Declan made me scared. Before I knew what was happening I was on a plane to London. Declan's cousin met me and then I went to stay with an aunt in Reading.'

'And would she have been a Roche?' Moira interrupted. Carol stared at her. How could that be her mother's only question after all they had heard?

'No, a Molloy. My father's side,' Joan replied as if it had been an entirely reasonable question.

'OK, but why not come back? After people thought that Cathal had done away with himself?'

Joan didn't seem especially emotional, but tears were rolling down her face. She wiped them away.

'It was always something. First, he was protecting me, then it was too soon, it would arouse suspicion. Later he began to use the children as an excuse. It would upset them too much. Killian had an exam or whatever.'

Carol thought back to Declan deciding that they should keep their relationship a secret. He had blamed that on Sally's exams. It felt like there was something cold and heavy in her stomach.

'Finally, it must have been nearly two years later, I was desperate. Not for him' – another glance at the bed – 'but for the kids. I was in hell. I remember, it was a Sunday night, I wasn't supposed to phone, it was one of his rules, but I just wanted to hear the children. I thought he might let me speak to them, but he was so angry. You know what he can be like?' She looked at Carol for confirmation, but Carol had no idea how to respond. She was not ready to accept that her Declan, the man she loved and shared a home with, was anything to do with the man Joan was describing.

'He was never . . . like that, with me.' Carol tripped over her words and her mother gave a snort.

'Well, he was furious. He shouted at me for using the phone.

I tried to reason with him, you know, just asking to speak to the children, begging him to explain why I couldn't come back. Well, he was having none of it. He made it clear that if I ever tried to come back, he would go to the guards himself. He had the body. Apparently he'd even kept the iron with my prints on it. There was no Ballytoor for me, only jail. I knew he meant it.' She swiped at her tears once more.

Carol was in shock. Could this be true? Joan seemed sincere but Carol refused to believe that her Declan had ever been this man.

'Why? Why would he threaten you?'

'At the time I thought it was as simple as him hating me. He was just trying to punish me. Later on, I figured out that he had probably met someone else and didn't want a wife messing it up for him.'

'I never—' Carol began quickly.

'Not you,' Joan reassured her. 'It would have been before your time. I thought it might have been the little Orla one from the shop.'

Carol's first impulse was to tell Joan that Declan hadn't been with anyone else between the two of them, but then she realised how foolish she would sound. She only had Declan's word for it, and what was that worth now? Carol didn't know what or who to believe. Out of the corner of her eye, she caught sight of her mother. Moira's mouth was drawn tight. Carol's heart sank. Her mother had been proved right yet again.

'And Sally?' asked Moira. 'Does she remember any of this? What went on with your brother?'

'No. We spoke to her that night. But no. Afterwards, when I thought about it, she was one of those kids, you know, running around after her bath. It was always a job to get her into her pyjamas, so she mightn't have noticed anything out of the ordinary, but to take pictures of her like that, there's no excuse.'

'Awful,' Moira agreed. 'At least he did no real harm.'

In the silence that followed, Carol thought about Sally, strange withdrawn Sally, living in her bleak little cottage. It struck her that somewhere along the line some harm had been done.

'And that was it?' Moira asked. 'You never reasoned with Declan again, never tried to come home without telling him?'

Joan nodded slowly. 'Oh, I did. It got so that I didn't care if I ended up behind bars. I just needed to—' Her voice cracked. 'I had to see my children no matter what.' She found a crumpled tissue and dabbed at her eyes.

'And?' Moira prompted her to continue.

'He explained what would happen to Sally.'

'Sally?' Carol wasn't following.

'If I came back, the body would be found and Sally would find out what had happened to her. He told me that she wasn't strong enough to know the truth and I believed him.'

Moira and Carol exchanged a look. They agreed.

'So it was decided. I couldn't come back. It was my fault that it happened to Sally in the first place and it would be my fault if she found out she had been abused. I knew it would destroy her. At that point me wanting to see my kids seemed selfish, if Sally was going to be the price I paid. Do you understand now?'

'Yes, yes.' Moira handed her a box of tissues from the table. Joan took them gratefully and blew her nose. She looked at Declan.

'It's so strange being in a room with him. That night you found me in here with him . . .'

240

'Yes?'

'I . . . I half thought that I might hurt him in some way – put a pillow over his face or something, I don't know. Just punish him. But when I got here, I realised it was too late for all of that. Look at him.'

The three women turned towards the bed.

'You'd feel sorry for another man like that, but this is his happy ending. He got everything he wanted and never paid the price . . .' Her voice trailed away and she kept looking at the sleeping body.

Carol wanted to defend him. She had been with him as he slipped away. That had felt like some form of punishment. How much would you have to hate someone to see this as their happy ending?

Joan was surprised at how this evening had gone. She had never intended to reveal so much, but now that she had, she was glad. It wasn't as if she had been seeking forgiveness, but to share her darkest secret and have these two women sit and listen, seemingly without judgement, made her feel slightly giddy. The weight of her burden revealed to be imaginary.

'Well, over to you two, I suppose,' Joan said brightly. 'I've just confessed to killing someone. My fate is in your hands.' She held them out as if awaiting invisible handcuffs.

Moira shifted in her chair. 'Well, I think Carol will agree with me,' she didn't even bother to glance at her daughter, 'when I say that there is no point opening up this can of worms now. Your brother is long gone, Declan is in a world of his own, and you've suffered enough, more than enough. It's time you came home.' Moira spoke with an almost regal assurance. Making decisions was what she enjoyed, it was what she did best.

'So are you just going to leave him there?' Joan sounded doubtful.

'No.' The *don't be stupid* was silent. 'We need to sell the house. No, we have a plan.'

Carol groaned and put her head in her hands. 'You. You have a plan.'

'Yes I do.' Moira was indignant. 'And it's a good plan.'

Joan leaned forward, anxious to hear it.

'I have a friend with a trawler, and a van.'

Carol looked up. She hadn't heard about the van before.

'The plan is to take the body and dump it far enough out at sea that the currents will take it further out and it will be lost – or if we're unlucky and anything comes to shore, it'll be far enough away from here that no one will come asking any questions in Ballytoor.' She wiped her hands in a gesture of a job being well done.

'OK,' Joan said slowly. 'And you can trust your friend?'

'Of course.'

'Right. And when are you planning to do this?'

'Well, it needs to be done at night. The forecast is too bad for tomorrow, so the next night I'd say.'

'What?' Carol was alarmed. This seemed so soon.

Suddenly the door opened and a slightly startled face appeared. At first Carol thought it must be a new nurse she didn't recognise, but then she realised she did. The startled stranger was Sally.

Killian was not asleep. How could he be? Beside him Colin was breathing not quite noisily enough to qualify as snoring, and occasionally smacking his lips, as if in his dreams he was a baby being fed. Maybe that actually was his dream? Killian stared up at the ceiling. He had driven around the town for nearly an hour, parking under the cold bright lights of the bypass to gather his thoughts. He felt like a prisoner planning his escape route, and the more he considered it, the easier it seemed.

He had to leave before the baby arrived. That was obvious. After that it would be too messy. Initially he imagined selling Brook Drive and splitting the money with Colin, but then he decided against it. He was sick of being the bad guy. Money would come later; for the moment he didn't want to be the man who made a baby homeless. Besides, he had to admit that this baby was at least partly his fault. OK, it had never been his idea, but at the same time he hadn't stopped it. Cath would be over the moon. Her and Colin together at last. Maybe she'd move into Brook Drive?

The insurance firm had offices everywhere. Surely he could get a job in one of them. England or Scotland. That was the way to go. Make a clean break of it. As he drove back home, ready to face Colin, his mind was whirring with all the possibilities the future seemed to hold. Killian wouldn't have said he was looking forward to telling Colin, but at the same time, once Colin understood that he didn't have to leave the house, Killian found it hard to imagine him being that upset. He'd soon find someone else to cook a tagine for. The thought of it made Killian smile. He'd never have to eat couscous again.

Of course, as soon as he had walked in the door, the tables had been turned. It was Colin who had the shocking news. All the missed calls hadn't been to find out where Killian had been but to tell him who he had missed. His mother was in Ballytoor. As he lay in this bed, she was somewhere nearby. At first he thought that Colin had got the message wrong somehow. Maybe the woman at the door had been someone who knew his mother or had information about her, but then he had called the number.

'This is Joan's phone.' The little laugh on the recorded message to acknowledge the rhyme. At the tone he had opened his mouth to speak but all at once realised that he couldn't. He knew that his voice would be overwhelmed by tears. He hung up quickly and bent forward, his body heaving with great rolling sobs. It was too much. He felt ambushed by his own feelings. Colin stroked his back and Killian wasn't annoyed.

Even the sight of Colin wiping the dust out of their only two brandy balloons didn't make him breathe through his nose the way he felt it usually would.

'For the shock,' Colin whispered as he darted around the room like a butler on the *Titanic*.

'Just give it to me. I can drink it out of the bottle, for God's sake.'

'Killian!' The level of shock and horror in Colin's voice brought

Killian comfort. It was so expected. The dull, dependable presence of his husband was more soothing than the brandy.

They had sat together on the sofa, Killian asking questions that Colin couldn't answer. What was she wearing? Did she look like me? Did she seem rich or poor? Colin didn't like to admit that for most of the time she had been at the house, he had been looking for a pen. Instead he offered up theories about her return. It had to be about Declan going into the home, but who had told her? Did Killian think she had been coming back all along, checking on him and Sally?

It wasn't really a conversation so much as two people spouting self-contained thought bubbles. Eventually Colin's head began to droop wearily. He had also been drinking hefty amounts of brandy. Sympathy shock.

'I'm sorry – I've got to get to bed,' Colin announced, heaving himself up from the sofa. 'Will you take care of the candles?'

Killian glanced around at the glitter and glow of the room.

'I will.' He reached out, took Colin's hand and pressed it to his lips. Colin bent down and kissed him. 'Good night. Don't be too long.'

'I won't.'

Killian must have fallen asleep eventually because he had awoken to find daylight edging the curtains and Colin propped on his pillows, scrolling through his phone. Killian's brow felt tight – the emotional hangover from all the crying of the night before. He knew he had to get out of bed and start the search for his mother, but first he had something to say.

'Colin.'

'Yes,' his husband muttered, not taking his eyes from the phone.

'This is important, Colin.'

'OK.' Colin placed the phone in his lap. A look of uncertainty played across his face.

'I have two things to tell you.' Killian pulled himself up in the bed and looked into Colin's eyes.

'I love you, and I don't want a baby.'

The bad weather Rory Lynch had warned Moira about had arrived. The rain was drumming across the wall of glass in the bungalow as Dave struggled to unblock the milk steamer with the end of a fork.

'You were fierce late. Everything all right?' he called over his shoulder to Carol, who was sitting at the kitchen table. It seemed Moira was still asleep.

'Declan wouldn't settle, so we ended up staying on for a while.'

This explanation seemed to satisfy her father.

'I'm going to microwave the milk. Will that do you?'

'Grand. Have you seen this, Daddy?' Carol pointed at a pool of water gathering on the floor beneath one of the hinges in the glass door.

'What? Oh, yeah, it does that when the wind is coming from the south. Can you grab an old towel?'

Carol got up to go to the airing cupboard. 'Has it always done that?'

'I think so. Do you not remember it?'

'No. I don't think so.'

The middle shelf of the hot press had an array of thick new towels in pale peach, but on the shelf above were the well-worn towels of Carol's childhood. She reached for the one covered in large graphic slices of lemon. Linda and she used to fight over it when they went to the beach. She bent forward to smell the familiar scent of her mother's ironing. Carol had the urge to just rest her head against the rough material and fall asleep standing up in the corridor. She felt tired but in a way that reached far beyond the night of tossing and turning she had just endured.

She was exhausted by all the uncertainty, the weight of the things she had assumed were true but now seemed to be a burden of her own creation. Who was Declan? What sort of man had he been?

Carol had managed not to engage with her mother's questions on the drive home and Moira must have sensed how close her daughter was to breaking and hadn't pushed very hard. Alone in her room, however, Carol couldn't evade the things she knew she must ask. She told herself the story of her life with Declan through the lens of what Joan had revealed in St Brendan's. What she had always thought of as her own happiness she could now see as living her life purely in order to make sure that Declan was happy. Things had only gone well when they were going the way Declan wanted. Had he controlled her? Bullied her? No. It had never felt like that. Yes, he had lost his temper sometimes, but she had never been frightened of him, not what you would actually call fear. She loved him, so it was only natural that she didn't want to do or say anything to upset him. She knew it was wrong to blame Joan, but what if she had provoked him, what if she hadn't loved him the way that Carol did? It was all too easy to blame Declan for everything, now when he couldn't defend himself.

She thought about her friends, the ones she used to have. Carol couldn't deny that they had faded from her life, but had that really been because of Declan? She knew that he wasn't fond of many of them, and seen from his perspective she often understood why. They were a bit boring or critical or whatever, so it would have seemed perverse to prioritise them over Declan. And there was Eimear. Declan had liked Eimear, hadn't he? But then she remembered that Eimear gave Declan legal advice at discount prices.

So maybe he was a bit controlling, or perhaps Carol was the sort of person who sought that out in a partner, she didn't know. What she was certain of, though, was that the Declan she knew didn't have the capacity for the cruelty that Joan had described. She wondered if it was possible a man could change that much. Only the children might know, but then she thought about their relationship with Declan. Carol had always assumed she had been the one to drive them away, place a barrier between them and their father, but maybe that wasn't the case. Perhaps they had never been close to him. It would certainly explain the way they were able to bundle him into St Brendan's without a second thought.

Carol hated this. After everything she had endured, she was now having to consider the possibility that the villain in her story had been recast as the man she loved. What made it worse was the realisation that she would never know for certain; all was lost in a fog of medication and confusion. It just seemed so unfair that it was Joan Barry who was now in control of the story. She'd killed someone, her own brother, so how the hell did she get to be swanning around on the moral high ground?

'What are you doing with that?' It was Moira, striding down the corridor, her oversized dressing gown making her look like a child in a nativity play. Carol jerked her head up from the towel.

'Daddy said to put it down for the rain.'

'This house,' Moira announced to no one in particular, before making her way into the kitchen. 'Good morning, love. I hear we're leaking.'

Dave was now at the table, reading a paper. He looked up.

'Have you heard from your friend Eimear?'

Carol was bent over pressing the towels against the wet glass.

'No. I owe her a text. Why?'

'Have you not seen the paper? She's in a spot of bother.'

Over her shoulder Carol could see her father folding the paper to show her something. She got to her feet and took it from him. There was a picture of Eimear looking glamorous, at some charity do, Carol guessed. Everyone else had been cut out of the frame so it was just Eimear beaming at the camera, her hair swept back, elaborate earrings emphasising her long neck.

'What is it?' Moira was anxious to hear the news.

Carol read the headline out: 'West Cork solicitor faces disciplinary tribunal.'

'Eimear? What in God's name has she done?'

'Shh, Mammy, I'm trying to see.' Carol's eyes raced along the type, trying to get to the point. 'Complaints made to the Law Society . . . concerns with land registry . . . financial impropriety . . . illegal changes to property boundaries . . . fraudulent wills . . . Jesus, this can't be true, this is terrible.' Her heart was beating fast and somehow she already knew what she was going to find next. '. . . and a number of Enduring Power of Attorney orders backdated and falsified.' She read it again, and looked up from the paper. Her parents were staring at her in horrified silence. Dave shook his head slowly in disbelief and Moira finally spoke, her voice crisp with indignation. 'That little bitch.'

'Ah now,' Dave began, 'we don't know if—'

'We don't in our hole, Dave Crottie,' Moira interrupted him. 'You know full well a backhander from Killian Barry is how they got that bit of paper signed off.'

'Carol!' Dave called as his daughter grabbed her car keys from the kitchen counter and headed for the front door.

'Where are you going, love?' Moira asked the back of Carol's head.

'I'm going to see my friend.' And then the sound of a door slamming.

Moira looked at Dave.

'Some friend.'

In the square a small crowd was gathered in front of Eimear's office, attracted by the presence of an RTE news van and a morbid interest in the improprieties of a local solicitor. Carol stood at the back, wondering what her options were. She had tried calling and texting but, as she had expected, got no response. The office door was firmly closed and remained so despite various people knocking and ringing the bell. Carol was beginning to question if Eimear was in the office. Maybe it made more sense for her to be hiding out at home? But before she could head back to her car, the heavy wooden door opened. The crowd hushed and waited to see what might emerge from the dark gap of the open door.

Eimear stepped out in her full solicitor's armour. A dark suit, a crisp blue shirt and the sort of high heels that looked more like weapons than footwear. Carol pushed herself forward. 'Eimear, Eimear, it's me, Carol.' Two photographers had appeared and Eimear was now shielding her face with a bundle of folders as she made her way to a waiting car. Her initial poise had crumbled and she now crouched, trying and failing to grab the door handle, her vision blocked by the folders.

'Eimear!' Carol was within touching distance of her friend and her voice seemed unnecessarily loud. The folders slipped and Carol caught a glimpse of Eimear's face. Her eyes seemed almost entirely white, wide and filled with fear. She looked like a wild animal caught in a trap as she threw herself into the back seat of the car. She pulled the door shut. Carol lunged forward and tapped on the glass.

'Not your fault! You told me that none of this was your fault.'

There was something in the way Eimear's body tensed that told Carol she had heard her, but she didn't turn to look at her as the car glided away.

Joan had spent the night in Sally's cottage. After the surprise visit in the nursing home, it seemed easier than saying goodbye in the car park or, more likely, sitting together in a cold car talking late into the night.

When Sally had walked into the room, Joan had immediately thought of the phrase 'cat among the pigeons'. She and Carol Crottie had jumped from their seats. Only Moira remained calm, greeting Sally with what sounded like a very arch 'Hello again.' Clearly there was history.

Sally just stood for a moment, looking at one face after the other, her eyes bulging. Finally she managed to speak.

'What's going on? Why are you all here?'

Carol was the first to respond. 'It's very late for a visit, Sally. Why are you here?'

'Yes,' Joan chimed in. 'Why are you here so late?'

They could see Sally trying to think of an answer but after a moment or two her shoulders dropped and she confessed.

'I was following you.' She raised her hand slightly to indicate Joan.

'Why? Why would you do that?' Joan went to her and touched her arm.

'I thought you were going to go away again. I don't know, after you left, I just thought I'd never see you again.'

On her chair by the bed, Moira rolled her eyes, but nobody noticed.

'Oh pet. I'm sorry.' Joan tried to pull Sally into an embrace but she resisted.

'I still want to know what this is about. What's going on?'

Joan had glanced at the other women before she replied, 'We were just leaving. Come on away and I'll explain everything. Good night, ladies.' With that she had shepherded her daughter back out to the car park and home.

The morning wasn't as awkward as Joan had feared it might be. Sally had insisted that her mother took the bed, while an extra duvet was found to cover the sofa for herself. Joan woke to noise from the kitchen below. She lay under the thin covers, surprised that she had managed to get a good night's sleep but also at how calm she felt after the night before. She had to keep reminding herself that she had confessed to murder. Carol and her mother could easily tell the police. If it was just Declan they were worried about, then her reappearance and full confession solved all of that. For whatever reason Joan found that she trusted Moira and Carol. She was confident that the women weren't going to tell anyone. Maybe it was as simple as they felt they would have done the same thing in her place, or perhaps it was the guilt Carol must have felt, hearing how the man she loved had banished Joan from her own children. Her bladder was full. She'd have to get up soon. Oddly she felt she had more energy today than since she had arrived in Ballytoor. Drama obviously suited her.

When she padded down the stairs in her socks, she found Sally making toast. A pot of tea was poured and the two women sat, their knees touching, at the small kitchen table. Sally talked about what she might do now that she had quit her job. She seemed energised and positive. Joan suspected that it was simply the effect of having some company. Neither her daughter nor the cottage gave many signs of a social life.

The night before, Joan hadn't lied, but that was not to say she had told the whole truth. She had considered telling Sally that the meeting at St Brendan's was simply a coincidence, after all it had happened only once, but eventually she had opted for a version of the truth. They had been talking about Declan and what to do with Stable Row. Practical things. Happily Sally had not asked her why such things were any of her business, considering that she had abandoned the family twenty-five years earlier. Joan made no mention of the basement or of Moira Crottie's plan.

Studying her daughter across the table, Joan felt a strange sense of consolation. Her daughter had grown to be a fragile thing. Protecting her from what Cathal might have done had been the right thing to do. Declan might have said it because it suited him, but that didn't make it any less true. Whatever happened next with the Crotties was all about trying to spare Sally.

'I forgot to ask,' Sally said as she ripped off a piece of toast with her teeth, 'did you see Killian yesterday?'

Killian. Joan was ashamed to admit that she had completely forgotten about her son.

'No. Not in the end, no. I called up but I just met the husband.' Joan paused, thinking of adding some comment about Colin, but everything had the danger of coming out as a gay slur so she said nothing.

'What's today? Saturday. You should go round this morning. Will I make us more tea?'

As Joan drove along Brook Drive, she could see Colin outside the house, getting soaked by the rain as he struggled with a large suitcase on wheels. She parked and crossed the road as Colin was putting the case in the boot of a car. A pregnant woman with an umbrella was standing to the side, watching.

'Morning,' Joan called.

Colin turned to look at her. Clearly, he had been crying. His eyes were red and swollen and his whole face looked raw.

'Is everything all right?' She was concerned.

'Ask your son.' Colin almost spat the words at her. He slammed the boot shut and then he and the woman got into the car and drove off. Joan watched the car disappear around the corner. She wondered if she should do the same thing. Pulling the collar of her coat up against the elements, she made her way to the front door.

'Did you forget—' Killian stood in the hallway. A look of surprise at it not being Colin quickly turned to puzzlement and then his face crumpled and he threw himself against Joan, nearly knocking her to the ground. She clutched him back and strained against his weight as he emitted a thin, high-pitched wail. After what seemed to Joan like a reasonable pause she gently pushed the man-sized version of her child back into the hall, shushing him as she used to do all those years before.

Swallowing sobs, he led her through the house into the kitchen. He sat heavily in a chair and wrapped his arms around his head. Joan felt a familiar pressure behind her nose, and tears sprang into her eyes. It was as if she was watching someone doing an impression of her little boy.

'Colin's after leaving me.'

Joan had momentarily forgotten the drama she had witnessed outside, but this explained it. She wasn't sure how to respond. After all, she didn't know Colin and while she didn't like to see her son upset, she couldn't help feeling that the moment should be more about, well, her.

She patted his shoulder awkwardly and offered a vague 'You'll be OK. You'll get through this.'

He looked up at her, suddenly aware that his mother, the woman he hadn't seen for over two decades, was in the room and that he needed to acknowledge her in some way.

'Sorry. I tried to call you.'

'I know. I got your message. I should have called you back but Sally said she was sure you'd be in this morning and I felt all of this was too much for the phone, so here I am.' She shrugged apologetically.

'Here you are.' Killian gave a weak smile.

'Not great timing. Sorry. Should I leave you and come back later?'

'No, don't be mad.' He stood. 'Will you have a coffee or something?'

Joan was still awash with tea, but she felt she had to accept this offer from her son.

'Lovely, thanks.'

Joan watched him move around the kitchen easily, his hands reaching to find what he wanted. The line of his shoulders, the way he seemed to stand on the balls of his feet reminded her of Declan when he had been that age. He seemed confident, efficient, the sort of man you could rely on. She knew it was foolish but it gave her pleasure, an undeserved mother's pride.

'How . . . How did you feel when you heard that I'd called round?'

Killian looked at his mother over his shoulder and then back to the coffee machine.

'A bit of a mindfuck, if I'm being honest.'

'I'm sorry. I just didn't know what to do for the best.'

Killian turned and leaned against the counter.

'Like, what's the story? Where are you? Have you got some other family? What?'

Joan took a beat before replying. 'England, a town called Salisbury. I never remarried. You and Sally are still my only kids.'

'Jesus, Sally. What sort of state is she in?'

'She's OK. Like yourself, she has a lot of questions and I'm doing my best to answer them.'

Killian nodded. 'Sorry, will you have a seat. Sorry.' He pulled out one of the chairs from the table. 'And let me take your coat, it's soaking. God, I'm an awful host.'

Joan slipped off her coat and handed it to her son, who ferried it off to some other part of the house.

When he came back into the kitchen he sat opposite Joan at the table.

'So the big question has to be why. Why did you do it?' There was almost a laugh in his voice, a twinkle in his eye. Joan took comfort in how little her children had changed over the years. Killian and Sally still so different from one another.

'Thanks for looking out for Sally. She told me you took care of her after I left.'

Killian leaned back in his chair and gave his mother a long quizzical stare.

'Seriously?'

'What?'

'You're going to come back into our lives after all these years, and you're seriously not going to tell us why?'

Joan hated this. Who was she protecting by not telling the truth? Herself, yes, but also the children. It still wasn't the right time. Telling Carol and Moira the truth had been the only option, but it hadn't made Joan feel any more at peace with what had happened. If anything, it had made her feel stupid in addition to the guilt she had always carried with her.

'Oh Killian. I'm sorry. There are things it's best I don't tell you.'

'Still?' he interjected.

'Still. But just know that I never wanted to leave and I always wanted to come back. I know it felt like I abandoned you and Sally but I never stopped thinking about you. I never stopped loving you.'

Killian seemed unmoved by her speech.

'So you loved us. Great. Nice to know. If it wasn't about us, then was it about Daddy?'

Joan winced slightly. 'Yes.'

Killian looked shocked. 'Did Daddy make you go away?'

Joan twisted a lock of hair in her fingers. 'It's not as simple as that. I'm sorry, Killian, but it's a mess. I don't know if it will ever be fixed.' Her voice faded away to a whisper.

Killian's face hardened. 'Coffee's ready.'

At the counter with his back to Joan, he continued, 'You know, I never allowed myself to miss you. I saw what it did to Sally, so I figured I'd be the strong one. I'm not sure how I did it, but I did. I managed to box away my feelings. Then, last night, it was hearing your voice on the phone, I guess I wasn't prepared or whatever, but it broke me.'

Joan saw him wipe his sleeve across his face and there was a tremble in his voice.

'It sounded like love to me, or, I don't know, the possibility of love. Someone who would love me like no one else. But now that you're here . . . it's just not – is there something wrong with me, because I'm not feeling what I wanted to feel and Colin warned me . . .'

Killian bowed his head and braced himself against the counter, clearly overcome.

Joan stood slowly and went to him. Her impulse was to comfort him, but she worried that she might just make him more upset. She placed her hand flat against his back and held it there without speaking. He turned, and although his face was contorted with tears he began to laugh.

'This isn't me. I never cry and now I'm crying all the fucking time. It's too much.'

Joan took her son in her arms. 'It'll do you good. You just cry.'

After a few moments she led him gently to the table and sat him down.

'Now, do you take milk in your coffee?' Her voice was soft.

He looked up. 'I'll do that.'

'No, you just sit there. I can pour out a mug of coffee.'

'Thanks. Just a drop.'

Joan joined her son at the table and they both wrapped their hands around the warm coffee mugs.

'So how did you leave things with Colin? Will he be back?' It was an ungainly change of subject, but Joan hoped she might get away with it. Killian didn't reply. He didn't even look up.

'Sorry,' Joan said quickly. 'I don't mean to pry. If you don't feel comfortable—'

'No, it's not that,' Killian assured her. 'I suppose I just don't know. We don't really have rows. Didn't really have rows,' he corrected himself. 'I've never seen Colin the way he was this morning.'

'Right. Well, maybe give him a day or two. Let the dust settle.'

Killian drank some of his coffee.

'Is it too strong for you?' he asked his mother.

'No, lovely. Thanks.'

'The weird thing is that I was coming home last night to leave him.'

'Oh.' Then Joan didn't see the problem. Hadn't Killian now got what he wanted?

'But when I heard your voice, it made me want to hold on to Colin. You know what I mean? Does that make any sense?'

'I think so.' Joan reached out and stroked his arm.

'He can be annoying. God, so annoying!' He threw his head back. 'But he's someone I could always rely on. There are never any surprises with Colin. I mean he's a travel agent and he never goes anywhere. That's the sort of guy he is, and I thought that was a bad thing but then last night, I don't know, it seemed like a good thing, a great thing. Having something solid in my life, you know?'

Joan just nodded, horribly aware of why this man might need a love he could rely on in his life. She hated that she had done this to her son.

'Well then, it sounds like he'll be back.'

Killian shook his head.

'What happened? What changed in a few hours?'

'I changed. I changed my mind.' He paused and then pushed his chair away from the table. 'You know what? If you can have secrets, so can I. Fair?'

'Very,' Joan said but decided to push her luck, thinking back to the pregnant woman she had seen outside earlier. 'Is it anything to do with the baby?'

Killian rolled his eyes. 'Sally?'

'Sally. Sorry. Is it a secret?'

'Apparently not, though we're trying to keep it quiet. Sally only found out by accident.'

'And what's the problem? Is it to do with the mother? Was that her outside?'

'Cath. Yes, that was her. No, she's not the problem. I am.' Killian picked at something on his knee. 'I don't know how this will sound out loud. God, I can't believe you've just walked back into my life and now I'm telling you this.' He paused and looked at Joan as if he was assessing her in some way.

'What is it?'

Killian let out a long sigh. 'I've changed my mind.'

'Changed your mind?' Joan wasn't clear about what he meant.

Killian's voice was small and tinged with embarrassment. 'I don't want a baby any more.' He kept looking at Joan for her reaction. She wasn't sure what to say.

'Do you get to change your mind, Killian? That woman looked fairly pregnant to me.'

'I'm not suggesting anything awful. The baby will still happen. Of course it will. It just won't have me as a father.' He shrugged.

It was a strange feeling for Joan, being reunited with her son and almost at once taking someone else's side against him in an argument. She remembered Sally indignantly pointing out that Killian and Colin hadn't even bothered with trying a dog before going straight for a baby. Best to keep that to herself.

'But is that fair, making Colin a single parent?' she asked, as tactfully as she felt able.

'Well, you'd know all about that, wouldn't you?' Killian shot back at her.

'Oh God, I know you think that's what happened but I swear it was never my choice. This is different. You're going to be forcing this on Colin.'

'There's Cath,' he replied defensively.

'Did she not think she was giving the child to you?'

'She was always going to be around. There was never any way she was just going to hand over the baby and get out of our lives. I mean the only reason she agreed to the whole thing is because she's in love with Colin. It's obvious.'

'Right.' The whole plan sounded ill-conceived to Joan. It might as well collapse now, before the baby was born.

'I thought I could give them money to help with the child and start my life again somewhere else, but then last night I realised I don't want to lose Colin, but now I have. It's a fucking disaster.'

He drained his mug.

Something was bothering Joan. It was like hearing a snatch of a song you couldn't identify, or not knowing what memory made a certain smell so special. Suddenly it came to her. She knew how Killian's mind worked because she had dealt with it before. Joan felt she had to say something.

'You remind me of your father.'

Killian looked at her, perplexed.

'I don't mean it as a compliment.' She said this with a smile, hoping her son understood that she wasn't blaming him, or accusing him of anything.

'You know I don't want to get into it all but, well, your father saw the world the way you seem to.'

'What do you mean?' Killian had never seen himself in his father. He'd always thought that was why they had never been close.

'That way of seeing things in a way that suits you. That only suits you.'

'That's not fair. Why should I make a mistake because—'

'Look, Killian,' his mother cut him off, 'I'm just saying that some of the ways that your father acted towards me were cruel, but the older I get the more I think that your father wasn't like that deliberately. It was just convenient. If something got him what he wanted then he wasn't worried about who got hurt, what the collateral damage was. Don't be that man.'

Killian was outraged. This woman, his mother, who didn't know anything about him was lecturing him about how to live his life.

'That is not who I am. I don't know what the fuck went on with you and Daddy but don't try and drag me into it.'

'Oh Killian, can't you see it? Kicking Carol out of the house, putting your father in a home, now this baby, an entire human being that only exists because of you, is just going to be dumped. I know it's too late in the day for me to swan in here and play Mammy, but, well, I needed to say that. And now I have.' Joan sat very still, waiting to see how her son was going to react.

Killian's face twitched. Part of him wanted to frogmarch this woman to the door and throw her into the street but, reluctantly, he conceded some of what she was saying. Not all of it. He wasn't a monster, but he was aware that he had to remind himself of that more often than perhaps he should.

'For the best.' His voice was little more than a whisper. 'Everything I do is because I want things to turn out for the best.' He looked at his mother and she nodded.

'I know I can be a bit impatient, but I don't mean people to get hurt. Never.'

'I know. I know that. That's what I'm saying. You don't want that to happen but it does.' Joan was surprised Killian was handling this conversation as well as he was.

'The good news is that it sounds like Colin is going to be a rock for that baby, and to be honest that's the way it should be.' She had more to say, much more, but stopped herself. It was grotesque for her to lecture a child she had abandoned about the importance of being there for your children.

Killian cocked his head to one side. 'I hadn't thought of it like that. It's just the idea of starting again. All the time it took to get to the place I was with Colin last night. Will I ever be able to build it back again?'

Joan didn't know what to say. Her life between leaving and this return had been spent treading water. She had never wanted to build something new because what she had walked away from was unfinished. She looked at her son. Was it too late? What had they to offer each other at this point in their lives?

Moira couldn't decide. Sometimes she thought her plan was a neat solution to something that could have turned very messy, but then there were times when she couldn't believe that her daughter, and now this Joan Barry woman, were going along with her risky scheme. All she knew for sure was that every time she considered doing the sensible thing, and involving the police, she immediately had an irresistible gut reaction. Dave was somehow involved, or knew something or was covering something up. Moira knew that giving up now would lead to disaster. She told herself that she had no other choice, she had to solve things her own way.

It was still raining but the wind had died down. Tonight was the night. Moira had dispatched Dave to Dublin. She had found an auction that was happening early the next morning and invented a story about wanting Dave to check out some paintings and then bid on them for her. He had protested, trying to make Moira go herself, or bid on the phone, but she had insisted, and Dave, as she knew he would, had eventually bent to her will. Moira hoped he was outbid, because she didn't actually want any of the pictures. It might prove to be a very expensive plan, but it got her husband out of the way and that was the most important thing.

At least Carol seemed calm again. Moira had worried that all the drama with Eimear might have ruined everything. When her daughter had got back to the house from her confrontation in the square, she had gone straight to her room. Moira and Dave had silently agreed to leave her there undisturbed.

The *Six One* news had just started when Carol emerged and began moving around the kitchen, making a cup of tea. It was as if she was daring her parents to say something, so they both chose not to.

The kettle had just boiled when the report from Ballytoor began. There were views of the town as a reporter with a nasal Cork accent described the allegations against Eimear and how she would now face being struck off. The screen cut to the scene outside the office on the square and Carol recognised her own arm banging on the car window. Back to the studio and the newsreader was describing a tree-planting initiative organised by children. Dave hit the mute button.

'So, what are you going to do?' he asked.

'What can I do?' Carol replied flatly.

Moira swivelled in her chair. 'Do? Killian had no right to sell that house. Isn't that right, Dave?' She looked to her husband.

'As far as I know,' he confirmed.

Carol was dunking a teabag in a mug. She seemed strangely calm.

'And what? So, Declan still owns the house?'

'Yes.' Moira was frustrated that her daughter didn't seem more enthused about this news.

'OK. Well, if that's the case, the person with the biggest claim on Stable Row would be his wife. One Joan Barry.'

Moira and Carol exchanged a conspiratorial look. Dave was not to know that Joan Barry had unexpectedly turned up on the scene.

'Oh.' Dave sounded confused.

'It was Eimear who explained it to me. Turns out it was the only good bit of legal advice she ever gave me.'

'That one.' Moira spat out her disapproval.

'So, look at it like this,' Carol continued, 'Killian isn't going to challenge it, so if we don't, then at least we are the undisputed owners of the house. I say we leave it.'

Her parents considered this.

'Fair enough.' Moira was quietly impressed by her daughter's logic.

Now she was crashing around the bungalow, gathering everything she thought they might need for their – well, *her* – plan. Mostly this involved barking orders at Carol.

'Right. Head outside and get the cover off the barbecue.'

'What? What for?'

'The body. It'll cover the body and it has a drawstring thing around the end.'

'Won't Daddy wonder where the cover has gone?'

'No. It will have blown away. They're always blowing away. We get through two or three a year.'

Carol was still incredulous that her mother had thought all this through and it was actually happening. She pulled on her coat and headed for the patio doors.

'You do that and I'll gather up the hairdryers.'

It crossed Carol's mind to ask why they'd need hairdryers but she thought better of it.

Carol wrestled with the black vinyl cover and finally managed to drag it back to the door.

'No, no,' Moira called from across the room. 'That thing is soaking. Don't be bringing it through here. You'll destroy the place. Leave it around at the car. I'm making flasks of soup.'

Carol gathered the wet cover in her arms and struggled one step at a time around the side of the house. Soup? When were they going to need soup?

The full flasks safely stowed in a canvas tote, Moira was now busy forking lumps of butter into two baked potatoes.

'Will tuna and a bit of sweetcorn do you?'

Just the steamy smell of the freshly cut potatoes straight from the oven made Carol feel full.

'To be honest, Mammy, I'm not that hungry now.'

The forking was paused momentarily and an icy glare was thrown in Carol's direction.

'Carol Crottie, you will eat this potato and you'll be very glad of it later on.'

'Not if I get sick, I won't,' she muttered under her breath.

'I heard that,' Moira snapped. 'You have very good sea legs. Always have. Remember going out when your Uncle Frank had the cabin cruiser. Linda and Brian were spewing like fountains. You? Not a drop.'

Carol had no such recollection of ever being on a boat with her siblings but she knew better than to share this information.

'There's salt on the table.' Moira placed a large steaming potato in front of her daughter.

'This evening we'll drive out to Stranach and leave your car there. We'll bring Rory's van back into town with us.'

'What?' Carol had forgotten this part of the plan.

'Well, the ice-man fella will never fit in the boot of your car.'

Carol was feeling panicked. 'But I can't drive a van. It's been years since I've driven anything but an automatic.'

Moira waved her fears away. 'You passed your test in a manual. You'll be fine. No bother.'

Carol poked at the mound of tuna on her potato. She hoped her mother was right.

'Do we have to do it tonight? Can't we wait and do it during the day?'

Moira put down her knife and fork.

'Honestly, Carol. Do you not understand the word "plan"? This is what we're doing because it's what we decided we were doing. If we're carrying a body around it makes sense to do it at night. Rory says the tide is good for us just after eleven and besides, I've already got your father out of the way, so yes, it does need to be tonight.' She returned to her baked potato.

Carol had more questions. How long would they be on the trawler for? Did they all have to get on the boat? But her phone pinged.

'It's Joan Barry. She wants to know what time to meet.'

Moira considered this.

'I'd say, tell her to meet us here at half eight. That'll give us plenty of time. We'll all go in the van together and then when we get back, her car will be here.'

Carol obediently texted this information to Joan.

'Would we not be better off just doing it by ourselves – not involving anyone else?'

'Plan Carol. P.L.A.N. Jesus. I'm not the woman I was, so unless you fancy humping your man into the van on your own, you'll include Joan Barry. Besides, and I don't mean to be insensitive, but she made this mess, so the least she can do is help us clean it up.'

Made this mess. The phrase didn't sit well with Carol. Joan had killed her brother and yet somehow her mother didn't seem to have a problem with that. Yes, he had taken a few dodgy photos, but it didn't sound as if he had ever laid a hand on Sally.

'I'm piling everything here by the door,' Moira called from the hall. Carol pushed her chair away from the table and scraped her untouched potato into the bin. It seemed the time for questions was over.

It was happening. Carol was driving to Stranach. Then they would be driving Rory Lynch's van back to the bungalow to meet Joan Barry. As Carol leaned into the steering wheel on every turn of the road it felt as if they were travelling further away from the point of no return. The light was fading and it seemed that on this side of the headland the wind was still quite strong.

'Do you think he'll go out in this, Mammy?'

Moira stared out at the dark banks of clouds and the churn of the ocean. She chewed her cheek anxiously.

'Tonight was his choice. I suppose he might tell us different now. It doesn't look great right enough.'

Stranach appeared to be deserted when they arrived. No one was on the pier and only the scattered lights from houses on the hill suggested anyone lived there. Rory Lynch's cottage was in darkness as Carol slowed the car at the gate. She looked at her mother, awaiting further instruction.

'Pull in around the back. That's the door they use all the time.'

Sure enough, when Carol rounded the cottage a pool of light was spilling across a semi-circular patch of well-worn gravel. There was also a tall white van. She pulled up beside it and switched off the engine. She peered at the large panel on the side of the van and then turned to her mother.

'Did you know about that?'

'What?'

'That our getaway vehicle has his address and phone number on the side of it.'

Moira bent forward to peer past her daughter. She wasn't wrong. There on the side, in dark blue cursive script, was a promise of fresh fish and crab or lobster on request with a phone number and the address for Stranach Pier.

Moira snorted. 'It's a disguise. People will just think we're delivering fish.'

'In the middle of the night to an empty house? Oh, Mammy.' Carol pressed her forehead against the steering wheel.

'Your problem is you worry too much,' Moira said. It was too late for second thoughts now. Hesitation was their enemy at this point. Moira felt certain of that.

'Come on away in. We'll get the keys off Rory.' Moira threw open her door and swung her legs out. With much less enthusiasm, Carol did the same.

The man who opened the door looked very different than he had from a distance. What had looked like the healthy tanned face of someone who worked in all weathers was actually the colour and texture of a walnut. Carol had to stop herself from reacting when he smiled at her mother. The only two teeth that still seemed to reside in his mouth were fang-like and pointed upwards from his bottom lip like an inverted vampire's.

'Moira.' He sounded hoarse. Carol wondered if it was from a lifetime of shouting to be heard over howling winds and engines.

'Rory, this is one of my girls, Carol.'

She got a brief repeat of the upside-down vampiric grin.

'You'll come in,' he rasped and led them through the low doorway into a bright clean kitchen. The windows were steamed up and the air felt damp. Clearly, when it came to cooking, Rory favoured things boiled.

'Will we be all right to go out tonight, Rory?' Moira asked. 'There's still quite a swell out there.'

'I'd say so. I was listening to the forecast there and it's passing. What time do you think you'd be back out to me?'

'No later than half eleven, I hope. It'll all depend how long it takes us and if people are around, that sort of thing.' Moira sounded as if she did this sort of thing regularly.

'We should be grand so. Will I wet the pot?'

'Ah, you're very good, but no. We should be off. We have to load the van and you never know if there's going to be hold-ups in Ballytoor.'

Rory nodded vigorously in agreement. This was a man who avoided the metropolitan mayhem of Ballytoor as much as he was able.

'Is it yourself who's doing the driving?' He was talking to Carol.

'Yes, that's right. Mother's orders!' She felt awkward and self-conscious, the way she had as a girl when her mother had brought her to a neighbour's house. She had to remind herself that she was an adult.

'There you go.' He picked up a set of keys from the table and held them out. 'She can be a bit sticky in first but other than that she's grand.'

This was not what Carol wanted to hear. She took the keys without comment.

'We'll call if there are any problems,' Moira said as she opened the door.

'And you have the number?' Rory confirmed.

'Yes, yes, yes,' Moira called as she strode out into the wind. And if she didn't, it was written on the side of the van, Carol thought to herself.

At the van the realisation of how high the doors were off the ground made Moira pause, but before Rory or Carol could offer to help she had pulled herself up onto the seat. As Carol settled herself at the wheel she noticed that the sudden exertion had left her mother breathless. Carol hated moments like this when she was reminded of her mother's mortality, the promise of a world without Moira Crottie in it. Quickly banishing such thoughts, she leaned down and started the engine. Rory stood in the bright doorway, waving as the van shuddered and hopped its way to the gate. In the wing mirror a stressed Carol thought she could see Rory laughing.

It was their routine. After the news and weather, Mrs Buttimer went out into the hall and took the dog's lead off the chair by the phone table. If Margo hadn't followed her, she rattled the lead and the old terrier would rouse herself from the mat in front of the hearth and trot obediently to find her owner by the door. Then they made a couple of circuits of the small front garden, allowing Margo to do her business. This happened no matter the weather. Mrs Buttimer enjoyed filling her lungs with the chill night air. She had come to believe that it helped her to sleep.

The sky was clearing after the rain and Mrs Buttimer looked up at the stars. Her husband had known the names of all the constellations but she had forgotten them long ago. She remembered the first night he had walked her home and the way he had pointed them all out to her. She had fallen in love with him so easily. Bookish and serious, he was different from all the other boys. He hadn't tried to rub his hard thing against her hip on the dance floor and hadn't ended the night drunk as a lord after swigging from some hidden hip flask he'd smuggled into the dance with his friends. When people asked her about her late husband she always said the same thing: 'He was a gentleman, a real gentle man.'

It was only on the steps, as Margo and Mrs Buttimer were heading in for the night, that she noticed the white van. She wondered who it belonged to and why it was here at this time of night. Probably some tradesman who couldn't get parked on the quay or in the square. She made a mental note to resume her campaign to have Stable Row reserved for residents' parking only. Margo pulled at the lead, anxious to head to bed, but Mrs Buttimer stood still for a moment or two to see if she could see or hear anything. Nothing. She went inside, double-locked the door and slid the security chain across. You couldn't be too careful.

Six doors down, three women were hard at work. Per Moira's instructions only the light in the basement had been turned on, so that they wouldn't arouse suspicion or attract unwanted attention. Carol had opened the back doors of the van and herself and Joan had carried the equipment up the path wordlessly. Moira supervised, standing by the door, dressed in an outfit that might have doubled as a French resistance fighter at a fancy dress party. A thick black polo-neck sweater with a matching beret pulled down low over her ears, all worn with her customary padded gilet. Carol wondered if she had bought the beret specially, but didn't dare ask.

The barbecue cover lay to one side and an old sheet was pressed against the base of the freezer. An extension cord snaked down the stairs and three hairdryers were plugged into a multi-socket adapter.

Joan stood back, peering up the stairwell, as if expecting someone to storm into the basement and arrest them all. It was all proving much harder for her to cope with than she had imagined. It was only when she had been sitting in the van, pressed up against Moira, that the full horror of what she was going to have to confront really dawned on her. She felt she needed to address things before they were actually in the moment.

'The body . . .' she began.

Moira looked at her sharply.

'I know, obviously, I'll help carry it and that, but do you think that maybe I wouldn't have to look at it?'

Moira's shoulders relaxed. 'Not a problem. I thought about that. We have a cover so you won't have to look at your . . .' Her voice trailed away, Moira aware of not upsetting Joan at this early stage of the evening.

The freezer had been switched off and the hairdryers were aimed around the edges of the body. Moira had produced two chisels, and she and Carol were chipping into the ice as it softened under the hot air. They were making fast progress.

'Are you hungry?' Moira called over her shoulder to Joan.

Joan looked at her in horror. What was the old woman suggesting?

'Soup. I have flasks of soup. I thought we'd have it on the trawler to keep us warm but we're making good time here, so if you wanted some, help yourself.'

'No thanks. I'll wait,' Joan called over the noise of the hairdryers.

'We just need to get under him now,' Carol said, rocking the body from side to side to demonstrate that it had been freed from the walls of the freezer.

'Use this.' Moira handed her daughter a broom handle.

Carol edged the thin wooden pole down the inside of the freezer and then pushed. There was a loud cracking sound.

'That's working. Go again.'

Carol jiggled the broom handle down further and pressed her weight against it. Another loud crack echoed through the small basement room.

Joan couldn't help but look over to see what was going on. Moira was at one end of the freezer, lifting what must be the feet. It was really just a shapeless piece of ice but it contained a dark shadow. It wasn't anywhere near as graphic or shocking as Joan had imagined.

'I'd say we're ready for you.' It was Moira, beckoning Joan to the freezer.

'Give me a hand with this, Carol,' she added, tugging at the barbecue cover. The two women quickly spread the black nylon material over the frozen mound and tucked it in, like busy nurses.

'You take that end.' Moira pointed towards the feet and Joan did as she was told. Carol braced herself at the other end of the freezer.

'Ready?'

Joan nodded.

The two women gathered the cover around the icy form and began to lift. It scraped and snagged against the icy sides but rose slowly from the chest. Carol was making a groaning sound, and then as if by prior agreement both she and Joan dropped their load.

'Jesus, that's heavy.' Carol was breathing hard.

'It is,' Joan agreed, trying not to think about what *it* was.

'Will you get it out at all?' Moira sounded worried.

'We will, I'd say. Now we know what to expect. Ready, Joan?'

Another nod.

This time they both made their efforts vocal, groaning in unison as the freezer slowly released its contents. The moment most of the frozen form had cleared the top of the chest, Carol leaned it towards the floor and they let it down as carefully as they could. It still landed with a heavy thud and the cover slipped away from the top half of the body. Joan stared. She couldn't look away. In her imagination Cathal's face had been trapped behind a wall of clear ice, his eyes open, his hair slightly raised as if he was under water. This ice wasn't clear, and what it contained bore no relation to Cathal. It was a series of shadowy black blotches, more like a body found in a bog than a perfectly preserved young man. Maybe it was the result of him being defrosted recently, Joan thought, but whatever the reason, she was glad.

Carol looked around.

'Have we something to put him in or on? Anything with wheels?'

'No,' Moira said with the air of someone who had been expecting this foolish question. 'There wasn't any point because of the stairs.'

'Yeah. Of course.' Carol could see her mother's logic.

'Just take your time. There's no rush. You'll be grand.'

Margo was already curled up on the threadbare towel Mrs Buttimer left on the bed to spare the duvet cover. The smell of Pond's Cold Cream was heavy in the air and the old lady was winding her alarm clock. The West Highland terrier let out a contented snore that made Mrs Buttimer wish that she was already asleep. She stood and peeled back the bedcovers. She wasn't sure what prompted it, but she suddenly remembered the white van. Was it still there?

She crossed to the window and nudged the curtain open. It was. She gave a small indignant snort. If it was still there in the morning she would put a note under the windscreen wiper. People needed to know what was and wasn't acceptable. She was just about to turn away and go back to bed when a light caught her eye. It was bobbing in the darkness. She pressed her face to the glass to get a better look. Another light! She counted the hedges and fences. Number seven. What was going on? She craned as far as she could, but was unable to see the house, just the edge of the garden as it met the road. Now she could make out figures. They were dressed in dark clothes and were stooped over for some reason. They were carrying something. It was obviously heavy. They were at the van. The back doors were open. All at once she realised what she must do. She went down the stairs as quickly as she dared to call the guards.

'Ballytoor Garda barracks.' The voice on the other end of the phone sounded as if it was chewing.

'Hello, hello.' She was breathless from the stairs and the excitement. 'It's Mrs Buttimer here from number one Stable Row.'

'Mrs Buttimer. Sergeant Draper here. Bit late for you, isn't it?'

This relaxed, untroubled response did not seem at all appropriate. For all he knew she might have just been violently assaulted.

'Well, Sergeant Draper. There's something going on in number seven.'

'Oh?'

'Something bad!' Mrs Buttimer wanted to give this guard a good shake. 'There are people creeping around in the dark and they've just loaded something into the back of a van. Dark clothes, flashlights. This is a police matter!'

'Oh, right. I see.' Sergeant Draper sounded as if he was paying attention at last. 'And are they still there?'

'I'm not sure. Oh wait. Wait.' There was the sound of an engine outside. Mrs Buttimer rushed to the door as the van moved slowly past. The gears let out a shriek of protest. Under the streetlights, the old woman couldn't make out the phone number but she could clearly see Rory Lynch's promise of fresh fish from Stranach Pier. Mrs Buttimer slammed the front door and almost threw herself at the phone.

Maybe it was her nerves, or perhaps she was overtired, but Carol was struggling with Rory's van more than she had on the way into town. At the bottom of the hill, turning in to the Back Quay the engine had stalled. After she had managed to restart it, they had shuddered their way over the bridge. Carol almost wished Moira would say something. Somehow her mother sitting tight-lipped in her ridiculous black beret staring straight ahead was even more infuriating. Every time she tried to change gears they made the sound of an ancient dungeon gate being forced open.

After they had passed the entrance to Castle Heights, they made their way down the long hill towards the coast road. The engine seemed distraught and Carol was trying to wipe the sweat from her eyes at the same time as wrestling with the gearstick. Finally, it was Joan who spoke.

'Are you OK there, Carol?'

'Not really, no,' she said through gritted teeth. 'I told my mother I haven't driven a manual for years.' Carol glanced at her mother, but Moira wasn't taking the bait.

'Well I drive a manual all the time at home – well, my other home. Do you want me to have a go?'

'Yes!' Carol could have kissed Joan. 'It will take all night with me driving and I'd be scared we'd just break down altogether and that would ruin everything.'

'Pull in there.' It was Moira, pointing at a small layby up ahead.

The cold wind from the sea whipping at Carol's face felt good after the stress of the driving. The night was quiet and her feet crunched loudly through the gravel to open the side door to let Joan out.

'Thanks for this. I blame my mother.' Carol smiled. 'But then I blame her for most things.'

'She's some woman for her age. I hope I'm as good.' Joan arched her back and groaned. 'It's not very comfortable back there. Good luck.'

'Jesus, we have a trawler after this.'

The two women exchanged a look that seemed to say 'too late now', and then Joan walked around to the driver's side. Carol was just stepping into the back of the van when she stopped. What was that noise? Was it a faraway siren? She looked around and there, in the distance, she thought she could see the flashing red and blue glow in the night sky. Her heart immediately began to race. It might be an ambulance but she felt certain that it wasn't. She jumped into the back of the van and slammed the door.

'Go. Just go. I think it's the guards.'

'What?' 'Where?' Joan and Moira were speaking at once and then the van roared across the gravel back onto the road.

'It's probably nothing to do with us,' Moira said over the noise of the engine. Joan was driving as fast as she dared. All three of the women could hear the siren now. It must be getting closer. In the side mirror, Joan caught a glimpse of the flashing lights, still quite far away but clearly on the same road.

'Just drive. That's a good girl,' Moira said encouragingly. Carol couldn't believe how calm her mother sounded. She felt like she might throw up. She clung on to the back of her mother's seat, pressing her head into the stinking upholstery. She was too frightened to even think of indulging in some panic prayers. The van snaked along the coast road, the siren and lights getting closer all the time.

'The trouble is no cover, no trees, nothing. Do you think they can see us yet?' Moira asked.

Joan looked in the side mirror again. 'No, not yet. Oh fuck, yes,' she corrected herself as she saw a flash of headlights on the bend before the car disappeared again. 'It's not an ambulance, I can tell you that.'

The van roared on. Moira leaned forward, peering into the night.

'Here's what we do. In a minute we'll get to that stretch of straight road and at the end of it there's a turn up to the right, where that German couple had the pottery.'

'OK.' Joan didn't remember this road very well and was fairly certain she had never known about any German potters.

'Right, so when we hit the straight, turn the lights off.'

'What are you talking about?' Carol protested from the back. 'You'll get us killed.'

'We'll be grand. We can see every other car, they'll have their lights on but we'll vanish and then nip up the hill to the right and the gardai can get on with whatever it is they're doing without bothering us. Agreed?'

Joan said nothing. She could see the logic but also agreed with Carol about the danger.

The van made the corner and the road lay straight ahead of them. Moira sat back in her seat and lifted her chin slightly.

'Lights!' she commanded, and Joan found herself reaching out and plunging them into darkness.

The sudden shock of the night silenced them. Joan steeled herself not to slow down too much because if the garda car got too close this plan was never going to work.

'Steady,' Moira said quietly as if she was working with an animal.

After a moment or two, the darkness seemed less impenetrable. What had just been a wall of blackness began to break into different shades and textures. They could see the outline of the hedgerow on the land side of the road, and where the hillside met the night sky. It was still unnerving to be hurtling through the night with no lights, but the fear of sudden death receded slightly.

'The right is coming up in a bit,' Moira warned.

Joan reached for the indicator. 'No,' the older woman snapped and slapped at Joan's arm.

'Sorry, sorry.'

Carol silently enjoyed someone else suffering her mother's wrath.

'Here, here it is now. Quick.'

Joan heaved the steering wheel and the van turned up a steep narrow road.

'How far?'

'Slow down, right down. I don't know this road.'

Joan did as she was told.

'Pull in here.' Moira waved at a break in the hedge where a gate had been set back from the road.

The engine off, Moira rolled down her window. They could hear the siren mixed in with the noise of the ocean and the wind stroking the hillside. They listened as it got louder and closer. It would be passing the end of the road soon, but before it did, the siren stopped abruptly. The women looked at each other in alarm.

'Have they spotted us?' Carol whispered hoarsely.

'I don't know.' It was a phrase Moira didn't use often. Joan was eyeing the gate through her window. Should she climb it and make a run for it? What was the point? They'd find her car at the Crotties' and Moira and Carol were hardly going to keep her secret if they were arrested themselves. Joan's mouth was dry and she gripped the steering wheel tightly. The seconds turned to minutes and still they sat undisturbed in silence. Where were the guards? Had they been after someone else? There were no other houses on that stretch of the road. It made no sense.

'I think we're safe.' Moira didn't sound at all certain.

'What should we do?' Joan asked.

Moira shrugged. 'Turn the van and head out to Stranach, I suppose.'

'But if they've seen the van they know that's where we're going.'

'Well they didn't go by the end of this road so that's not where they're heading. I'd say the coast is clear.'

'What if they're waiting for us at the end of the road? What if they're on foot or something? It hasn't been that long.' Carol cursed herself for not objecting more forcefully to this whole insane plan. They were all going to jail, and it was their own stupid fault.

'Well we can't stay here all night.' Moira had had enough. She used her head to indicate towards the black nylon mound at Carol's feet.

Without further discussion, Joan started the engine, switched the lights back on, and began the slow process of turning the van around on the narrow road. Carol found a sliver of comfort in the fact that she was no longer driving. Joan inched slowly down the hill to the coast road. The windows were both down but there were no engine sounds or any lights to be seen. All three of the women braced themselves as the vehicle turned onto the main road. Would there be alarms and bright lights, police in high-vis jackets running towards them?

Nothing. The road was empty. They drove on, the tension they had all shared slowly melting away. Carol realised that she had been holding her breath. She let it go and leaned against the side of the van. Moira readjusted her beret and seemed to be about to speak before changing her mind. Soon they began to catch glimpses of the sparse lights marking Stranach, and then they were turning onto the pier.

Rory was at the far end, waving a torch slowly. Joan inched the van forward, careful not to crush the stacks of lobster pots or small wooden boats leaning against the high sea wall.

'Nearly there now,' Moira said quietly, as if trying to reassure herself that her plan was still on track.

'You made it, then,' Rory greeted them. 'All good?'

'Bit of bother on the coast road but sure, we're here now.' Moira smiled. 'Still a bit of wind around. Will we be all right?'

'Tide's on the turn. Shouldn't be too choppy once we get out, I'd say.' Rory turned and looked out at the endless black of the ocean. Carol felt a strange shift in her stomach.

'Where's your friend?' Rory slapped his hands together, signalling that it was time to get to work.

Moira and Carol glanced at Joan. He was no friend of theirs.

'In the back. He's fairly heavy.'

'No bother.' Rory's voice trailed behind him as he strode off to the back of the van.

The doors open, and the interior lit with Rory's torch, the women gathered around. The dark cover was on one side of the van, the floor stained by a pool of water seeping from beneath the black nylon. Rory, moving much more nimbly than his age suggested, jumped into the back and started to push the frozen body towards the women. Moira stepped back, while Joan and Carol braced themselves.

Having a third pair of hands made the job much easier and their load was quickly dumped unceremoniously over the side of the trawler, hitting the deck with a loud crunch. Carol and Joan helped Moira onto the metal ladder on the side of the pier and then all of them were on board the trawler. Rory looked them up and down and then went into the small cabin. He returned with large, stiff raincoats.

'You'll need these when we get out further.'

It crossed Moira's mind to argue the point. She had thought through her outfit very carefully. But she took the giant coat obedi-ently. There was no mistaking that it belonged to a fisher-man. The stench was overwhelming. Joan gave a series of little coughs. Carol tried to recall when she had last smelled something so awful, but then she remembered and remained silent.

Rory went into the cabin, pulling his heavy yellow jacket closed, and started the engine. He let it idle and then returned to the deck to begin untying ropes. He moved quickly, throwing the released ropes up to the pier, where they landed with a wet slap. He turned to the two younger women.

'When I give you the nod, you need to push off the pier. There's a pole there.'

Carol stepped forward and picked it up.

Rory revved up the engine and then gave a shout. Joan and Carol assumed that was their signal and pushed as hard as they could against the wall. Slowly the trawler edged away and Carol prodded the wall with the pole until the boat was clear of the end of the pier. The trawler chugged away from land, passing a few pleasure boats and yachts dotted around the shore.

Rory stuck his head out of the cabin.

'You better squeeze in here.'

The three women held on to the side of the boat and made their wide-legged, bent-kneed way towards the cabin. Already the wind had grown sharp and all of them were happy to find some shelter.

The four of them were a tight fit. Moira stood beside Rory while Joan and Carol leaned against the back wall, which was covered with ancient Page Three girls and *Sunday World* beauties. Once the boat rounded the small promontory and hit open water they all had to find something to hold on to. The noise of the engine and the constant crashing as the trawler bullied its way through the waves meant conversation was unnecessary.

The clouds had cleared and the reflection of a large moon was smeared across the waves. Its light gave shape to the headland on the other side of the bay as the little trawler made its way out towards the open sea. Rory, conscious of his delicate cargo, wasn't going at full speed, but still the boat was tossing the women around like a dog playing with a stuffed toy. Moira could feel the saliva building in her mouth. She was glad she had forgotten the bag with the flasks of soup in the van.

The air in the little cabin was thick with fuel and fish. Carol angled her face towards the open door, allowing the night air to refresh her senses. Joan kept her head bent low and tried to brace herself with her feet spread apart. She didn't feel well, but she wasn't sure if it was because of the motion of the trawler or the gathering dread of what they were about to do.

Rory stabbed a finger into the darkness and called over the engine, 'Once we clear land, we'll head east along. With a bit of luck the currents there will take him out.' Moira nodded as vigorously as she dared. Joan winced at the mention of *him*. The others had been so careful all night to never gender or humanise what they were transporting, but she couldn't forget that it was her brother Cathal out there on the deck, covered in black nylon. She felt a sudden impulse to just slip over the side of the boat herself, into the oily waves. Old

Mrs Crottie had made this plan sound so simple and sanitised, but the reality of what they were actually doing felt like an assault. The thought of an abrupt escape was very appealing.

Time and the trawler both seemed to be going very slowly. The looming shadow of the headland was still alongside them. Moira felt a light sheen of sweat on her face. She would never have admitted it to anyone but she felt overcome by tiredness. She didn't mind standing, but this was more than that. Her arms ached from holding on and a familiar pain was tightening its grip on her knees. Staring into the night, she could see Carol and Joan standing behind her, reflected in the window of the little cabin. If Declan Barry had a type then it wasn't obvious. Superficially the two women had little in common. Yet, Moira thought, they had both allowed the same man to wreck their lives. Maybe his type was anyone who could put up with him? It seemed so unfair that fate had intervened to give Declan no responsibility for clearing up this mess. She wondered if they would really succeed in getting away with this plan. That business with the police earlier had been very odd. It couldn't have been a coincidence. Still, even if the worst happened, at least now they had Joan Barry. Surely the law would deal with her more severely than an old lady who was just trying to help her daughter, no matter how misguided she had been. Moira felt a little less nauseous.

The moon was moving faster than they were. Carol just wanted this insane night to be over. The throbbing of the engine and the battering of the waves were so violent, and yet Carol found herself getting sleepy. She stuck her head out of the cabin and let the cold wind and sea spray revive her. Turning back, she noticed Joan had bowed her head. Was she praying? There was something about Joan

Barry that Carol couldn't understand. She seemed so capable and independent, and yet she had allowed herself to be manipulated for so many years. Carol wondered if she was telling the whole truth. Yes, Declan could be controlling, but was he really the monster that Joan described? Why had she come back now? Was it just to see her children or was it something to do with Stable Row? Carol couldn't remember exactly what Eimear had said, but surely Joan would have a claim on the house. Could that be right? Without warning, Joan looked up and caught Carol staring at her. She blushed and looked away.

The pitch of the engine changed and the trawler slowed to a swaying stop. Rory turned from the wheel.

'This is good.'

Carol and Joan followed him out onto the deck. Moira stayed in the doorway, holding on as the boat was slapped by the waves. She watched the others make their way to the black mound. Joan half fell and pulled herself up the side of the cabin. Rory took her arm to steady her. Finally the trio surrounded the frozen body in its nylon shroud. They reached down and dragged it to the side of the boat. Moira could hear snatches of Rory's voice shouting instructions as they were carried on the breeze. She saw them all take a firm grip of the barbecue cover. This was it. She had a sudden urge to stop them, so that one of them might say a prayer. This was a body, after all. But before Moira could say anything, the black shape had been raised in one swift movement and then disappeared over the side. Moira rushed forward to get a better look.

Joan stepped back from the side, arms outstretched, trying to keep her balance. She let out a small whimper and then Carol turned to see her face contorted with ugly tears. A low wail was taken by the wind. Going to her and wrapping her in a comforting embrace felt like the natural thing to do. There was no resistance. Joan fell into her arms and hugged Carol tightly. The movement of the boat and Joan's sobs coursed through them both. Then a voice cut through the night air.

'Oh for fuck's sake!'

It was Moira. Carol turned to see her leaning over the side of the boat. Leaving Joan, she went to her mother.

'Look at him! He's just bobbing around like an ice cube in your drink.'

Not far from the boat Carol could make out the ghostly shape moving on the surface of the sea. The barbecue cover had been lost and now the uneven grey figure was being rocked by the waves, like a sunbather on a hammock. It seemed to be heading back towards the boat. Without saying anything, Moira reached down and picked up the pole that Carol had used to push the trawler away from the pier earlier. Holding the end of it tightly, she swung the pole over the side of the boat and landed it with a heavy thud on the frozen figure. Carol thought she heard the scrape of ice. Her mother lifted the pole and hit again. This time a lump of ice fell away into the water. Another blow and a bit more ice was removed. Moira was gasping for air and in the light from the cabin, Carol could see her mother's face flushed red and covered in sweat. She was brought back to her senses.

'Mammy! Stop it.' She grabbed the pole away from her mother and flailed at the body, but it had drifted out of reach. More than half of it was now submerged, and the rest was protruding from the water at an awkward angle. Carol thought she recognised the feet.

'Christ! What are you doing?' It was Joan, rushing to the side of the boat.

'He's, it's just floating. We didn't think about the ice.'

'That'll melt fast enough in the salt water. Don't worry.' Rory Lynch appeared at their side. 'We can sit tight to be certain. If you have the time, like.'

'We'll wait,' Moira said, still breathless, one hand on her chest.

Carol looked around. 'Is there anywhere for Mammy to sit?'

Rory walked away and came back with a wooden box that he set on its side. 'Will that do you?'

'Lovely. Oh, that's better.' Moira lowered herself down.

The four of them turned and watched the murky grey object in the waves. Occasionally it vanished from view behind a wave, only to reappear a moment later. Carol thought that there was slightly less of it above the surface now. Hopefully it wouldn't take too long.

'I can boil a kettle. Anyone?' Rory looked at his passengers.

'Oh, a hot cup of tea. You're a life-saver.' Moira rubbed her hands together.

'No milk,' Rory warned her.

'We'll manage, I'd say,' she replied.

'Anyone else?'

'No thanks,' said Carol while Joan just shook her head, the lack of milk less concerning to her than the thought of where fresh water and a clean cup might be coming from.

While Rory headed into the cabin, Carol bent down and zipped Moira's padded gilet right up to her chin, and then buttoned the stiff yellow coat that she had been given. Moira peered out at her daughter as if she had been swallowed by a wide-mouthed yellow monster.

'Don't be fussing, pet,' Moira protested weakly. She longed to be back in the bungalow under the weight of the double duvet and Dave rubbing her back as she fell asleep.

The boat was still being pushed from side to side by the waves, but the wind had died down. The three women were lost in their thoughts, looking out into the dark ocean or up into the dusting of stars above them. It was only when Rory returned with a steaming mug of tea for Moira and remarked, 'That's it gone then,' that they noticed the ragged outline had slipped beneath the surface of the water forever.

Was it early or late? Sally wasn't sure at first. Outside the kitchen window she could see the light beginning to change. The trees that lined one side of the field opposite her cottage were picked out against the first smudge of daylight. It wasn't that much earlier than when she had been working at the hospital kitchens, but unlike those early mornings, today she felt alert and clear-headed. She was awake in a way she couldn't remember being before. She had energy and a feeling that anything and everything was possible.

She had already filled three bin bags. It was unclear to her if what she was doing should be described as cleaning or packing up. She tried to recall if she had ever had a clear-out like this in the entire time she had lived in the cottage. She didn't think so. Magazines that she had been saving for . . . for what? It was as if a switch had been flipped and suddenly she had no attachments, no unnamed days in the future when she might need ten space-saving solutions for bathrooms or the best recipes for butternut squash. The magazines were piled into a black bin bag. She had a confounding certainty that there was nothing in any of them she needed. This new version of herself found no problem in discarding old post and grease-stained takeaway menus. All were swept into a bag. It was a wonderful feeling. She was already imagining the old, no-longer-worn clothes that she would be heaping into piles upstairs.

It felt like she was hacking her way through a jungle, clearing a path for herself.

Something was going to happen. Sally wasn't sure what, but she was confident that very soon, she would not be living in this cottage. She literally gasped when she realised that she was going to leave Ballytoor. All this stuff being loaded into plastic sacks was like the ballast being thrown from a hot-air balloon. She was untethered, finally able to float free. Was this what enlightenment felt like? Everything so clear, so obvious, so straightforward.

Sally threw open the front door and walked out into the dawn. The spongy moss of the small lawn was cold and wet on her bare feet but she didn't care. The faint traces of her breath hung in the air and she threw her arms wide to greet the day. Sally knew she was being foolish, putting on a performance for no one to see, and yet standing outside her cottage, shivers beginning to take her limbs, she felt special. She felt seen.

All the years of thinking that she was lazy or settling for less than she wanted were over now. Finally, she understood that what she had really been doing was waiting. Her life had been a long wait for her mother to return. How could she begin to live her life when there was such a big piece of it missing? Oddly she had been right, but not in the way she'd expected. Seeing Joan again had set her free, but only because she realised that her mother wasn't the final clue, or the lost key to unlock everything. Joan Barry seemed like a nice woman, but she wasn't going to fix Sally's life. She had no explanations or solutions. It was as simple as that. No more waiting. Sally was half laughing, half crying as she hurried out of the morning chill and back into the cottage.

She glanced into the little sitting room. Books. She would need a cardboard box for those. She picked up a few. Unread novels. Annuals from when she was a child. Textbooks. It was then she saw it, Emily Brontë's dusty face peering up at her. It was the notebook Carol had given her years before. Sally was surprised that she had kept it and not thrown it away when everything had changed. Picking it up, she flicked through the pages, the blue loops of her schoolgirl writing floating by. Notes from her classes, bits of essays, and then at the back she found long-forgotten lists.

She tried to remember who she had been when she had sat in her bedroom trying to figure out her life. Her heart broke for herself as she read.

People Who Love Me

Mammy

Daddy

Killian

Uncle Cathal

Debbie

Carol

Darragh?

An angry line had been scribbled through Daddy and Carol. Sally could feel the rage burnt into the page. Strange that she'd still thought her mother loved her, despite her disappearance. She didn't remember who Debbie was and Darragh was the one who had changed his mind about the debs. How had he avoided being crossed out? Sad to see Uncle Cathal on the list. She remembered how happy he had made her. His death had sort of been brushed to one side. She supposed because of how he died, people wanted to protect her, especially because it happened so soon after her mother had left them.

Uncle Cathal had made her feel so special. Weirdly, even after all this time she could recall being certain that she was his favourite. He had made a fuss over her and she remembered they'd played games without Killian. She folded the notebook and held it to her chest. It had been so long since she had thought about Cathal. How had his death affected her, she wondered. God, when she thought about her childhood it was so completely fucked up. It was amazing she was as normal as she was.

As she replaced the book on the pile, she noticed the corner of a Polaroid photograph sticking out of another book. She pulled it out and smiled. She hadn't seen it for years. Who had taken it? She couldn't imagine it had been her father, so it must have been Joan before she left. It was a picture of Sally as a very little girl, standing on the stairs. She was wearing a pair of her mother's heels and nothing else. Her face seemed to be one enormous smile and her hands were raised in the air as if she was celebrating everything, her whole life. What had happened to that child? Sally wondered if she could ever find her way back to that sort of joy again.

The first glow of the sun was just tipping over the horizon as the little trawler made its way back down the bay towards the pier at Stranach. The sky loomed vast and grey. Another day had begun. The return journey had been without incident and the three women hadn't really spoken since their mission had been completed. Moira sat on her wooden box clutching an emptied mug while Joan and Carol leaned against the back wall of the cabin.

As land drew closer, Moira pulled herself up and studied the shore. She squinted and then turned to call her daughter over.

'Carol, is that your father's car?'

The shape of a vehicle was clearly visible at the start of the pier, close to where Carol herself had parked when they had first come to talk to Rory.

'I don't think so. I mean it might be, but what would he be doing out here?'

'That's what I'd like to know,' Moira said in a way that suggested she already did.

The two women kept their eyes trained on the car as the trawler inched closer.

'That is Dave's car. I'm sure of it.'

'Is it?'

'It is.'

'Maybe.'

'Oh God.'

'What is it, Mammy?'

Moira clutched her daughter's arm and pointed.

'There he is. That's him.'

Carol could see the dark silhouette of a man walking towards the pier. His back had a familiar slant. 'Christ, I think you might be right.'

'And he's wearing that stupid cap.'

Carol began to speak very quickly. 'What are we going to do? How can we explain that we're on this boat? What we were doing out here? Oh Mammy. We're fucked. Fucked.'

Moira snapped at her daughter. 'Would you stop? Let me hear myself think.'

Carol stopped speaking but an involuntary whimper continued.

'Dave's on the pier,' Moira called to Rory.

'Your Dave?'

'Yes, my Dave.' Why was she surrounded by idiots?

'Right.' Rory pulled a lever and the tone of the engine changed as the boat slowed to a stop. Joan was very still, waiting to see what might happen next. Her sense of dread had returned.

'What are you doing?' Moira hissed at Rory. He shrugged.

'I was going to wait a bit.'

'Wait? For what? Dave to die? He's seen us now, we have to keep going. We don't have a choice.'

Without bothering to defend himself Rory eased the lever up and the trawler lurched forward again. The women could feel the air change, less of the sea on it.

Carol twisted around to face her mother.

'What's our story? What are we going to tell him?'

Moira jutted her chin forward.

'We tell him no story. Nothing. He's not here by accident. Your father knows something, so let's find out what.'

Not wanting to say more, Moira made her way to the front of the boat, swaying unsteadily. She had been right. It seemed that Dave Crottie was involved after all.

Dave was waiting on the pier. Carol struggled to make out the expression on his face. When the trawler was finally close enough to make out his features, they gave nothing away. At least he wasn't glowering or shaking his fist. He waved at Carol and then helped as Rory threw some ropes ashore.

Moira held out her hand for assistance and smiled like a visiting politician as she stepped as lightly as she could onto the pier. Dave tried to lean in for a kiss on the cheek but Moira turned away.

'Oh, Rory – your coat! I forgot.' She shuffled out of her borrowed rain jacket and Carol and Joan did the same. Rory collected them all and stepped into the cabin.

'Well, this is a surprise, Dave. What brings you out here at this time of the morning?' The smile on Moira's face didn't falter. Carol froze. She didn't appreciate this direct approach.

'Well, I thought you'd be tired and could do with a lift. I'd say you don't fancy driving all the way into town and there's a strange car at the bungalow.' As he mentioned the car he looked at Joan, who had just stepped onto the pier.

'Dave Crottie.' He offered a hand.

'Sorry. Joan, Joan Barry. Nice to meet you.'

The brief flash of bewilderment on Dave's face told them that however much of the story he knew, he hadn't been privy to the news of Declan's wife's return.

'And you remember Rory, don't you, Dave?' Moira continued breezily as if hosting a pier-side cocktail party.

'I do, of course,' Dave said, nodding his acknowledgement as Rory was still on the deck of the trawler. 'Good to see you again.'

Dave clapped his hands together. 'Now, I'd say we should get you ladies home. Nice hot coffees is what you'll be needing. Do you need any more help tying up the boat?'

'No, no. You're grand. I'll finish up here. You head away home.'

Moira stepped away from her husband, back towards the trawler.

'Thanks, Rory. Thanks for everything.'

'Ah . . .' He waved away her gratitude and began winding some wet rope.

Carol and Joan both called their thank yous, and Rory, without pausing his work, just said, 'Safe home to you now. Safe home.'

The mismatched group of travellers walked slowly along the pier till they reached Dave's car. Moira had begun to shiver.

'Are you all right, Mammy?'

'Yes, yes. Just get me into the car and turn the heater on.'

'There's a rug on the back seat there.' Dave opened the door to show Carol and then helped Moira into the front. Her daughter draped the blanket over her shoulders and Moira tightened it around herself.

Carol and Joan sat on the back seat like children, while Dave drove back along the coast road, where just a few hours earlier they had been chased by the police. Apart from the dense roar of the heater working hard, the car was silent. Moira yawned and then they all did. Eventually, Dave spoke.

'So, have you anything to tell me?' His voice gave nothing away but at least, Carol thought, he didn't sound angry.

'We'll talk when we get home.' Moira had spoken.

It wasn't a big house and Colin hadn't been a huge presence, so why then did Brook Drive seem so cavernous without him? Killian felt as if the house was mocking him. The way his footsteps echoed, or a door closing sounded like thunder. It seemed the house had decided it was uninhabited now that it was no longer a happy home. Even the clink of Killian's spoon as it stirred his morning coffee sounded amplified and ludicrous.

He was looking forward to going to work. There, at least, Killian knew who he was. It wasn't as if he loved his job, but he knew he was good at it and for now, that was enough. The feeling of getting something right, while he was being eaten away by the fear that he had got everything else monumentally wrong. He had left messages for Colin. He had texted him. Nothing. It was disorientating, the tables turning so fast. Colin was the one who always complained that Killian didn't respond to messages fast enough; now he wasn't reacting at all. How could he plead his case if Colin refused to speak to him? So far Killian had managed to keep his messages calm and neutral. He didn't want to beg, and yet he was running out of ways to get through to Colin. Killian had toyed with the idea of going to see him, but then Cath would be there, with her mother-of-Christ smirk. The Cath that got the cream. At least that made Killian chuckle at his own joke.

The house was listening to him, but there was nothing else to hear. Killian hadn't played music or switched on the television since

305

Colin had left. The only sound was his thoughts. He kept thinking about what his mother had said to him. Was he really like his father? And was his father as ruthless as Joan thought? It didn't seem likely. Cutthroat people didn't live like Declan, they didn't end up in nursing homes. If his father would do anything to get what he wanted, surely he would have more than he did. Joan was wrong. She had to be. He didn't care what he looked like to her because he knew he did care about other people. It was thinking about other people that had led him to this miserable lonely place.

He wanted Colin back. No – what he wanted was their old life, the one they could pretend was full of possibilities. But that was gone. Even if Colin walked back through the door and told Killian that he loved him, things could never be the same as before. Cath and the baby would see to that. Was accepting fatherhood worth it to get Colin back? Killian didn't think so and it was too late for that now. He had laid his cards on the table for all to see. Who would fall for his bluff? No one.

So, that was that. No more messages or voicemails. Killian had damaged his life, seemingly, beyond repair. He cursed himself for letting Colin sweep him up in the excitement of being daddies. If only he had pushed back. Colin would have grumbled and sulked but in the end, he wouldn't have left Killian because of it. Then he wouldn't be sitting alone, listening to the sound of the buttons on his jacket click against the edge of the table. He sighed. Sometimes knowing where or when things went wrong didn't mean you could fix them. It just meant you could beat yourself up over them more effectively.

Through the wall he heard the muffled thump of the hot-tub filter switching itself on.

Joan made her excuses as quickly as she could. She didn't want coffee. All she desired was to get out of Ballytoor as fast as possible before something changed and she was forced to face long-overdue consequences. She knew that the further she was from the body if it was discovered, the better the chances of Sally being kept in the dark. There was a late-morning flight from Cork to London and Joan was going to be on it.

'Seems nice enough,' Dave commented as he came back from showing their unexpected visitor to the door. Carol was standing by the kitchen island, staring at her coffee. Moira was in her armchair, still wrapped in the blanket, her beret pulled down low. She had the air of a very old French student.

Dave stood at the top of the two steps that led from the hall down into the kitchen. He put his hands on his hips.

'Who am I?'

The two women looked at him but didn't reply.

'Who am I?' he asked again. This time Carol shrugged and Moira made a face that suggested her husband had just asked her to examine some unpleasant medical condition.

'I'm your daddy. I've been married to you for nearly sixty years. I'm not the enemy here. Why all the secrets? What did you think would happen?' He looked genuinely upset. Hurt.

Carol looked at her mother. Surely she had to be the one to answer this?

Moira slowly pulled the beret from her head and smoothed it out on the coffee table in front of her.

'So how are you mixed up in all of this?' she asked, looking up at Dave. She seemed apprehensive and unsure of herself. This wasn't a Moira that Carol had seen before.

'Mixed up? In what? You think I'm involved in this? I thought you were the ones that were going to explain it all to me.'

'You didn't know anything?' Moira wanted to be clear.

'No!' Dave said with a trace of exasperation. 'Well, I did but only later on. After you.'

'So this was nothing to do with you? Oh, I'm so glad!' Moira let out a breathy laugh of relief. She wanted to explain but knew that Dave and Carol would think she had been a fool. She did feel embarrassed to think she had ever believed that Dave was part of some murder plot. 'I thought – oh, it doesn't matter what I thought! But you knew about the freezer?'

'Only from the day after you. Did the pair of you really think I wouldn't notice a bloody great hole in the basement?'

Moira stood, indignant and defensive all at once. 'But if you weren't involved, how did you know about the basement? I never knew about it.'

'Carol had me down there to look at the dryer one time when it was acting up.'

Moira glared at her daughter. Carol bit her lip. She had completely forgotten that she had shown her father down the narrow stairs.

'Well, why didn't you say something?' Moira demanded.

'Because I was waiting for you to say something!' Dave said as if this was reasonable.

'But we couldn't. We couldn't tell anyone. I mean, do you know,' she hesitated, 'what was in the freezer?'

Dave threw his arms up in frustration. 'Of course I do! But' – he held one finger aloft – 'I don't know who it was. I thought it was your one just gone out the door.'

'So did I!' Moira almost shrieked. 'Didn't I, Carol? Didn't I say the very same?'

'Yes, Mammy,' she said quietly, glad to see some common ground between her parents. This mess was bad enough without them falling out over it.

'So who was it then?' Dave stepped forward into the room and took the chair opposite Moira as she sat back down.

There was a long pause.

'It was Joan Barry's brother.' Having built up the suspense, Moira let each word slip from her mouth like a boiled sweet she wanted to savour.

'No!' Dave's reaction was very pleasing to his wife. 'The lad that killed himself?'

Moira shot a glance at Carol. 'The very same.'

'But how did he end up in the freezer?'

'Oh, it's a long story,' Moira said as if it was a tale she had grown tired of telling over the years. 'Suffice to say the boy was no good, some class of a pervert. Anyway, it was an accident. Joan Barry never meant to actually kill him—'

'It was Joan, not Declan, that killed him?' Dave interjected.

'Will you whist. I'm trying to tell you.' Moira regrouped her thoughts. 'So anyway, Joan Barry dispatched the brother, and when she did, well, I don't want to upset you Carol love, but it sounds like Declan seized the moment to get shot of her. I mean, to force a woman to leave her own children. It's monstrous. I'm sorry, Carol, but it just is.'

Carol studied the kitchen counter, not wanting to respond.

'Jesus Christ. That's awful altogether. But why not tell me? I was waiting for you to come to me for help.'

Moira pulled up one side of her mouth. 'We were worried you'd just go to the guards.'

Dave gave a bark of a laugh. 'And then I did go to the guards!'

Moira joined in with his laughter. 'You did. I could have cheerfully strangled you. And you knew when you had him up to the house. Were you mad?'

'I bumped into him and he knew the house from when the wife had disappeared. He just wanted to have a nose around, but then he tried to dress it up as if he was on some sort of official business. I never asked him up.' He suddenly grinned widely. 'The look on your faces when you opened the door! I wish I'd had a camera. I thought after that fright, you'd come to me for sure. But no.' A shadow crossed his face. 'It wasn't me you went to for help.'

Moira reached out and took his hand.

'And you knew all these years that I was friends with Rory Lynch?'

An almost imperceptible nod of the head. 'I did.'

Carol leaned forward. This was the part of the story she wanted to know.

'Well, you met him a few times over the years.'

'I did. And he was your boyfriend before we were stepping out.'

'He was not!' Moira protested.

'Well, that's the story I was told. And I knew you'd stayed in touch.'

Moira squirmed. 'How did you know that?'

'Well, a few years after we were married, I remember you spending a lot of money buying a load of fish week after week, and we weren't eating a load of fish, so I supposed something was going on.'

'I didn't know you checked the books.' Moira had picked up her beret and was twisting it nervously.

'Amn't I running a business, pet? Of course I check the books.' Dave said this as kindly as he could.

'Why didn't you say anything?'

'I was waiting for you to say something.'

Leaning on the counter, Carol felt she was getting a very clear understanding of her parents' marriage.

Moira put down the beret again and shifted in her seat so that she was directly facing Dave.

'He owed me a favour. A big one.' Moira tilted her head back slightly, trying to sort out the facts before she began.

'Rory wasn't married long at the time. You remember my friend Teresa, the one with the long red hair? A bit wild.'

'I do.'

'Well they had been sweethearts when we were all in school. He was going out with her, not me.' Moira wanted to underline this point.

'All right, all right.'

'Well, I don't know what they were playing at, but it seems after Rory was wed, well, himself and Teresa were still carrying on.'

'Right,' Dave said to let Moira know that he was following the story so far.

Carol struggled to imagine the fanged Rory from the trawler involved in a love triangle, or indeed a romance of any shape at all.

'Anyway, the fun stopped when Teresa found herself in the family way and her with no family. Neither of them had a penny to their name but they needed to get her over to England to take care of things.'

Dave gave a little sigh of understanding. It had been a familiar tale at the time.

'They'd no choice. Him with a new wife, Teresa with nothing and less than that if she disgraced herself. So they came to me for help. We were starting to do well at the time. I didn't think we'd miss it and it saved their lives.' Her voice went up as she spoke. She was presenting her case and she hoped to be found not guilty.

'I just wish you could have told me.'

'I'm sorry.' Moira's face seemed to lose its age. Her eyes were clear. She was a young bride asking her husband for forgiveness. Carol looked away, embarrassed by such intimacy.

'Well, you can thank your lucky stars I did know, because that's what saved you last night.' Dave seemed eager to move on and avoid any displays of emotion.

'What do you mean, Daddy?' Carol chipped in, also keen to return to less personal territory.

'Well, when Sergeant Draper called me to tell me about the break-in at the house and the van he was pursuing, I put two and two together. I made up some story about Rory shifting a few bits of furniture. I'd say old Draper smelled a rat but he called off the chase any road.'

'Thank God for that,' Carol said. 'The panic. You should have seen the state of us.'

Moira put up her hand. She had a question.

'How did you get back from Dublin so fast?'

Dave grinned.

'I never went to Dublin.'

'What!' Moira was genuinely shocked. 'But why?'

'I knew full well you were up to something. You didn't want those paintings. I showed you that Percy French one months ago and you said you wouldn't let it through the door.'

At first Moira seemed crestfallen that her husband had seen through her plan so easily, but then a smile slowly spread across her face. She reached out and took both of Dave's hands.

'You're a marvel, David Crottie. That's what you are. A marvel.'

She leaned towards him and he met her halfway with a kiss. They rested their foreheads against one another and hugged tightly. Carol wiped away her tears, hoping they hadn't seen her cry.

Dave broke the embrace and got to his feet with a burst of energy.

'Do you know what we'll do now?' Without waiting for an answer, he went to the heavy pine dresser and picked up a bottle.

'A little nip of Baileys! What do you say?'

'Dave, it isn't even ten o'clock in the morning!' Moira said, but she was already on her feet getting glasses.

Two Years Later

Sometimes she forgot, but then some silly thing would bring it all back. The smell of clothes left too long in the washing machine might remind Carol of that first day in the basement. A news report on EU fishing quotas and suddenly she was standing on the deck of Rory's trawler in darkness, comforting Joan Barry.

Nervous days had become tense weeks. Then slightly more relaxed months. Now years had passed. They had got away with it. The Crotties had bought the papers every day, Carol googled dead bodies almost every time she opened her laptop, but there had never been a mention of any remains washing ashore. Cathal had disappeared, just as he had all those years earlier, but this time it seemed it was forever. As Dave put it, on the rare occasion the subject came up, 'He'd be long gone by now.'

Having eventually run out of reasons not to, Carol had returned to work. At first just two or three days a week, but before too long it was full time. She knew that she was an object of pity, not just in the staff room but also with students. There was a group of girls in her sixth-year class that seemed particularly anxious to befriend an actual real-life tragic figure. She was making an effort to involve herself more in school life – any life, really. She was on a couple of committees and she had volunteered to help out at the drama club. It felt good to have demands on her time. People expecting her to be somewhere and paying her to show up.

The next thing she needed to tackle – and she would soon, she swore to herself – was to finally move out of her parents' bungalow. She wasn't exactly sure why she was still there. At first she told herself that it was to keep an eye on her mother, but Moira had bounced back from her long night on the trawler in just a few days. So many things about sharing a house with her parents drove her crazy, but she had to admit that there was something about being with people who shared her secret that made life easier. She imagined that if she lived alone the burden of what they had done would weigh far more heavily on her. Soon though, soon, she would load up her car and head to her very own home. She would.

It was late one afternoon in that last week of the summer term when the whole mood of the school shifts. Pupils are cheekier, teachers more relaxed. On sunny afternoons whole classes would sit sprawled on the lawn that banked around one side of the school. Their books open, uniforms loose, the pupils would pretend to listen, when really all they were thinking about was the coming months of freedom. On this day, classes were over and Carol was in her classroom packing some books into her bag. Her phone was on silent but out of the corner of her eye she saw the flash of some activity on the screen. It was a message. From Sally. Carol hadn't thought about her in months. All she knew was that she was living in Edinburgh now, working for some huge catering company. Carol got any updates on Sally's life from Joan. She opened the message.

Daddy's gone.

Of course she knew what it meant, but just for a moment Carol allowed herself to imagine that perhaps Declan was merely missing. He had wandered off. He was just lost in the grounds somewhere. Carol didn't reply. Her whole body felt tight. She sat, her breath coming in short snatches, and called St Brendan's.

The voice was familiar, but Carol couldn't put a name to it.

'Hello, hello, it's Carol Crottie here. I was ringing about Declan Barry.'

There was the briefest of pauses and then the voice just said, 'Oh, Carol.'

Her heart cracked in two. Tears burst from her eyes. It was true. He was gone. Declan was dead.

Through sobs, she asked a few questions. How? She had seen him only the day before. It had been sudden. An infection. He hadn't been in any pain. They thought it was his lungs. Yes, she could come and see him.

Carol had managed to curb her emotions enough to drive to St Brendan's, but when she had got out of the car and approached the steps to the entrance she had been overcome. Her body was bent double with grief. It was the finality of it all. She would never come here again. This was the last time. No more sitting by a bed, stroking a waxy hand, wondering what Declan knew, or what his thoughts might be. She felt so alone as she leaned against the railing of the wheelchair ramp. Not because Declan was gone, she had got used to that loneliness long ago; no, this was different. She was alone in her grief. As far as her parents were concerned, Declan was officially a despicable man who had ruined their daughter's life. There had been times when Carol had wondered if that was true; maybe it was, but she found she hadn't been able to see everything through the filter of Joan's pain. She remembered good times. She wasn't wrong. Their life together might have had its challenges but they had been happy. They had been in love, she was certain of it. Now Declan was gone, really and finally gone, she was the only person who believed that love had ever existed.

Nurses who recognised her gave her sad looks as she made her way down the corridor. The red-haired one from Kerry had hugged her. Carol had had to stop herself from clutching him too tightly. She stood outside Declan's room and took a couple of deep breaths to compose herself, then pushed the door gently open. Before she saw Declan, she was confronted by a red-eyed Killian. Carol silently raged. This was not the way she wanted to say goodbye.

'Carol.' And then without warning he was giving her an awkward hug. Happily his effort was brief, and the two of them were left standing side by side looking at the figure on the bed. Carol had seen him only the previous afternoon, but Declan seemed so changed. The shape of his head was different and his hair seemed thinner. It struck Carol that it was as if he was fading away in front of their eyes. There was already less of him.

'I only just got here,' Killian said. His voice was hushed.

'Sally let me know,' Carol said as tersely as she dared. She didn't want to have an argument.

'Me too. She was the point of contact. We forgot to change it when she left.' He shrugged.

Carol focused on Declan's face. She didn't want to hear Killian's excuses, further proof of how little he had cared for his father.

'They said it was very peaceful.'

'Good. That's good. Was there anyone with him?'

'At the end? I'm not sure. I think they just found him.'

Carol began to weep again. She didn't care that Killian could see her. What did it matter?

Killian shifted uncomfortably. He didn't want to be in this room with the body of his father and his weeping girlfriend. He was sad, of course he was. He had shed a few tears when he had arrived, but mostly what he felt was relief. This hell was over. Not just for his father but also for himself. He would no longer have to feel guilty for not visiting, or awkward and ashamed when he did. He glanced at Carol. She was pulling old tissues out of her pockets and blowing her nose. He should go. It was the right thing to do.

'I'll leave you to it.'

Carol looked at him, and her face nearly made him cry again. She looked so stricken and heartbroken. That was probably what his face should look like. He considered telling Carol details of the undertakers and the time of the removal but he thought better of it.

'I'll text you later with all the arrangements.'

'Thank you.' Carol looked back to Declan's body.

She heard the door click shut and then she was alone. They were alone. Carol approached the bed and knelt beside it. She touched Declan's face. It was so cool. When Killian had been in the room, her mind had been full of all the things she had wanted to say to Declan, but now that it was just him and her, she found she had only one.

'I love you. Rest well, Mr Barry.'

She pulled herself up and kissed him on the lips. A step back, another glance, and then she was gone.

———

After the funeral, people had been asked back to Brook Drive. Carol didn't mind. She couldn't imagine her parents hosting a send-off for Declan, and his precious Stable Row had been sold the year before. A widow from Dublin had bought it. She wanted to be nearer her daughter in Clonakilty. The house had looked well after the work, every room painted a colour called 'String'. Moira had dressed the rooms with bits of furniture and Carol had been impressed. It turned out that Dave and Moira's taste was much better suited to Stable Row than their own bungalow. They'd even made a small profit. They were lucky because since then two more houses had come on the market. The couple in number six were on the move already, and old Mrs Buttimer had died. An accident. She had tripped over Margo on the stairs and fallen badly. Sad, really, and yet Carol and Moira had laughed for a very long time when they heard the news.

Craig had come back for the funeral. He had looked so handsome in his dark suit. After the drinks and platters of things in breadcrumbs at Brook Drive, Carol had given Craig and his girlfriend Harpreet a lift back to the bungalow. Carol studied the young woman on the back seat through the rear-view mirror. She was very beautiful; Carol could see why Craig was attracted to her. She seemed nice enough, if quiet almost to the point of silent. Carol supposed it must be serious if he had brought her to this funeral, and Harpreet must be keen if she had said yes. As happy as she was for Craig, Carol did find it all a little stressful. Having an Asian girl staying with Moira and Dave was like living with a time bomb. What would they say to embarrass themselves? So far they had been on their best behaviour.

319

Craig and Harpreet had even been allowed to share a room. It made Carol feel old that she didn't entirely approve.

Later, after her parents and Harpreet had gone to bed, Carol and Craig had sat at the kitchen table, finishing a bottle of red wine.

'I can't believe you're still living here.'

'Staying here,' Carol corrected him. 'I'm moving out soon. I swear to God. I can't believe it's been this long.'

Craig looked around the room he knew so well from his childhood, the whole scene reflected in the patio doors.

'I've something to tell you, Mammy.'

'Yes.' A fear gripped Carol. Was Harpreet pregnant? Were they going to get married? They were so young.

'Harpreet and I are living together.' He looked at his mother, awaiting her reaction, and then smiled when she did.

'That's lovely for you. She seems really sweet. I feel sorry for her though, being dragged to the wilds of West Cork. Has she met your father yet?'

'Tomorrow.'

'Nice.'

Neither of them knew how to get around the subject of Alex, so they sipped their wine.

'Who was that couple with the baby? They seemed to know me.'

Carol snorted. 'Oh, they're not a couple. That's Killian's ex and the mother of that child. I mean Killian or Colin is the father. To be honest, I don't know how it works.'

Craig shook his head. 'God, I would never have put those two together.'

'In fairness, since the break-up, Killian has really hit the gym and

Colin seems to think he's still eating for two. They used to look more like a couple. Will we finish this?' Carol held the bottle aloft to show how much wine remained.

'Go on so.' Craig pushed his glass towards her.

'Sally looked so well. Blonde hair, short. You could see her face and she's ditched the cardigans. She has a figure now.'

'Declan's daughter? Blue dress? Yes, I did see her. Pretty.'

Carol pulled a face. 'I wouldn't go that far.'

'Mammy!' Craig feigned shock.

'It's the wine talking!' A small chuckle. This felt so comfortable. Just what she needed after her awful day. Not a grieving widow, just a woman sat in the pew behind the family crying more than anyone else. She thought she must have looked deranged.

'Why weren't Granny and Grandad at the funeral?'

Carol thought for a moment. 'They weren't Declan's biggest fans.'

'Why not?'

Carol heard the surprise in his voice but she well remembered how judgemental he had been when she and Declan had started their relationship. No point bringing that up now. 'They never approved. You know what it's like. They worry about me, the way I worry about you.' She smiled and reached out to stroke his face.

'You don't need to worry about me,' he said quietly.

Carol drained the last of her wine and then looked into her son's eyes.

'Know this . . .' Maybe she was a little tipsy. 'Nothing lasts forever, so if you see a chance for happiness, grab it. Do you hear me?'

'I do, Mammy. I do.' He gave her an indulgent smile and finished his drink. 'I'm off to bed and I think you should be too.'

They both stood.

'I will, I will. I'll just lock up here and do the lights. Good night, son. I love you.'

She kissed him on the cheek.

'Night Mam, love you.'

Carol took the glasses to the sink. The dishwasher gave a little beep. It was done with the dishes from dinner. She walked away; she'd deal with it in the morning. She looked out into the night and gave a loud sigh. She was so tired. Checking to see if the patio doors were locked, she found that they weren't and she slid them open and stepped into the night air. It was a beautiful evening. Just the lightest of breezes and no clouds to obscure the stars.

In the distance she could hear the waves slapping against the rocks. She crossed the patio and walked down the grassy slope till she was nearly at the water's edge. Not for the first time that day, she found herself thinking about Joan Barry. There had been one brief mention of her name by the priest when he had delivered the eulogy, but other than that she had been entirely absent from proceedings. Carol knew that Joan was still in contact with Sally. She had visited her in Edinburgh, and there was talk of them going on holiday together. Killian hadn't stayed in touch. Carol wished she could tell Declan's children the truth about what had happened all those years ago. They deserved to know, but it wasn't her secret to share. It was Joan's and she had chosen silence.

Carol sat where the grass met the rocks and lost herself in the vastness of the night sky and the sea stretching away into the distance. The memory of a tune drifted through her mind and she wanted to hear it. Her phone was in her pocket so she scrolled through her music and then pressed play. Somehow the tinny speaker suited the hurdy-gurdy rhythms of the music and Leonard Cohen's low rasping voice: *Dance me to the end of love . . .*

Carol was weeping again, but this felt different. It wasn't the hot, tight tears of earlier in the day. This felt more like a release. She was letting go of it all. Declan, the body, Joan, Killian, Eimear . . . none of it mattered tonight. Just the music and the soft rustling of the waves on the shore.

Acknowledgments

This book may be set in a small, fictional Irish town, but it took a real-life village to get it into your hands. I can never thank these people enough for all their help and support. First and foremost, my greatest gratitude must go to my editor Hannah Black at Coronet. She has worked on all my novels and is the perfect combination of cheerleader and taskmaster. Her assistant Erika Koljonen is a tireless steward for the book.

Others in the world of Hodder & Stoughton that do trojan work are Catherine Worsley and Richard Peters in UK Sales, Emma Knight and Steven Cooper for publicity, alongside Alice Morley in marketing. Dominic Gribben took care of the audio book, while Rebecca Folland and her team dealt with all the US and foreign rights. Alasdair Oliver and Kate Brunt made the book look gorgeous using the artistic talents of Tom Haugomat. Claudette Morris was in charge of producing the book, and I mustn't forget the copyeditor and proofreader, Amber Burlinson and Jacqui Lewis respectively.

I'm also indebted to fantastic teams of people working in Hachette Australia, New Zealand and Ireland. Their enthusiasm and support means the world.

ACKNOWLEDGMENTS

My agent Melanie Rockcliffe at YMU, alongside Rebecca Taylor, Flo Helsby and Erin Johnston manage the rest of my career and ensure I have enough time to write a novel.

Enormous thanks to my personal assistant Rebecca Nicholass for thinking of everything and never letting the train come off the tracks.

To my first reader Jono, thanks your feedback. You've made this book and everything else much better.

Finally, thanks to you for choosing to read this book. Inventing a story is a particular sort of pleasure, but sharing it with others is the best feeling in the world.

Here ends Graham Norton's
Forever Home.

This edition of this book was printed
and bound at LSC Communications in
Harrisonburg, Virginia, August 2023.

A NOTE ON THE TYPE

The text of this novel was set in Guardi, a typeface designed by Reinhard Haus and published by Linotype in 1986. Haus drew inspiration from the Venetian Old Face styles of the fifteenth century used by Nicolas Jenson. Guardi embraces the characteristics of the Venetian Old Face style while meeting modern standards of fluidity and weight, producing an open, clean look on the page that is both graceful and distinguished. Guardi was named for Francesco Guardi, the eighteenth-century Italian painter.

HARPERVIA

An imprint dedicated to publishing international voices, offering readers a chance to encounter other lives and other points of view via the language of the imagination.